RESCUING HALIN

HISSA WARRIOR
BOOK 1

DISCLAIMER

This is a work of fiction. Names, characters, businesses, places, events and incidents are either the products of the author's imagination or used in a fictitious manner. Any resemblance to actual persons, living or dead, or actual events is purely coincidental.

All rights reserved:

Translation:

Don't steal the stories I worked so hard on, and occasionally cried over. Don't get upset at the absolutely made-up story lines: this is a romance, so of course it isn't realistic, duh! Don't be petty and hate on it because it isn't not your kink. We've all got different tastes and there's no shame in that.

ISBN-13: 978-1-962699-05-1
Copyright: RK Munin, 2021
Cover Illustration: Natasha Snow Designs
Profession Editing: Jenny Sliger, Owl Eyes Proofs and Edits

Warning: Author is dyslexic as hell.

Feel free to contact me with questions, requests, or comments:
author@rk-munin.com

Pick up some free novella by signing up for my newsletter. You can find the sign-up links on my website:
www.rk-munin.com

And, as with many writers, your reviews on Amazon, Goodreads, and/or Kindle help immeasurably, even if it's just clicking on the stars.

Thank you to all my readers!

CONTENT WARNING

-This novel contains assault between the two main characters when they get into a fight. Please note, the heroine gives as good as she gets. Mian is no helpless damsel in distress.
-There is talk of losing parents and loved ones due to attack or disease in the past, nothing on page.
-There is a chapter involving combated both ship to ship and person to person.

DEDICATION

I dedicate this book to my mom, whom I quote here: "You're my most favorite child. I can't believe I gave birth to someone so talented and wonderful but still modest and kind to everyone. I'm truly blessed to have you in my life."

CHAPTER

1

Halin watches the two sleep pods launch, knowing the expensive, well-engineered pods will also act as lifeboats to carry his friends and crewmates to safety. Well, he hopes it's to safety because with the three raider ships on his tail, he can't be sure of anything at the moment.

Another impact makes the ship quake around him. Cursing, he pushes the engines even harder. He knows the ship can't take much more. This is a basic tier-one civilian transport. No extra shielding and no guns. The engines are already suffering but throttling back will only get him captured sooner.

If he were flying anything else, he'd turn around and do battle. Even the smallest ship in the Hissa military could take down at least one of those raiders. But instead of being on a military ship, he's on a slightly modified civilian transport. The ship shakes again, causing the reinforced box sitting on the floor to bump his leg. In that box is the reason he's currently on a ship with no weapons. He wishes he'd argued more strenuously with command. He wishes he just went against their orders and had the ship retrofitted with a few guns as soon as he was outside Hissa-controlled space.

So many wishes and nothing to show for it, as his mother would say.

No point in pining for what he doesn't have; he's got raiders to get away from. He surveys the ship's controls, status display, and holo-chart. There's not a single port, station, or planet close enough to reach. His only hope is the well-known fact that raider ships are almost always in a pitiable condition. Their engines are so poorly maintained that there are stories of them suffering catastrophic failure during a chase. The one thing this shuttle has going for it is strong engines, despite the beating they're taking from weapons fire.

Right now, he's staying ahead of his pursuers, barely, but enough to challenge their targeting system. Most of the hits are glancing with little to no real damage.

An alarm shows up on the console display. The engines are maxed out, and fuel is getting low. The transport wasn't designed for this kind of hard burn for so long. He won't have much longer before he's dangerously low on fuel.

His ship takes another hit, but this time it's a direct hit to an engine. He feels the ship shift violently around him, and then there's intense burning pain in his leg. He ignores it as he watches the control console display. The ship's computer automatically starts an emergency shut down of the damaged engine. With only one engine burning now there is no way he will be able to evade the raiders. It looks like running out of fuel is about to become the second most critical issue.

"Transport ship designation Hope, throttle back your engines." The voice over the open com is garbled and says something else he can't quite catch.

Halin scrambles to the com and smacks it on, adjusting the signal with his other hand. "Who is this?" he demands.

"Gunship Fortune," a female voice tells him, the sound clear and distinct now. "Cut your engines and don't maneuver."

Halin slams the throttle to the off position and cuts power to the maneuvering thrusters. "Hope is no longer under power or maneuvering," he tells her.

Let this be real, he thinks. *Please don't be a ploy by some clever raiders.*

The moment he cuts power to his engines, Fortune appears on his console display. It's small for a gunship, but bristling with weapons, many of which look like they were installed long after the ship was manufactured. Could he be lucky enough to have a gunship appear just in the nick of time and save him? He's always been told he has incredible fortune. Is this aptly named gunship more proof? His comrades back home won't believe him, if he manages to survive to tell them the tale, that is.

To his immense relief, the gun ship flies right past him and hurls itself at the three raider ships. With a brilliant strafing run, it fires on two of the raider ships with guns on either side of its hull and evades fire from the third. Rolling on its side as it passes, weapon fire from the third raider just misses the gunship and hits the broadside of the second raider ship, causing a few minor explosions. Both the pilot and the gunner on Fortune need to be complimented on their skills.

He hears a crow of delight issue from the com and realizes the Fortune never cut the communication link with him. Halin remains silent, not wanting to accidentally distract the crew of the gunship during battle.

Instead of making a long-winded burn to come around again for another run at the raiders, the Fortune shuts both engines off and hits all maneuvering thrusters on one side, making the ship cartwheel violently. When its nose is pointed in the right direction, all engines come on at full burn, shooting the ship back toward the raiders, who are only now turning enough to train their weapons on the smaller craft.

He expects another strafing run, but the Fortune doesn't do that. Instead, it barrels at one of the raider's ships, then hits its back thrusters just before the two ships would collide. It jerks to a halt on the far side of the cluster and then flies so close to one of the raider ships; he expects to see impact debris.

Weapons from the raider ships are firing, but more of them are impacting each other rather than the heavily armored gunship.

Suddenly the Fortune pulls away, burning hard from the raider ship for no apparent reason. Halin can't understand what the gunship's strategy is until the raider explodes and he understands the Fortune tossed a bomb on the ship and ran.

Raiders are opportunistic cowards, so it comes as no surprise to Halin when the two remaining ships turn around and run. He expects the gunship to go after them, but it wheels around and flies back to him.

"Transport ship Hope, you're unstable. Remain calm and you'll be rescued. How many souls aboard?"

"Only one," Halin replies and looks down at his display. Fortune is correct, he can see the damaged engine compromised the ship's hull integrity before it was shut down. It's only a matter of time before the entire ship succumbs and probably implodes first and then explodes. He'd rather not be onboard for either event.

"Brace," the woman on the Fortune tells him. "I don't have time to be gentle."

Halin isn't sure what she means, but suddenly the entire ship jolts. He hears the scream of metal being grabbed and ripped. He looks over to see cutters making fast work of one side of his ship, and then there's a hole just large enough for him to slide through.

"Move it!" a voice calls out over the com. "The seal is good, but we only have seconds! Get your ass in here!"

Halin scrambles to get out of the pilot's chair and grabs the box on the floor near him. He dives through the small hole and slides down the short connecting tube into the waiting gunship. No sooner are his feet clear than the iris door of the emergency slide shuts, and he hears metal shriek as it rips and gives way.

The Fortune shakes around him as the engines are powered up. Grabbing a nearby rail, he pulls himself to his feet. A small window allows him to watch Hope disintegrate.

First, she buckles in as the grav drive fails; then she explodes out as the fuel mixes within the ship instead of the engine. They're just far enough away to catch a ripple from the explosion. But all it does is shake the ship around him as Gunship Fortune races away. He looks down at the box in his arm as Fortune settles. He almost died. He doesn't know where his crewmates are, and his ship is gone, but all he can think is: *That could've gone much worse.*

He waits a few moments, making sure the ship isn't going to move abruptly and knock him off his feet. When he's reassured the gunship is done with quick maneuvering, he starts making his way to the fore, hoping to find the cockpit. He's eager to meet the crew. Maybe he can hire them to help him find his missing people and persuade them to help him finish his mission. Or at least get him to a place where his homeworld can send reinforcements.

The ship's cramped and crowded. Boxes of ammunition, parts, and supplies are crammed everywhere. He's forced to move boxes just to make it down the corridor. His leg is bothering him, but he ignores it. He estimates he's about halfway to his destination when a small female figure appears in front of him.

The helmet on her chest piece isn't engaged, exposing her head, so he can see her face and recognizes her as a human female. They might be on the rarer side, but he's interacted with enough of them to not mistake her for any other species.

The armor she's wearing is old but well-kept and cared for. She has large green eyes, full of concern as she takes in his appearance. Her generous lips are turned down in a frown and her blonde hair is pulled into a short ponytail at the back of her head that doesn't even brush the armor's wide neck.

The armor isn't the only thing she's wearing that is battle-ready. There are blasters in holsters on her hips, several knives in sheaths on her thighs, and a sword secured at her back. None of that startles him. He's met plenty of female warriors armed to the teeth, but what does cause him to stare is the red bundle tucked just inside the neck of her armor.

It's a PKB, personal kill bomb, used by soldiers who fear capture and torture. As long as a warrior can move their head, they can activate the PKB and end their life along with those around them. He can understand the need for it. Anyone dealing with raiders runs the risk of capture and suffering a horrible captivity. He knows the logic but finds he has an almost overwhelming urge to rip the small device away from her, along with the rest of her weapons and armor. His instincts scream at him to tuck her away some place safe where those things will never be needed.

He probably feels that way because of the state of the Hissa civilization. Otherwise, he's sure he wouldn't be so interested in this human female. Humans are too small. Too delicate for a Hissa warrior.

Except she did just help save him. And he's fighting an almost irresistible urge to find out firsthand how soft her skin is. That leads him to wonder how this little human would like to be touched. What sounds would she make?

He shakes his head, trying to dislodge those distracting thoughts.

While he was busy letting his mind wander far afield, she's closed the distance between them, shoving several boxes out of her way until she's within arm's reach.

"Are you injured? Did you take a blow to the head?" she asks, and he realizes she's been talking to him for a while now. What's wrong with his head that he's having intimate thoughts about this female when there are so many more important matters to attend to? Maybe he did take a blow to the head and doesn't remember.

"I don't think so," he grunts, answering her in Space Standard as he assesses the state of his body. His head doesn't hurt. His body feels strangely free of pain. "I think I'm fine," he says as he looks down. That's when he notices a red stain running down the length of his leg.

"I don't think your assessment is correct," she mutters and hurries forward, pulling out one of her knives. When his ship was attacked, he only had time to put the top part of his armor on over his torso, he didn't have time to put on the leg or arm pieces. The burning pain he felt when the engine was hit must have been this injury.

He watches, bemused, as she uses the knife to rip his pant leg apart and with a strange detachment notices that there's a chunk of metal protruding from his thigh. "Shouldn't that hurt more?"

"It will," she promises him grimly. "I don't have a medical suite, but I do have med supplies. I need you to walk to the bridge before you collapse. You're too big for me to carry, and my hover cart stopped working a while back." She cuts off the rest of the pant leg and wraps it tightly above the wound. He can feel the pressure but is surprised there's still no pain.

His brain is starting to feel a little fuzzy, and he reaches out to touch a wall to steady himself. "I can walk," he assures her, taking a step forward. "I won't collapse."

He stumbles, and she grabs his right arm and puts it over her shoulder to help steady him. His boot makes a strange squelching sound, and he realizes his shoe is full of his blood.

"Yeah, keep telling yourself that," she grumbles. "One step at a time. Come on. Don't stop."

"I'm moving, female," Halin assures her, even though he's not sure he is moving.

He's uncertain how long they spend walking. Their progress is hampered not only by his stumbling gait but also by all the boxes she's forced to kick out of the way to allow them to pass side by side. Finally, they reach the small control room, and she props him up against a wall.

"Stand here," she instructs him. "Give me just a few minutes."

"I can stand," he retorts. "Just help me up."

"You are up," she tells him in a strangled voice, and he opens his eyes to find that he is indeed standing, but the room doesn't seem to want to be still.

"Right, I'm standing. Go about your business, female," he commands. "I'll wait here."

He closes his eyes again and concentrates on keeping himself upright. He can feel the pain now. Fire is burning his leg from the inside out. As a Hissa warrior, he's felt his fair share of pain and injury, but this is beyond anything he's experienced before.

"Just a step," the woman tells him, her hands drawing his arm over her shoulders again. Shame at his weakness fills him, but he's also surprised by the human's strength. She might be small compared to him, but it's obvious she is used to labor because she thinks nothing of grunting under his weight. She's not as delicate as he first thought.

She's trying to get him to a fold-out bunk on the far side of the control room. The room's so small the bed takes up a third of the space, so it isn't too far away. He takes a step, but his legs start to give out from under him. She manages to guide his bulk into the bed, and with a hard thump, he crashes onto the small but sturdy bunk. He rolls to his back, clasping the box tightly to his chest as the woman helps him pull his legs up into the bed. Then she lifts his wounded leg and unceremoniously shoves pillows under it.

"That's a lot of blood," the woman mutters darkly. Should he apologize for making such a mess on her ship? He wants to tell her how grateful he is for her assistance but can't seem to form words anymore. The pain is overwhelming. It's all he can do to remain still and quiet.

He feels a tug on the box. Without opening his eyes, he growls and shows fang, clutching the box tightly to his chest. He hears a little gasp, and the tugging stops. His eyes must have slid closed again. He didn't mean to close them, but now his lids feel too heavy to open back up.

"Right, fine. You can hold on to that," the woman tells him. Then he feels her hands on his leg. Struggling, he manages to wedge his eyes open just enough to see her examining his wound. "I'm going to have to use my nanos on you," she tells him, eyes still focused on his injury. "I hope you can pay me back for them later because they're expensive. Well, pay me back if you live. Otherwise, there's no charge."

Her face is grim, and she looks upset but in control. He wants to reach out and comfort her, tell her that he can buy her anything she needs, not to worry about money. "No concern," is all he manages to croak out.

"Oh, I'm very concerned," she tells him. "Now be quiet so I can work."

I can do that, he thinks. *I can be quiet for her as the pain consumes me.*

She mumbles a few things he can't quite hear and then leaves his side. He wonders if she's disgusted by his weakness. *Give me time,* he wants to tell her. *Let me lie here for a bit to rest, and I'll be better. Don't leave me. I can prove myself a worthy male.* Then he hears her return, and he feels calmer. She came back for him. That's good. Now he can tell her how beautiful she is and how he wants to buy her things. He thinks of the words he wants to say, but nothing is verbalized. When did he lose the power of speech?

"This is going to hurt," she warns him. "But I can't give you anything for the pain until the nanos get to work. Can you not move? Or do I need to tie you down?" She asks such simple things of him. Of course, he can grant her this easy request.

"I'll be still," he assures her. Anything this female needs he'll provide, as long as he doesn't need to stand up again. He's not sure he can do that.

A shock of pain comes from his leg, making him roar. He manages to keep himself from pulling his leg away from the brutal female, but why is she hurting him? Did he insult her in some way? If she just told him what he did, he'd apologize and make amends.

He hears a clatter as she tosses something away and she mumbles, "That was in there deep."

"Stop," he grits out between clenched teeth. "Please stop. Just stop."

"I know, big guy," she tells him. He manages to get one eye open to find her looking at him with tears in her eyes. "It'll be better soon. I promise." She is touching his face and he smells blood. Is she bleeding? No, it smells like Hissa blood. He's bleeding. When did he start bleeding?

She turns her attention back to his leg and opens a small tube and dumps the contents into a wound on his leg and then slams her hands back down over the wound, physically holding the edges together.

I'm wounded and I'm dying, he realizes and that sends a wave of panic through him.

"Box," he tells her desperately.

"I won't take your box," she assures him quickly, making him growl in frustration.

"Box needs to go," he tries to tell her. She needs to get the box to Bicoma. She needs to help him.

"Right, your box is important. I get it. Just hold onto it, and when you're feeling better you can take it where it needs to go."

"You take," he tells her. "Bicoma."

He feels her hands relax their grip on his leg, and she gives a little sigh. "Damn. I knew those nanos were worth the price." He wants to open his eyes and look, but that seems much too hard. He can feel the pain starting to retreat and tries one more time.

"Save us," he mumbles out. "Bicoma."

He feels her hand on his face. Her touch is soft and gentle. "You're safe, handsome."

He can smell his blood all over her, and under that, he can smell her. Sweet, feminine, and perfect. For a moment he thinks she smells like a Hissa, not human, and dreams he's found a female of his own.

At least I'll die with her scent to usher me to the afterlife, he thinks and slips into unconsciousness.

CHAPTER 2

Mian flops down into her pilot chair and lets out a big breath of air. This isn't the first time she's rescued people after a raider attack, but this is the first time it's put her through an emotional ringer. Usually, when she rescues people, they're alive and well, maybe bumps and bruises, but none of them have tried to die on her. At least none that were on a ship that hadn't been boarded yet. When raiders physically take over a civilian transport, all bets are off as to what she'll find when she retakes the ship. And she's seen some pretty bad things over the years.

She's never pulled someone onto her ship that was actively trying to die on her. This roaring, growly, green, hulking male is a first for her.

All she can do is sit there and stare at the big guy as she lets her system calm down. She's never seen anyone bleed that much and still be alive. There's a trail of blood leading down the length of the ship. There's also a pool of blood where he stood leaning against the wall. Finally, there's a small puddle of blood under her bunk. The sheet under him is soaked, and his pants are bright red. She's pretty sure one of his boots is full of blood also.

What a mess.

One of the rounds the raider fired must have sent a piece of shrapnel into his leg. She's amazed he made it as far through her ship as he did. Whatever species this guy belongs to, they're a tough people.

Which raises another question, what was this guy doing in a ship with no weapons flying through Raider Alley without any kind of escort? It's like he was trying to get attacked.

She got a good look at his ship when she'd passed by the first time and noticed it had no defensive weapons at all. Nothing. Not even a fuel discharge port to mix and disgorge fuel. It's the only defense some cheaper vessels have, but it can be effective if the attacking ship is close enough. Mixed fuel landing on a hull and eating away a ship's integrity has managed to make more than a few raiders back off.

But this guy's ship didn't even have that inexpensive form of attack. Sure, the ship was well made and sturdy as hell. It lasted a lot longer under raider fire than an average shuttle that size normally would. But being well built doesn't mean anything if you have no weapons to defend with.

"You got lucky, handsome," she tells him. "Whoever put you in this sector in a ship with no guns almost got you killed. I wasn't even planning to patrol here today. I was going to take the day off."

She thinks about the uneasy feeling that settled in her gut when she woke from her sleep cycle earlier. A feeling that pushed her to fire up her engines and take a tour around the system. Happy to jump into any fight with raiders, she didn't hesitate when she saw Hope under fire, but she hates to think what would've happened if she'd been even a minute later.

Looking down, she notices the blood on her hands and wrinkles her nose. She needs to clean both of them up. And the control room. And the hallway. And probably the rescue tube. This guy painted her ship in his blood.

Her eyes fall to the box now loosely clutched to his chest. Whatever's inside is important enough that this male wouldn't let go of it, even while she tortured him by pulling out that piece of metal without any numbing agent or pain killer.

Then, he changed his tune and tried to ask her to take the box somewhere. What kind of precious items are inside to make him so protective and then so insistent? He mentioned he wanted the box to go to Bicoma, but she couldn't imagine a reason for anyone to visit that unfriendly system. She leans forward in the chair and gently tugs the box away from him and hangs it up by one of the handles on the wall just above his head. She doesn't want him to panic if he wakes up and finds it missing.

She examines his armor. It's fancy and advanced, at least three generations newer than her battered gear. She gently starts pulling it off, revealing a sweat-soaked shirt under it. He's not wearing the arm or leg guards, and she can only assume he didn't have time to get them on.

She debates propriety for a moment, thinking about how she would want to be treated if she was unconscious. She certainly wouldn't want some stranger stripping her down. But she wants to get him cleaned up, not just the blood, but the drying sweat she's worried will give him a chill.

She's going to strip and clean him. If he's upset with her later, she can just return him to the debris field that's now his ship and tell him to find his way home.

Getting the chest armor off is a chore. After a lot of fighting and tugging, she finally manages to roll him back and forth enough to pull it completely free. The shirt under is soaking in sweat and hugs his body like a second skin. She's done wrestling, so instead of trying to get it off, she cuts the garment.

When faced with an unhindered view of his magnificent chest, she makes an involuntary sound of appreciation. He's nothing but muscles. She takes a moment to take a good look at this stranger. Obviously, he's not human. Not only are her kind rare outside the Earth's solar system, but his roar, the light green tint to his skin, blue scale pattern on his head, and massive size are dead giveaways.

She gently lifts one of his lips to get a closer look at his teeth. He's got large, sharp-looking canines on top and smaller, but just as sharp canines on the bottom. The two pairs of long teeth are slightly offset so when his jaws meet, the fangs don't inhibit chewing. Or biting. She releases his lips and sets her gaze on the rest of his face.

He's got high, sharp cheek bones and a narrow face, and even relaxed in sleep he looks fierce. There's a scar that runs from his forehead down the side on the edge of his face and ends just below his ear. Judging by how much it blends with the rest of his skin, she can only assume it's from an old injury. The width of the scar tells her the original injury was substantial. No wonder he was able to walk so far while bleeding out and with a piece of shrapnel in his leg. This guy has had practice with being severely wounded.

Unlike a human, there's no hair on his head. A scale-like pattern starts at a point on his forehead, and V's out from there, encompassing most of his head by the time it gets to the back of his neck. She can't tell if they are overlapping scales or a pattern on his skin. Her hands itch to touch him there and find out, but she resists the urge. She's already pushing the boundaries of decorum by stripping him while he can't refuse her or give consent.

And ogling him doesn't seem appropriate either. Where is her usual iron self-control? She forces herself to concentrate, to be clinical. He's a wounded warrior in need of care. That's all she should see him as. Straightening up, she looks down at his pants.

"It'll be easier just to cut the damn things off," she mutters and reaches for a knife, then stops. He's probably not wearing anything under the pants, and her face flushes a little at the thought.

She looks around and grabs one of the blankets she'd tossed off the bunk when she'd pulled it down earlier. She lays it across his lap and then goes to work cutting his pants off. She makes sure not to upset the blanket as she cuts the fabric starting at the hip and then all the way down. Once both sides are cut, she's able to tug the pants off him and toss the ruined clothing aside. His legs are completely bare now and just like his chest, they're nothing but muscles.

When her eyes fall on the wound, all lustful thoughts vanish. She knows there's a chance he won't wake up, even with those expensive nanos working hard to heal him. She needs to clean off the leg and bind it tightly, giving the nanos the best conditions to work in. She wishes she had bought synthetic blood last time she had the chance, but just buying the nanos broke her budget.

She pulls a cleaning cloth out of the med kit and starts wiping away the blood on his leg. Once it's gone and she can see the wound clearly, she grimaces. It stretches almost from his groin to his knee. She glances over at the piece of metal she pulled out of him. It's still covered in his blood and looks to be a shredded piece of engine shielding.

Pulling out a large bandage, she wraps the wound tightly, making sure the skin on either side of the cut meets. When the nanos are ready to seal the outer area of the wound, it will be easier if both sides line up. If the merchant who sold the nanos is to be believed, within one cycle the wound will be sealed and within two cycles the damaged muscles and other tissue will be good as new. Although he will be left with one hell of a scar. The literature on the nanos made it very clear that they aren't programmed to minimize scar tissue. She has a strong suspicion this guy won't mind the scar.

Finished with that part of her duties, she turns to cleaning off the rest of him. He's got blood on his face where she touched him, and his chest is still damp from sweat. She carefully cleans off the blood, then grabs a towel and dries his chest. Finally, she pulls off his boots, blanching when one makes a sucking noise as it comes off because it's so full of blood. She'll clean the boot later. For now, she concentrates on getting the last of the blood off his body.

After she's done, she fetches one of her blankets from her cabin and tucks it around him. "That's all I can do," she tells him with a soft pat on his chest. "The rest is up to you and the nanos. Try not to die on me, you're too pretty to leave this world and I'd hate to think I wasted my nanos." She's not surprised when he doesn't react to her words.

Flopping down in the pilot's chair with a sigh, she turns her attention to the navigation system and checks their progress. It'll be a full cycle before they are within hailing range of the nearest station. Thoughtfully, she looks back at the sleeping giant and wonders what she'll do if he's poor. His ship was expensive, and his armor is top of the line, but the lack of weapons on the ship, and no crew makes her think he might have stolen it. Is he AWOL from his military unit? A deserter? A thief?

If he's a thief, then there's probably a bounty on him and she might make back some credits. But the thought of him being a criminal fills her with disappointment.

Her eyes wander up to the box, and her imagination takes over. Maybe he's on a secret mission. That would make much more sense and explain a ship with no weapons and why he's alone. Probably something to do with the contents of his box and the Bicoma system.

He was strong and brave when she had to tend to his wound. Unlike his stoic silence, she would've been screaming if he had to pull a hunk of sharp metal out of her leg. And there's no way she could be still. She knows that for a fact. She punched out a med tech once when he tried to treat a wound years ago. She still feels bad about that, but he should have warned her before he touched her.

Wincing at the memory, she finds herself studying the stranger's face. She knows she shouldn't touch him. He's unconscious and under her care, but she reaches out to cup the male's jaw with her hand anyway. Muscles move under her hand, and it looks like he's trying to talk. He must be dreaming; she thinks and leans over.

"Don't leave me," he whispers in his sleep, his deep voice so faint she strains to make out the words. "Sweet female, don't make me beg." His head turns slightly, and his soft lips kiss the inside of her wrist. "You smell so good. Ask for anything but let me hold you."

She rears back and feels her face flush. He's dreaming about a lover. Despite feeling like she intruded on something very personal, she can't help but wonder what it would be like to be the woman he begs to stay.

Mortified by her wayward thoughts, she turns her attention back to her computer console and focuses on the few tasks she needs to do there. Once finished, she fetches another blanket from her room and settles back down in the chair. She can't leave him alone and not just because he's healing and vulnerable. But also, because there is no way she's going to let a stranger wake up alone in the control room of her ship where he could easily lock her out and take over.

She wiggles around in the chair a bit. She really should have paid to get the better chair last time she put in for repairs. "It's going to be an uncomfortable cycle," she mutters to herself, her gaze still focused on him.

He whispers something else in his sleep, and she's amazed to see the blanket over his crotch rise a little.

Well, she thinks, *at least he's got enough blood to have an erection. That's got to be a good sign.*

She grins at him. "I guess this is going to be an uncomfortable cycle for both of us."

CHAPTER 3

Halin wakes suddenly and jerks to a sitting position. He hits his head on the blunt corner of something. With a roar of pain, he falls back, clutching his head with both hands.

"Oh crap!" a startled female voice exclaims, and he feels warm hands tugging his hands away from his head. "Let me see, damn it!" she demands. He lets her pull his hands away but only so he can better look at the owner of the voice. Recent events flood back to him when he sees her face and despite the pain, he smiles. Not only is he alive, but the lovely creature from his dreams is real and hovering over him with a concerned expression on her beautiful face.

"You didn't break the skin, but you're going to have a bruise," she tells him, examining his head. She pokes the spot, and he gives a little growl of pain.

"That didn't help," he mutters and pushes her hand away. He looks up to see what he hit and finds the genetics box he fought so hard to save. "Moons preserve me. I didn't lose it with Hope."

"You sure had a death grip on that thing," she tells him following his gaze to the box. "I guess that wasn't the best place to put it. I just wanted to make sure you saw it when you woke up."

He looks back at the woman and notices her face looks pale and there are dark circles under her eyes. "How long have I been asleep?"

"About a full cycle and a half," she tells him, glancing over at the control console. He looks around and realizes he's sitting on a bunk in the control room of her small ship. The pilot's chair is turned to face the bunk, and a discarded bright green blanket hangs off one armrest. Did this female stay up for over a cycle to tend to him?

He feels a little dizzy. Maneuvering so he can lean his back against the bulkhead, he takes a few deep breaths. The blanket slides off him, revealing he's naked, but he doesn't reach to pull it back over himself. He's a Hissa warrior, and nothing in their culture is shy. He watches with amusement as she stares at his lap and then looks up to find him watching her. Her face turns an interesting shade of pink, and she looks away.

"I had to cut your pants off," she mumbles, looking anywhere but at him.

"Why would that be?" he asks with interest. He hopes the answer has something to do with her wishing to examine his worthiness as a bed partner. He hasn't bedded anyone in a long time, and this female isn't just lovely to look at but also smells so good his mouth is watering.

To his surprise, she drops back into the chair and leans forward, gently touching a scar on his thigh. "This," she states simply. "It looks like it's healing well," she murmurs and gently presses to test the scar tissue.

Distracted from the lush female, he leans forward to look at his leg. "That wasn't there before," he grunts.

"You don't remember the giant piece of shrapnel embedded in your thigh?"

He brings his eyes up to meet hers and feels caught by her gaze. Her eyes are an indescribable color. At best he'd compare them to gems, glittering green macko gems. But even that doesn't do them justice. He's not sure there's a word in either Hissa or Space Standard that accurately defines the color.

"Your eyes are like macko crystals," he whispers to her, leaning closer to her face. "But even lovelier. I've never seen such a color." She rears back, and he sits up, hoping he hasn't offended her.

"Thanks," she replies.

She seems wary of him and maybe slightly flustered. She shouldn't be. He's sure many males notice and comment on her loveliness.

"Let's, uh, concentrate on you though. Are you feeling a little dizzy or do you have a headache? I've got some basic pain relievers."

Taking his attention from her, he takes an inventory of his body. His leg doesn't hurt much. Mostly it feels sore, like he badly bruised it in a sparring match. He does have a headache, and he feels a little lightheaded, even though he's sitting down. If he's this weak after such a prolonged sleep, his wound must have been grievous.

"I don't remember getting hurt," he murmurs to her.

She gives a little shrug. "Considering you decorated a good portion of my ship with your blood, a little memory loss isn't surprising. I wasn't sure I got to you soon enough," she admits. "I don't have any synthetic blood, so you're going to be dizzy until your body recoups."

"How much did I, uh, decorate?" Halin asks, and she winces.

"Let's just say, the last time I saw someone bleed that much, he was already a corpse by the time I got there," she tells him bluntly. He tries to straighten up a little, puffs out his chest, and gives her a wide cocky grin.

"I need you to repeat that to a vid capture. I'm going to want to be able to have proof later that I heroically survived a severe injury," he says, and she looks puzzled.

"Is that so you don't get in trouble because the ship was destroyed?"

"No, so I can brag to my friends," he tells her and feels elated when she laughs. It's a clear, lovely sound, and it seems to have a particular effect on his cock. He grabs a blanket and drops it over his lap.

"My name is Halin," he tells her as he taps the fingers of his left hand just under his throat, a traditional greeting among warriors or competitors. "Second male of the family Tormid."

"I'm Mian," she responds with a smile and copies his tap. "I guess I'm the only female to the family Garmin, but now I go by the name Sorrow." He notes that she's no longer wearing her armor, and he can see the curvy outline of her body through her tight clothing.

"Mian," he murmurs, rolling the sound of her name on his tongue. "That's a lovely name." Her skin flushes again, and he wonders why but enjoys the effect. When she changes color, it makes her look even lovelier. Does she do that whenever she receives a compliment or is it just him?

"Uh, thanks," she responds.

He wants to ask if she changes color all over or just her face, but before he can speak, she asks him a question of her own.

"What were you doing in the middle of Raider Alley in a ship without guns?"

"Raider Alley?" Did he misunderstand the Space Standard words?

"That sector you were attacked in is called Raider Alley," she explains. "By your expression, I'm guessing you didn't know. It's gotten pretty bad recently, ever since the Polia system opened up trade. Now there's a ton of raiders preying on ships going between the Polia system and Wint. More of us bounty hunters show up every day, but there's still not enough of us to put a dent in the raider traffic."

"We didn't know this area was so dangerous," he explains. "But it makes no difference. We were instructed to travel in an unarmed ship. We didn't have a choice."

"Well, you ended up being a tasty target. You said we. Did you mean that there were others on the ship with you?"

Halin feels a shock of fear go through him. "Yes, my two crew mates. They were in sleep pods, and I launched them both to try and keep them safe. Did you see the pods?"

"I take it you had the sleep pods that can act as life pods?" Mian murmurs as she shakes her head sadly. "I'm sorry. I didn't see any pods. But we're close enough to Wint Station that I can check in there and see if any of the patrols picked them up or if there's chatter about ransom demands." She turns her chair to face the control console and starts fiddling. Soon she's talking as she scans her display.

"Looks like one pod landed safely on a small planet being geo mapped for mining. Your government has already arranged transport for that man back to your homeworld. Another Hissa was just sold at a slave auction. It doesn't look like your government knows about it yet. He might not be one of your crew mates, but I've never met a Hissa before in this sector. That means chances are, he's one of your guys.

"Slavery?" Halin is horrified. "Tiran or Lazil, sold as a slave?"

She nods absently as she keeps reading, then turns to look at him with a big grin. "I wouldn't worry too much. A hauler named Mara Lost bought him. She's human like me. I've never met her, but I know her by reputation. She was a slave herself, so if she bought him, then it's unlikely she'll abuse him. I can send a message to your government so they can contact her to buy him back."

"How can you be so sure she won't abuse my crewmate if you've never met this woman?" Halin demands.

"I keep a close eye on the civil disturbance reports. It can be a good way to find raiders trying to get parts or doing reconnaissance of a station or port. She's popped up a couple of times for fighting, and it's almost always because of slavery. Your guy is in good hands, I'm sure. And you shouldn't have a problem buying him back because he went cheap at auction. Only twenty credits. Damn, that's sad." She looks over at him with a grin. "If he looks anything like you, I'd pay at least thirty."

"That means I'm the last left to finish my mission," he murmurs, ignoring her innuendo for the moment. His mission isn't finished, and his entire race is in peril.

"I can drop you off at Wint, and you can contact your people," she tells him. "If you're going to try to make it back to Bicoma, I'd suggest a full military escort or at the very least a sturdy gunship like my Fortune." She absently strokes her hand across the control console and smiles.

Watching her delicate hand move over the shiny metal sends blood to inappropriate places.

Then her words register, and he scoots forward on the bunk until he's sitting right on the edge. She looks over and startles a little. They're so close their noses almost touch. He fights the overwhelming urge to just lean forward and put his lips on hers. Her eyes seem to darken, and she gives a little gasp as he draws even closer to her.

This female is perfect. Skilled, capable, and in possession of a well-outfitted gunship. And she's beautiful and smells delectable.

"You could take me," he whispers, overjoyed at the idea.

"To bed?" she asks. He notices her eyes are a little unfocused, and she seems like she's panting slightly. *I'm not the only one affected. Good to know.*

"I can hire you," he murmurs. "To take me to Bicoma."

As if a container of cold water was suddenly dumped over her head, she rears back. Her expression is incredulous. "I might be a bounty hunter, but I'm not insane," she declares.

"Why is going to Bicoma insane?"

She blinks at him for a moment. "You're asking me that question? Do you not know what happens when foreign ships enter Bicoma space?"

He shakes his head. None of the reports he read included descriptions of Bicoma defenses or weapons. He just knows they're well defended.

"Right, you don't know because no one knows!" she almost shouts and throws her hands up with exasperation. "Aggressive ships go in, and they never come out."

"That can't be right," Halin disagrees, thinking about the reports he's read. "I know delegations from other species have met the Bicoma and visited their home system."

"Sure, diplomats get to come and go, but you know what they report. Nothing! They never see anything. They can't explain how the Bicoma protect their space. Before I was born, the Anavac decided they were going to invade the Bicoma system. They all disappeared. The entire armada just vanished. Long-range scanners from the observation ships said they could see all the ships one moment and the next they were all just gone."

Halin's impressed but undaunted. "Then it's good I have permission to be there."

"But I don't," Mian emphasizes each word and jabs a finger into her chest. "And the Fortune doesn't have permission. Need I remind you she's a gunship? Not some innocent-looking civilian transport. She's made for one thing, going into battle. If we wander into Bicoma space, we're going to get disappeared fast. I'm not interested in dying, so thanks, but no thanks."

Before she can draw any further away from him, Halin grabs one of her hands and clasps it loosely between his. She doesn't struggle, just freezes and stares at her caged hand. Her hand feels small and delicate as he runs his thumb across her wrist.

"I can get permission for you and Fortune," he assures her with confidence although he's not sure that's true at all. "The fastest way there is through Raider Alley, and I'll need you. Getting Hissa ships here will take too much time. This mission is important for all my people."

He can see her hesitate, thinking about it. But then she shakes her head again. "I just can't risk it. If they get a look at Fortune and decide she's a threat, we go poof. We don't get a chance to explain or apologize. We just disappear."

She tugs at her hand, and he reluctantly releases her. He glances around, giving himself a moment to think. He notices his armor chest piece on the floor next to a neatly stacked pile of hers. He remembers the state of her armor, old and worn. The ship is an older model too, well maintained but still patched and run down.

He nods his head to his armor. "Your body armor is rather old."

She stiffens and scowls. "It works just fine."

"I have a business proposition for you." She looks like she's about to object, but he holds his hand up to silence her and is pleasantly surprised when it works. "There's no way for me to get to Bicoma without going through raider space." Halin attempts to appeal to the hunter in her. "I would get attacked again."

"You're correct," she agrees, now looking confused. "But I thought you said you couldn't arrive in a ship with weapons."

"Considering what happened, I'm sure they will grant me dispensation to arrive in whatever ship can get me there safely. If you take me there, I'll make sure Hissa pays you very well." He sweeps his eyes back to her armor. "Wouldn't it be nice to buy a new suit? The armor you have doesn't have the full 360 heads-up range-finding display in the helm or the advanced biometric system to seal wounds." He can see her eyes glimmer with interest, so he pushes his advantage and points to his own much newer chest armor. "I can buy you a suit just like it." He can see she's tempted and tries to sweeten the offer even more. "And perhaps a plasma rifle?"

Her eyes widen, and he knows he's got her. "With the extra-large recharge pack? And extra cartridges?"

He grins wide. He has nothing but admiration for a woman who knows her weapons. "Of course I wouldn't dream of not including recharge packs and cartridges," he tells her quickly. For other women, he might promise jewels and other precious items; for Mian, it's all about the weapons. "And I'm sure I can swing a few other things as well."

She's silent for a few moments, regarding him with an expression he can't quite read. He wonders if he should offer her a new ship. He knows there are several smaller gunships in the Hissa military, and it would be easy to get one of those for her. He has permission to utilize an extreme amount of credits and resources to accomplish his mission.

But the same intuition that hasn't led him astray yet and is the reason he's lead on this mission tells him to be quiet and just wait.

If I offer too much, she will assume I'm lying, he realizes as she glances over to his armor one more time and then turns back to him with a small, tight smile.

"Shiny new armor," he says with a broad grin, showing off his long canines, a sign of virility among his species. Some Hissa males have their canines artificially lengthened, but he's never had to. His have always been long.

She looks momentarily surprised at his fangs but recovers quickly and smiles. Her teeth are rather flat, but that doesn't detract from her beauty.

"You'll pay for fuel and docking fees?" she demands, and he nods his head.

"That's standard for contract transport," he agrees.

"Assuming the Bicoma don't make us vanish, where do I drop you to terminate the contract? I looked up Hissa, and it's much too far away from Raider Alley for my comfort. I'm already going to lose a lot of hunting time taking you to Bicoma."

Halin fights to keep from frowning. He wants her to take him back to Hissa but knows that's a losing battle. He does a quick calculation in his head. "You can take me back to Wint Station. I can arrange transport from there."

She nods in agreement. "That's a reasonable distance. I accept your terms." She holds out her hand to him, and he stares at it uncomprehendingly. "It's a human custom," she explains. "Hold out your hand like mine." He does and watches with interest as she voluntarily places her palm against his and clasps his hand. She moves the two hands up and down a few times and then releases her grip, but Halin doesn't.

Using her hand as an anchor, he leans closer to her and whispers, "Let's create a new human-Hissa tradition to mark the occasion."

He brushes his lips over hers, and when she doesn't struggle, he presses, sliding his tongue along the slit of her lips. She gives a little sound of surprise and opens her mouth to him. He's overwhelmed by the taste of her. If he thought her smell was pleasurable, it pales in comparison to her taste.

He bedded a human woman once. She worked on a brothel ship that traveled from planet to planet and made a stop in orbit around Hissa to service the female-deprived men. She commanded a small fortune for her time, as humans are so rare, and she was in great demand. She'd been kind and willing. His time with her was pleasant, but Mian is something else entirely. She might be a human woman also, but her smell and taste are nothing like the brothel worker. Mian is something he could become addicted to.

It's women like Mian that poets write about when they speak of perfection.

She makes another sound, and the smell of her arousal hits his nose. It's all he can do to keep from stripping her bare and pulling her under him.

Don't push her yet, his intuition tells him. *If you go too fast, she'll pull away. You might have her once, but she won't let you close again.*

With a level of willpower that he's sure would make every instructor he ever had in the military proud, he manages to pull away and release her hand. It's difficult, but he gives her an unconcerned smile as he casually leans back against the bulkhead.

"I don't suppose you've got any clothes I could wear?"

CHAPTER

4

Mian knows she's staring at Halin with her mouth open like a landed pessio fish, but her brain has temporarily gone off line. Her entire body feels on fire with a level of dampness between her legs she's never experienced.

She's always been a sexual creature. When her mother caught her masturbating as a young child, she sat her down and explained human sexuality to her and the basic rules of conduct. For a long time after her parents' death, she felt nothing. Years later when she was ready to experiment, she found a compatible male and gave sex a try. It hadn't been anything particularly memorable or even enjoyable. After a second try, she gave up and decided to stick to her own hands and toys instead.

But this is different. She wants to push this Hissa down on the small bunk, tear the sheet off him, and demand he put his mouth and hands all over her. When he'd deepened the kiss, she assumed that was what was about to happen, only to have him pull away, apparently unaffected by the interaction.

She looks down to where the sheet forms a tent over his erection and knows he's aroused. She looks back up at his face, and he shrugs his shoulders. She's silent for a moment and then just jumps in. She's never been a retiring, shy type of person.

"You seem ready to have sex," she points out softly, and he nods gravely.

"I'm eager to mate with you," he tells her simply. "But I wouldn't just bed a female. We must have discussions and know each other, or it won't be satisfying. We need to have a Knowing Period."

"Is this a Hissa custom?" she asks and can't help it when her eyes wander back down to his crotch.

"Yes," he tells her. "Mating without knowing isn't acceptable."

"You must not get laid very often," she mutters. "Your women put up with this?" His expression suddenly turns stony, and she knows she unwittingly hit a nerve.

"There are no Hissa women," he tells her flatly.

She takes a sharp breath. How can there be no Hissa women? The quick bit of research she did on Hissa shows they are a species with binary sexes, requiring one male and one female to produce offspring. Do they grow their children in vats like she was? Why would they only produce males?

He frowns and speaks before she can start riddling him with questions. "I didn't want this to be our first knowledge exchange, but I guess it's inevitable." He takes a deep breath and closes his eyes. His face looks like he's remembering something painful.

"When I was a child, there was a plague that hit Hissa. We call it the Great Death. Before we could develop a vaccine or cure, every single one of our females and half our male population succumbed to the disease."

She remains silent, so he continues. "In my family, my two sisters died first. They were so small, so fragile. In the last hour of their lives, they could barely breathe. They went so quickly that the mender didn't even make it to our house in time to examine them. They just closed their eyes and never opened them again."

"Then my mother fell ill, but she was stronger and that made it so much worse for her. By then, we knew the virus was a death sentence. Our menders and scientists were working night and day, but it takes time to find a cure or a vaccine. My father, brother, and I tried to comfort her, but she was so scared and in so much pain. At the end, she begged us to kill her to end her suffering. We couldn't. We were too selfish. We did everything to extend her life, to give us more time with her. A little more time for our scientists to find a way to save her. But she finally went into a coma. Not long after that, she crossed the starry veil."

Without giving herself time to think, she reaches out to take his hand in hers, clutching it gently with one hand and stroking her other hand up and down his forearm. He doesn't pull away from her embrace, and she's relieved he accepts her comfort.

"If no females survived, how will your species survive?"

"That's the problem we've been wrestling with almost my entire life. At first, the planet was in mourning. None of us could think outside of our pain. Not only did we lose all our women and numerous men, but many males who survived refused to live without the females they loved. Suicide became an epidemic. We lost so many so quickly. It was devastating."

"What about Decanted children?" she asks. "That's what we call children who are grown back in the Earth system. Human scientists figured out how to grow kids in vats. And while they're being grown, they can be programmed with language and knowledge before they're even decanted. You could potentially grow an entire generation of Hissa."

He shakes his head. "We've heard of that technology and even tried to replicate it, but all our efforts have failed. Hissa can't be Decanted." She frowns at his words, feeling nothing but empathy for the Hissa. When she lost her parents, her world was shattered. What would it be like to lose so many? To have an entire civilization decimated in such a way is unimaginable.

He jerks his head to the box hanging over the bunk, and she follows his gaze. "There are biological samples of tens of thousands of Hissa men and women in there," he explains. "It took us years of negotiating, but the Bicoma finally agreed to meet with us. We aren't sure they can help, but their technology is much farther advanced than any other species. I'm afraid they might be our last hope."

"What are they asking for in return?" she questions with real worry. The Bicoma rarely trade, and the few deals she's heard about were extreme.

"We don't know yet," he admits. "That's why the three of us were sent. Tiran is an expert programmer and our most valued computer engineer. Lazil is a scientist, one of our most brilliant. We hoped to trade some of their skills and Hissa wealth for answers."

"Your people sent an engineer and a scientist," she murmurs thoughtfully. "Why did they send you? What are your skills?" She sees his face flash surprise; then he smiles, and she knows he's about to tell her a half-truth.

"I'm a commander in the Hissa military," he explains. "I was sent to get them there and back safely."

She eyes him thoughtfully. "You were sent as protection?" She narrows her eyes. "I have a feeling you're not telling me everything."

He narrows his own eyes back at her. "You doubt my prowess as a warrior?" he asks, his tone full of mock outrage. "When I'm recovered, we can spar. I can show you my skill. I promise to be gentle with you."

She barks out a laugh. "I promise to take it easy on you too."

He chuckles at her comeback, but she notices strain showing on his face. His body is still recovering, and he needs rest. She pops up and strides over to a storage cabinet, then rummages around until she finds clothes that might fit him. She throws the bundle of clothing, which he easily catches.

"See if those will work for you," she commands, surprised when he just glares down at the clothes in his hand.

"Do these belong to your male?" he asks, looking up at her.

"I don't have a male or crew," she tells him quickly, wondering why it's important to her that he knows she's not in a relationship.

Because you want to climb on that dick and go for a ride, a little voice in her head states. She hopes she's not blushing because the Naughty Mian in her head has no filter.

He smiles and looks relieved. "That's good." He stands, and the blanket slides off him. She turns quickly, pretending to fiddle with organizing the cabinet. She knows if she looks at him in all his naked glory, there's no way he's getting out of the room unmolested.

"These will be adequate until I can buy something better," he grumbles.

She turns around and almost laughs. The shirt fits, but it's old and there are several holes in it she didn't notice before. But the pants are far from suitable. They are so tight the seams are stretching, and she can see the outline of him quite clearly. She has to force herself to swallow. She wonders how long it will take him to feel like he "knows" her well enough so they can have sex. Considering her reaction to him already, she's sure it's going to be hot, intense, and all kinds of enjoyable, unlike her past experiences.

Human compatible males are hard to come by in this section of the universe, and it's been a long time since she's had anyone in her bed but herself.

"We aren't far from Wint," she assures him. "It's a big station and there's a market area. I'm sure we can find everything we need there." He nods and sways a little on his feet. She rushes up, puts one of his arms over her shoulder, and grabs his chest to steady him. She ignores the wonderful smell of him and starts guiding him out of the cockpit and down the hall.

"I think I might need to rest some more," he mumbles.

"A big, soft bed is just down the corridor waiting for you," she promises. He nods, and she can tell he's concentrating on trying to stay upright, and not lean on her too much.

When they finally reach her quarters, he looks around the room with an expression of intense surprise.

Unlike the rest of the gray, utilitarian ship, this room is brightly decorated. The walls are painted in deep gold, with scarlet drapes of fabric falling from the ceiling and artfully gathered at the floor. Ornate bowls full of glowing crystals hang from the ceiling to light the room in a soft, warm, yellow glow. A cerulean blue rug takes up most of the floor space, so plush their feet sink into it as she helps him to the bed.

Thankfully, they reach the large, rectangular bed that overwhelms the small room without incident. Reaching out his fingers to touch the frame, his face is full of wonder.

"It's real wood," he exclaims softly. The bed is one of Mian's pride and joy. No small ship bunk for her. Instead, she commissioned an artist to build her a big wooden bed with an elaborate headboard covered in intricate carvings. She didn't stop there. She searched for the softest fabrics to cover it and a coverlet so plush she occasionally enjoys stretching out on it naked.

He carefully sits on the bed, and she can see he's sweating a little from the short journey. "Everything in here is so bright."

She looks around at all the vivid colors she's combined in the cabin and winces a little. "Sorry. I like bold colors."

"It's captivating," he assures her. "Hissa like bright colors too. When there were women, we showed our affection for them by buying them the softest, brightest, nicest fabrics we could. Women were the heart of us. They were our beauty, our love, and our souls. We're nothing without them." He glances around him. "My mother and sisters would have loved this room." He runs his hands over her coverlet and gives a small, sad smile. "And they would have adored this as well."

Mian's heart goes out to Halin and all the Hissa. "It's hard, losing so many in such a short period of time."

He looks up at her with eyes so troubled her breath catches. "How does a species survive when their heart is gone?"

Mian feels helpless at his question so she does what she always does when she can't solve one problem; she fixes another. "Let's get you into bed," she pulls back the covers and encourages him to slide in. "You'll feel a lot better after a long sleep." He clumsily wiggles himself over until she can pull the covers up to his chest.

He grins up at her. "This bed appears big enough for both of us. You could join me, and we could talk more."

"Rest," she commands. "We'll do more getting to know each other on our way to Bicoma after you're feeling better."

Nodding, he relaxes against her plush pillows and gives a sigh of contentment. "It smells like you," he murmurs. "It's very pleasurable." She's about to speak, but then she realizes he's asleep, so she tiptoes out of the room. She closes the hatch gently and makes her way back to the control room. This might prove to be the most interesting assignment she's ever had.

CHAPTER 5

By the time they reach Wint, Halin feels markedly better and impatient to get on the station. He crosses the dock with long strides, eager to reach the market and start buying things for the lovely creature—

Looking down, he finds she's no longer walking next to him. He stops and turns to search for her, only to have the small human run right into him with enough force to jolt him back a step. Flustered, she pulls away from him. Popping her hands on her hips, she gives him a little scowl.

"Where's the damn fire?" she growls.

"There's a fire?" he asks, looking around quickly, wondering if Wint is under attack.

"It's an old Earth expression." With a wave of her hand, her scowl disappears. "It means, why are you in such a rush?"

"There are things we must buy," he explains with a grin.

She gives him a skeptical look. "You want to go shopping?"

"Who doesn't like shopping for weapons and armor?" he responds.

She gives him an answering grin. "Good point."

"And we must buy you new clothes," he insists and takes her hand to tug her along as he starts walking again, but at a more sedate pace. He needs to remember her smaller stature. She'll need to jog to keep up with him if he walks too fast. He's elated when she doesn't try to tug her hand out from his, but she does voice a protest.

"I don't need clothes. You're the one that needs clothes, Mr. Tight Pants."

"Then we both need to buy clothes," he amends.

She shakes her head again and stops, forcing him to either drag her along or stop as well. He halts and regards her curiously when her expression turns tense.

"I don't need clothes," she tells him again. "I just want the armor and plasma rifle you promised."

"Of course," he answers, understanding dawning. "I'm not trying to replace one item for another. I'll buy the things we agreed on as part of the deal, but I wish to buy you clothing as part of our Knowledge Period. It's what a Hissa male does for his female."

She eyes him skeptically. "I thought we were going to talk."

"We'll do that also, but buying you clothing will make me happy," he explains, which is true. He doesn't add that the Knowing Period happens when the male and female in question live together and do everything a couple would. It was a common practice during the weeks when a male and female lived together to see if they were biologically and emotionally compatible. If they found each other desirable and compatible, they would form a Family Pact and potentially have children.

He doesn't want to spook her and mentioning anything more permanent than sharing a bed a few times might make her wary of him. He might be twisting Hissa customs a bit, but it doesn't matter.

He's not lying to her, just creating new customs to fit a new relationship. After all, there aren't any Hissa women to woo any longer, so creating new protocols seems appropriate.

"Don't you want to make me happy? I have credits and giving you clothing will make me happy," he presses.

"I guess we can buy me clothes too," she agrees hesitantly.

"Good," he says cheerily and tugs her along, keeping his strides short. "Let's get weapons first."

"Right over there," she points to a shop with several sets of armor displayed in the windows. Now it's her turn to be eager as she drags him forward, nearly running to get to the shop. "I wonder if they have the ones with the dimmerion components. I've read the advert and stats for it. The thing is almost rated for a class two hit, and the dimmerion components means it's resistant to electric fields, radiation, or magnetic interference."

She's so excited he's surprised she's not skipping. He chuckles as she pulls him into the shop, then drops his hand to start fondling armor. He starts looking too, knowing he needs to replace the missing legs and arm pieces to his set.

"Mian!" a voice exclaims, and a Fielden is suddenly grabbing her around the waist, nuzzling her with his bulbous, eyeless face. The entire top half of a Fielden's head is a translucent dome that acts both as their method of seeing and hearing. They can't speak with their mouths. Instead, he wears a small translation box that voices the meaning of the noises coming from inside his skull.

Acting on instinct, Halin grabs the Fielden by his thin arm and rips him away from Mian with a roar of displeasure. The Fielden stumbles back with a cry of surprise and pain, coming up hard against a display of weapons components.

Halin puts himself between Mian and this unknown male. "My female," he growls.

"Back off!" Mian yells at him, grabbing his arm and swinging him around.

He's surprised by her strength, but it doesn't stop him. He wraps his arms around her and pushes her back against a wall. Then he turns to put his body between her and the threat.

"Mine," he states again with another growl. He feels Mian become motionless, pinned between his big body and the wall. He thinks her stillness means she understands he's trying to protect her from potential danger.

He's wrong.

A sharp blow to the back of his knee along with a harsh shove sends him flying into a rack of clothing. He ends up on the ground, tangled in insulation suits. She takes a step forward to stand over him, her face full of fury. Maintaining eye contact with him, she points to the Fielden who's standing on shaking legs and making distressed chittering noises the translation box can't turn into words.

"That's Moriv," she tells him in a harsh voice. "He's a friend. You just attacked one of my dearest friends."

He looks back over to the Fielden and realizes the noises the creature is making are from fear. He acted out of instinct and now he's done damage.

His natural charm and charisma desert him as he gapes at Mian. "I'm sorry," he stammers. "I didn't think I—"

She cuts him off. "Out!" She points to the door of the shop. "I need to talk to Moriv. You get out!"

Halin stumbles to his feet and takes a small lurching step toward her. "Let me make amends."

She shakes her head adamantly. "No. What you did is inexcusable. Fieldens aren't hardy creatures. You could have hurt him." He feels his heart sink at her words. Will she sever the contract now? Will she leave him here on Wint? He's not ready to be parted yet. He opens his mouth to plead again, but the look of rage on her face makes him stop, drop his head, and shuffle out the door.

There's only one entrance to the shop, so he's sure when she finishes with Moriv she won't be able to slip past him and back to the ship. He paces outside the shop, furious with himself and silently berating his actions.

It was instinct to guard Mian against a perceived threat. The sight of Moriv touching her made him feel insane for a moment. He saw the Fielden as a threat to his precious female.

His female? Why was he thinking in terms of *his*?

That thought brings him up short. Is that what he wants, for her to love him? He delves into his mind and finds he already loves her. He fell in love with her the moment she touched him. The moment he realized the wonderful smell filling his lungs was her. He only vaguely remembers being wounded and feeling intense pain. But he remembers her touch with crystal clarity. Can love happen so fast?

He remembers his father telling him that it had only taken one day to fall in love with his mother.

"She smelled so good, and I couldn't imagine a life where I didn't wake up every morning and go to bed every night with her body in my arms, and her smell in my nose," his father explained during their mourning ceremony. "I knew the first day. I knew I could never love anyone else. We just know, son. The females take a little longer, but we males, we just know."

The more he thinks about it, the more he realizes that he wants this female to enter into a Family Pact with him, even though she's not Hissa. Could he talk her into it? Would it matter to her if they can't have any young together? He long ago accepted the fact he would never be able to have young of his own, but would Mian be content with that?

He'll have to interview her carefully. If she is dead set on raising children, perhaps they can find an orphan to adopt. Or even order a Decanted human to raise as their own. They could send Mian's genetics so the child would be half her. That is if she even wants to have children.

But it doesn't matter if she wants twenty or none. He's willing to accept just about anything to keep her in his life.

Of course, whether she wants children or not, he can't imagine she'd be content with living on Hissa without a job. But there's no reason she couldn't join the Hissa military. She's obviously skilled and they might even be able to command a ship together. He doesn't like the idea of her being in danger, but he can make sure they serve on a ship that's never sent into direct combat. The Hissa military is rarely needed now that they developed a deadly reputation. It would be a small matter to get them both assigned to ships used in the protection of convoys traveling to close trading partners.

He smiles at the thought. If she thinks the armor and plasma rifles are nice, he can't wait until she sees some of the Hissa battleships.

But none of that will happen if he can't keep his instincts from ruining everything before it's even begun. His intuition and bargaining skills are legendary among his people. He should be able to coax this female into loving him, especially if she's already physically attracted to him. If he could help a team of Hissa negotiate a visit to the Bicoma, convincing Mian to enter into a Family Pact with him should be possible.

He's thinking about seduction when she appears in the doorway of the shop with nothing in her hands. He watches her intensely, waiting to see what she'll do, but instead of glowering at him, she gives him a small smile and gestures him over.

"I just spent a ton of your credits," she tells him smugly. "Moriv tried to give me a good deal, but I demanded to be charged the full price plus a hefty percentage for extra profit."

Halin nods quickly. "Of course. It's the least I can do to make amends."

"And we are buying two plasma rifles and extra of everything," she continues, but he doesn't even blink an eye. The amount she spent is trivial compared to the budget he has access to.

"I can purchase all those things," he agrees.

"You're going to come in and apologize to Moriv in a very quiet, non-threatening way. Then you're going to try on some armor and pick out what you want."

He stands tall under her scrutiny. "I'll be polite," he assures her.

She turns and leads him in. The Fielden stands at the far end of the shop. He's stopped shaking but looks anxious, and it's obvious he doesn't want Halin to come too close. Knowing he needs to make amends, he locks his hands behind his back and drops his gaze to the floor, thinking he read somewhere that direct eye contact can make Fielden uncomfortable.

"Trader Moriv," he begins, hoping it's an appropriate term of respect for a Fielden. "I humbly beg your forgiveness. I acted hastily and out of fear for my m—" he just manages to keep from saying 'my mate.' That was close. He starts again. "Out of fear for the female Mian. I now know I acted erroneously, and you'd never hurt her, but I'm sure you would feel just as protective if an unknown male grasped a female near you."

A flurry of sound comes from the Fielden's dome, and the box takes time to start the translation. Halin waits patiently. "Warrior Halin, I know of the Hissa's plight and understand you might feel protective of females because of it. I would never hurt Mian. She's protected my family when we were most vulnerable. I owe her a debt I'll never be able to repay. She requested I forgive you, and I will do so. But you must understand this, you are not welcome in my shop without her present."

Considering Mian was the reason for his actions, he thinks the Fielden's request is a foolish one but doesn't say that out loud. "I readily agree to your terms and thank you for your forgiveness." Halin looks over to Mian, who's smiling.

"Well done," she nods and then points to a section of the shop. "Go find a suit you like. I've already picked out mine." That last sentence is delivered with a little gleeful smile. She's excited about the purchase of new armor.

Could this female be any more perfect?

"Certainly, but may I ask a question?" He turns his attention back to the Fielden who remains still and stiff next to a large display of small, edged weapons. "What did you mean when you said Mian protected you and your family?"

"We were coming back from our homeworld when we were attacked by raiders. She swooped in like an angry goddess and chased them away. She didn't leave us when they ran. She stayed with us until we got back here to Wint Station, even though that meant she lost her bounty. When I tried to pay her, she refused everything but some fuel. She won't let me give her the armor she wants. She won't let me give her weapons. Only lets me charge her for the cost of the weapons without profit added. I tried to get her to marry my son. I wished for her to join my family so she would also have financial protection. But she refused."

Halin can't help the shocked expression that crosses his face. The Fielden are only vaguely humanoid. There is no way they could be compatible with a human or Hissa.

"I can perceive your displeasure at the idea, but it would only be to make sure she had a family to care for her. Our kind believes in plural marriages. She would have married my son along with another Fielden female."

"You are my family," Mian tells him quickly. "And poor Tooval wouldn't last the ceremony. He's so scared of me."

"He adores you, just like the rest of the family. He's just intimidated by you," Moriv counters with a sound Halin thinks is a laugh. This must be an old joke between the two of them and for the first time, Halin honestly feels ashamed for attacking the kind Fielden who cares for Mian like a daughter.

"Thank you for appeasing my curiosity. I'll find the armor I wish to buy, and I would also like to buy any ammunition you might have for the guns on Fortune." The dome of Moriv's head turns a slight yellow color with interest.

"I have almost all that she requires. How much of each kind would you like?"

"At least two boxes of each," he answers easily and hears Mian choke.

"No," she intercedes quickly. "Just one box of each. I can't fit much more on Fortune." Her words remind Halin of the crowded corridors in the ship.

"Very well, two boxes of each and store one box here and send one box to the ship. When she comes back for supplies, you can have them ready for her."

Moriv's dome turns a deeper yellow, almost orange, and his body shakes a little. Halin wonders if he's managed to scare the Fielden again without meaning to. Then the thin creature starts rushing about, checking boxes and tagging items.

"Two of everything," he says as he rushes into the back. "Two of everything!"

"You just made him very happy." Mian laughs and gives Halin a gentle push. "Now go pick out gear. We still need to get food supplies and clothes, so hurry up."

It doesn't take long for Halin to decide on the pieces he wants and Mian arranges to have it all delivered to Fortune. The next stop is at a store that sells food and replicators. Mian buys a few boxes of ration packs using Halin's credit, but he's not happy and digs in his heels when she tries to leave.

"I want to buy something that tastes good," he demands. "Ration packs are barely edible."

"But they're nutritious and last forever. Look, I even got some of the chocolate-flavored ones. Those almost taste good."

"We will add to the order," he tells her and roams the shop. The shop owner eagerly follows him, making note of all his requests, both of them ignoring Mian's objections. He has no idea what chocolate is, but when he sees a few decorative boxes full of them, he has the owner add them too.

"You can't get those," Mian protests. "That stuff is real and expensive. It comes all the way from the Earth system. It's the only place it's cultivated. Besides, you don't even know if you like the flavor." She turns to the shop owner. "Take those last few items off. We don't need them."

"Don't listen to her. I'm paying, so I get to say what's on the list and what isn't," Halin retorts. He leans in close to Mian until his lips almost brush her ear. He deepens his voice and adds a slight purr. "I want to buy them for you. How am I to know you if I can't provide the things that you find most pleasurable?"

He can see her shiver with his words, clearly telling him that he's having the effect he wants. He leaves her there, her eyes a little glazed, and finishes the food order, then tugs her out of the shop, ignoring her slight frown.

"I don't know what game you're playing," she mutters as she stomps behind him. "But I better like the ending." Halin manages to keep from smirking at that comment and moves them quickly to the shop he saw earlier.

He sighs with happiness as they walk into the clothing store. All kinds of fabrics, styles, and colors surround them, and an eager clerk runs up to help. "I want to buy a gold soliman silk shirt and pants for her. Also, chovic cotton in deep purple, if you have it. I want them all fashioned in the Hissa style," he tells the clerk and notes the greedy look in the woman's eye.

"That's expensive," she warns.

"I have plenty of credits," he assures her. "And I want the same outfits in green, to match her eyes if you can."

"I thought we were here so you could get pants that aren't about to burst," she points out. "Not to buy me clothes I'll never wear."

"Why wouldn't you wear them?" he asks, feeling a little hurt. He wants to cover her lovely pale skin in soft fabrics. He wants to see the silk move against her body and watch it pool around her feet as she disrobes.

"I'm either in armor, insulation suits, or biosuits," she points out. "Or old maintenance clothes when I have to do chores. There's no reason for me to wear fancy outfits."

He shakes his head quickly. "There is a reason now. It would please me to see you wearing them. To watch the fabrics move against your skin." The fine hair on her arms is standing up on end. He's not sure, but he thinks this is a good reaction from her. "If you don't like them, you can sell them later," he promises.

"Fine. Sure, right." She makes a sound that might be part aggravation and part longing.

He buys a dozen sets of clothes for her, all in soft exotic fabrics and made in traditional Hissa styles. He buys himself a few dark brown sets of clothing and catches her frowning at him as he emerges from the fitting room.

"Why aren't you wearing bright blue, purple, scarlet, or gold?"

"I'm male," he explains simply.

She hazards a guess. "So, males don't do bright colors?"

"It's the females who are supposed to shine with lovely clothes, surrounded by bright colors," he says looking over at the drab shirt and trousers she's currently wearing. "Those colors do nothing to show your inner beauty. You should be wearing beautiful things to reflect your heart and soul to the world around you. You show great care to the most helpless. It's a noble trait showing you have a kind heart and a warrior's soul. I would have your clothes reflect your worth."

He looks up to see her eyes are slowly blinking at him, her mouth parted. "That was very…" She pauses and licks her lips. "That's very eloquent. Is that part of Hissa culture. The clothing thing?"

He shrugs his shoulders. "I'm Hissa."

She laughs. "I deserved that answer. Well, I think we've done enough damage to your credit accounts. Let's head back to the ship. We've got a lot of stuff to try and find room for."

Halin soon realizes she wasn't exaggerating. It takes them much longer than he likes to find places to store all the purchases on the already crowded gunship. The ammunition is by far the most difficult to stow. They end up stacking some of it in a way to act like stairs so it can be near the gun it feeds, but they can still get over it to go down the corridor.

When he takes the boxes of clothes to her room, he knows he's made the right decision as many of the colors he chose match the ones she used to decorate her personal space. She might be human, but she uses colors and textures like a Hissa female.

He drops the clothing boxes on the bed and hurries out to find her stowing the last of the food purchases. She turns to him with a big smile.

"We're fueled. And we're stocked with provisions and ammunition," she reports gleefully. "I'm ready to undock and set course for Bicoma."

Halin nods with a small frown, thinking about Bicoma and the plight of his people. She misunderstands his expression and places a reassuring hand on his arm.

"Don't worry. Unless the raiders form some kind of armada, there's no way they're stopping Fortune. I can get you to Bicoma easy." She gives him a reassuring squeeze, but then her smile turns wry. "Of course, the whole surviving in Bicoma space is your job."

He forces himself to smile at her. "Have faith, small human." He deliberately towers over her, knowing it will make her laugh. This woman isn't afraid of anything and finds challenges nothing but stimulating. There's not a chance he can intimidate her, only amuse her. "I will keep us safe in the Bicoma system."

"Why don't you take those to my cabin, and I'll meet you there once I get Fortune underway," she orders and pushes a few boxes of food items into his hands.

"You're going to join me in the cabin?" he asks carefully. She licks her lips. He's captivated by that small motion. Her plump lower lip glistens a little and he wants to draw it into his mouth and give her a nip. It takes effort, but he forces his gaze back up to her eyes.

"Yup, I'll be joining you. As soon as we are underway, I'm hoping we can do some more 'getting to know' each other," she confesses.

He meant to take everything slow. He meant to tease her until she's desperate. Then he planned to take his time and impress her with his bedroom skills. But teasing her means he's tormenting himself also, and there's no part of him that can wait any longer.

New tactic — get them naked and touching.

"Go on," he almost shouts, shooing Mian towards the cockpit. "Hurry and set our course. I'll be waiting."

She laughs and saunters off.

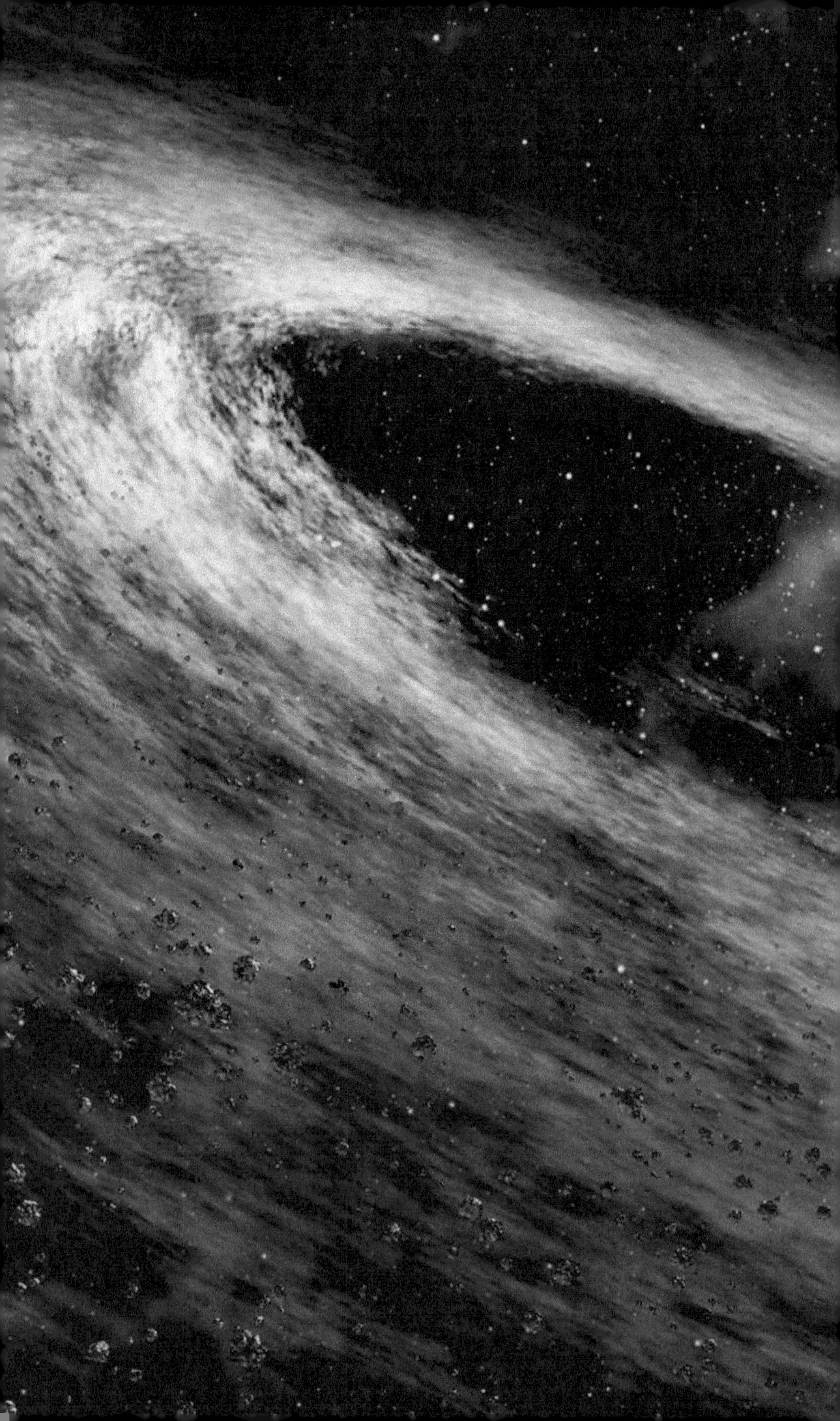

CHAPTER

6

Mian can't believe how nervous she is when she walks into her cabin. Halin's there, reading something on a data pad he purchased at a kiosk on Wint. He looks up as she walks in, then gives her a smile that makes her heart beat a little faster. She left her new armor charging in the control room and is just wearing the tight, one-piece insulation garment she always wears under the cold armor.

She suddenly feels very unattractive. She never really thought about her looks before. But with Halin staring up at her, all she can think about is all her most unflattering aspects. Her messy hair, the unappealing insulation garment, the fact that she hasn't bathed in several cycles.

"I'm going to use the cleansing unit," she squeaks out, surprised at the unusually high pitch of her voice. She can feel her face flushing and almost sprints through the cleansing unit door, slamming it shut behind her with more force than was necessary. *And now he thinks you're an idiot,* she berates herself silently. *And he's probably not wrong.*

She strips out of the insulation suit and starts up the cleaning unit, glad she splurged for one that uses water instead of subsonics. The hot water hits her, and she gives a little sigh, enjoying the feel of it for a moment before she starts working the soap into her short blonde hair.

She's just ready to start washing out the soap when Halin is suddenly there, crowding her back as he shoves his big body into the stall with her. With a gasp, she finds herself pressed between him and the wall.

She grunts as she wiggles around, eventually able to get her body turned around so she can face him. "What are you doing?"

"Furthering our knowing," he explains and grabs a small bottle of soap and examines the bottle. "What part of you does this cleanse?"

"It's for everything," she replies without thinking, too engrossed at staring at him to wonder at the odd question.

"That won't do," he grunts. "I wish I'd known. We could have picked up more products at Wint." He dumps an excessive amount into his hands. "My sisters were very particular about their cleansing products. I remember the bathing area being full of bottles and tubs of sweet-smelling things. Some were just for their head. Some for their hands. I'm sure humans have different cleansing needs for different parts of the body."

"Hey, not so much! I'm on a budget." She snatches the bottle away from him and turns to place it on a high shelf. As she reaches up, he puts his hands on her. Large hands, slippery with soap. He grips her at the waist, then runs his hands up until they're cupping her breasts. She can't help the small moan that escapes her lips.

"You have lovely, soft skin," he murmurs in her ear, and a small shiver goes down her spine. She tries to turn around, but he pushes her against the wall, pinning her in place. "No, don't touch me," he orders. "I'm worried I'll forget myself if you touch me. Put your hands against the wall."

Excited by the game, she slaps her palms on the cold metal, even with her head.

"Higher," he whispers, "stretch them up higher." She complies and feels the hard length of him all along the back of her body. His cock is a hard ridge line trapped against her lower back, and she wonders how they'll manage in such a small shower with their height difference.

His soapy hands start massaging her breasts and she groans with pleasure at the feel. It's been a long time since she's been touched, and none of her experiences so far have made her this aroused this quickly. The feel of him pressed against her is almost overwhelming.

He plucks her nipples, and her head falls forward until she's resting her forehead against the wall. Soap from her hair starts streaming down her face, and she closes her eyes to keep it from stinging. His hands slide lower until he's petting the thatch of hair at the apex of her legs.

"Give me permission." He makes it sound more like an order than a request.

"Keep going, or I'll break your legs," she growls, and he barks out a laugh.

"Part your legs for me," he demands. Eagerly, she edges her feet apart and gasps when he slides those big blunt fingers between her legs. One hand is still plucking at her nipple while the other parts the lips of her labia and lazily explores her sex. She growls and tries to move against him to put his fingers where she desperately wants them.

"Be still," he commands and starts to withdraw his hand. She freezes and hears a strange sound. With surprise, she realizes it's her making the sound. She's whimpering.

His hand returns to its slow movements, and she wants to scream when his fingers draw circles around her clit. He suddenly pulls both hands away and grabs her around the waist, pushing her under the water before she has time to protest.

"By the moons, female," he grinds out. "Why didn't you tell me you had soap on your face? No, don't open your eyes. Let me clean you off." She stands still and silent for his ministrations. He works his fingers into her hair, massaging the water in and the soap out. He runs gentle palms down her face until she can't smell or feel any soap on her skin. She opens her eyes to find him examining her head with care, his face frowning in concentration. When he notices her looking at him, he grins, showing off his fangs. The sight of those fangs sends fissures of desire through her belly.

"I'm going to kiss you," he warns and drops his mouth to hers. The taste of him, sweet and addicting, explodes in her mouth as his fangs graze her lips. She struggles against his hands, wanting to get closer to him. She wraps her arms around his neck and draws her body close, and she can feel him tense against her. His cock is a hard rod, pushing against her belly, a beast begging to be touched.

She reaches one hand down to feel the hard length of him but only manages to brush him with her fingers before he grabs her wrist and draws it over her head, pinning her hand against the wall.

"No touching," he growls, nipping her neck. "I'm doing my best right now. Don't make it harder."

"It's already hard. I just wanted to give it a little pet," she tells him and sees his confusion before he realizes what she meant.

She watches his eyes darken with need. He swiftly grabs her other hand and pushes her wrist into the same hand holding the other. Now both wrists are shackled above her head, held by only one of his hands.

She doesn't fight his hold on her. Pressing her belly forward, she rubs against the steel of his erection. "Don't tease," she pants. "You seem to know human bodies. If you're good to me, I'll be good to you." She can tell her words have an effect because he draws in a sharp breath.

She watches with fascination as a series of emotions cross his face that she can't identity except for the last one, determination. "This is by far the most difficult of trials," he confesses. "But I'll prove myself to you."

Before she can ask what he means by that, he slams his hand over the controls and shuts off the water. He steps away, kicking the door open with a casual movement of his heel. She feels a moment of disappointment, assuming he's done playing; then he leans over and pushes his shoulder into her hips.

Her body folds over his and he stands up, easily caring her weight over his shoulder like so much baggage.

"Hey!" she protests. "This isn't sexy."

He chuckles and slaps a hand down on her wet ass. The contact stings a little and to her shock, she feels her sex clench. He stops mid-stride, seeming to sense her arousal, and casually smacks her ass again. She hears him take a deep breath through his nose.

"I didn't expect that," he murmurs, and she's about to ask what he's referring to when suddenly she's flying through the air. She lands with a bounce on her bed and before she has a chance to recover, he's there, covering her with his body.

"You like a little bite to sex, don't you?" he asks, forcing her to lay under him with his larger, heavier frame. She notices he's careful to support enough of his weight, so he isn't crushing her, but he's making it impossible for her to move. She's never been interested in this kind of sex play before, but she finds Halin's actions are making her more aroused than she's ever been. Who knew she had a kinky side to her?

"I have no idea what you mean," she answers with half a grin, delighted to find out something new about herself. "But if you do it again, I probably won't put up much of a fight."

"Do you want to fight?" he asks, his tone serious.

"Maybe, a little," she admits. "But not right now. Right now, I want to climax. I feel like I've been teased enough."

"Fair," he declares and brings his head down to one of her breasts and clamps his mouth around her nipple. The sensation makes her gasp and bow under him. He pulls away from her nipple, and she tries to grab hold to pull his head back when he intercepts her hand and pulls it away.

"Put those hands behind your head, female," he orders gruffly. She complies quickly, hoping it will mean he brings his mouth back to her. Instead, he kisses down her chest and belly, until his breath fans the hair between her legs.

With almost brutal force, he grabs her thighs and forces them apart, pulling her legs over his shoulders. She gives a little start of surprise and then he's sucking her clit into his mouth. She gasps and tightens her legs around his head.

In no time, she's screaming and undulating her hips under him, unable to remain still as her climax tears through her. He keeps his mouth on her until she gives a small sob and tries to draw away from him. Only then does he lift his head and gaze into her eyes.

"Mine," he growls, and she freezes, her brain befuddled from pleasure. "Say it," he demands. "Tell me you're mine." To emphasize his point, he rubs a calloused thumb against her over sensitized clit, making her jolt and whimper.

"I'm yours," she whispers. His face is triumphant. He crawls up the bed and lays down next to her, pulling her tight against his body. With a contented sigh, he closes his eyes.

"Mine," he whispers and then he does something she absolutely doesn't expect.

He falls asleep.

Doesn't he want her to service him? Wouldn't he want to climax too?

She feels thoroughly confused by his actions and words. She moves her leg a little to get more comfortable and feels a wet spot far down on the bed. It takes her tired and content brain several moments to realize what must have caused the spot, and then she smiles.

I'm so good he climaxed just from a taste of me, she thinks with humor. She relaxes into his embrace and refuses to read anything into his declaration of ownership before he slept.

"It's just sex," she mutters and closes her own eyes. "The guy has probably been in space a while. It's nothing."

The last thing she needs is to get emotionally attached to someone who's going to leave her. Her job is here in Raider Alley or anywhere else people like her parents are being attacked. Falling for a Hissa with a planet full of obligations is a non-option.

CHAPTER

7

Halin sleeps so soundly that Mian has to work to wiggle her body out from underneath him. He never let go of her as he slept. Even though both of them changed positions several times. Now that she needs to get up, he keeps shifting, locking her in his arms as she attempts to get free of the bed.

"I've got to use the facility," she whispers to him. "You need to let go."

He grumbles in his sleep, but after a little more whispering and prodding, he eventually, reluctantly lets go. Then he murmurs something in Hissa before clutching one of her pillows to his chest and falling back to sleep with soft snores.

Once she's standing next to the bed, she looks down at him with a small grin. She gives herself a moment to examine his warrior's body. Compared to the few males she's been with, he's the most delectable. If she didn't know it would bother him, she might even call him beautiful.

Heck, maybe she would call him beautiful anyway. The consequences could be fun.

With that thought, she forces herself to dress and head to the cockpit to check on messages, reports, and run diagnostics. They're well into raider territory now, and it wouldn't do to be caught unprepared.

Of course, no raider has ever attacked Fortune. If anything, they burned hard to get away from her. She's built up such a reputation in the last year that it can be hard to flush out raiders until there is a tasty, vulnerable transport for them to attack. Maybe she needs to start changing her tactics and offer transport protection for free, on the understanding that they are the bait to bring the raiders out and she won't appear until they're attacked.

Contemplating this new strategy, she settles down in the pilot's chair and starts checking systems. She notices several of her guns need their ammunition topped off and one gun on the port side is reporting a possible jam. There are several other issues, but all of them are much too minor to bother with now, so she instructs the computer to send the list of guns needing maintenance to her data bracelet.

Then she turns her attention to her new armor. A big, fat smile curves her lips as she gazes at the shiny pieces of tech waiting for her. She gets up from the pilot's chair and takes the few steps to her new toys, then gracefully sinks into a cross-legged sitting position on the cold metal floor. With an expression of pure delight, she pulls the chest piece into her lap.

She's so absorbed in fiddling with her new toys she doesn't notice Halin's joined her until a hard body gently tackles her to the floor. A piece of leg armor goes flying as Halin quickly covers her body with his own.

"I woke up alone," he complains with a wicked grin, working a hand under her shirt to cup her breast. "I'm still recovering from a grievous wound, and you should spend all your waking hours caring for me. Soothing me from my worries and distracting me from my pain."

He tugs at her nipple, and she wraps her legs around his lean hips. "If you're still healing, then I don't think you should engage in any extreme physical activity," she teases him.

"You're correct," Halin agrees as he uses his immense strength to flip them over so she's on top. She draws herself up on her knees, her sex resting over his erection. It's then that she notices he isn't wearing clothes. He seems to dislike her state of being dressed because he plucks at her shirt and frowns.

"Why are you wearing these ugly things? You have all the silks and cottons I bought you at Wint." Before she can answer, he grabs the shirt in both hands and easily rips it down the front. She tries to glare at him but ends up laughing as he pulls the shredded shirt off her.

"I didn't think you wanted me wearing nice clothes to do chores. They'll all get ruined fast," she chuckles and then flushes when his eyes latch onto her breasts.

"Wear them to do everything," he growls as he reaches up with a hand to palm her breast. "It will make me happy to buy you more. You're mine. I'll make sure you never want for anything."

She ignores his possessive words and arches back, pushing herself against his hand. "That feels good," she moans. When his hand withdraws, she starts to protest, only to have him push her up on her knees. She looks down just in time to see him do the same thing to her pants that he did to her shirt. She ends up with the legs of her pants pooled around her knees, the crotch seam destroyed.

"You're going to have to stop doing that," she murmurs, bemused. He grunts and draws her back down.

"I find I have no patience," he tells her bluntly. "I need to be inside you. I can't wait."

"You don't need to wait," she tells him and reaches down between them to find his hard cock. He gives a strangled groan when she strokes him a few times; then she positions him at the mouth of her sex. She starts lowering her body, slowly impaling herself on him. He's larger than any male she's ever had, and his size is almost too much. She's panting by the time she's all the way down.

"You aren't ready," Halin growls. "Be still." He brings his hand between their bodies until he finds her clit and starts rubbing. He palms her breast with his other hand, and she finds herself opening to him, warming, and getting wet. It's not long before the uncomfortable changes to titillating. His fat cock stops being uncomfortable to the point of pain and starts making her feel filled and aroused.

She starts to move against him, enjoying the way his erection feels as it moves inside her. Halin increases the pressure on her clit with his fingers and starts plucking at her nipples, making her gasp with the sharp sensation.

She's not sure why, but something is missing. She can feel pressure starting to build, but she can't seem to find her release. Panting with need, she grinds herself against Halin even harder, hoping to find what she needs.

"Slower," Halin gasps. "Or I won't last. By the moons, you feel so good."

She ignores him until he pulls his hands away from her breast, and between her legs. She makes a needy sound when he grabs her hips. At first, she thinks he's going to force her to slow, but instead he lifts her off him. She gives a small cry of disappointment when he moves her, but with a fluid movement, he sets her on the floor and rolls over on top of her. He nestles his hips between her legs and guides himself back inside of her.

It was fun to be on top, but Mian likes this position much better. The weight of him on top of her feels good so she wraps her legs around his hips and urges him on with her heels digging into his muscular legs. He latches his mouth onto a nipple and suckles. When she wiggles under him, he looks up, his face contorted with need.

He reaches up and grabs a handful of hair, holding her head still so he can kiss her, and she finds that's what she needed. His forcefulness pushes her over the edge as he thrusts into her. She feels herself tighten on him, milking his hard shaft as she climaxes.

Shouting with pleasure, he stiffens, and liquid warmth fills her, making her quake as the last of her orgasm moves through her.

He rolls off, drawing her against him as they both try to catch their breath.

"That's not payment," she tells him with a small grin. "You're a good lay, but don't think this gets you out of paying me when this trip is over."

Halin barks out a laugh and hugs her tightly. "Give me more time to convince you," he begs with mock fear. "Don't push me out the airlock yet."

She raises an eyebrow at him. "You've got until we get to Bicoma, so you better work hard." Suddenly the good humor disappears from his face, and his arms tighten around her to the point of discomfort.

"Would you consider coming back to Hissa with me?" he asks, and she gives him a wary look.

"My job is here in raider space."

"We can come back to do more hunting," he tells her quickly. "And I'm sure I can get you some nice additions for your ship. We just replaced some of our older gunships, and they are sitting in the boneyard, decommissioned. It wouldn't take much for me to convince the Council to let you take parts from them for Fortune."

She's tempted by the offer, but she concentrates on something else first. "When we come back?"

He smiles and nuzzles her. "When I'm finished with my mission, if you don't wish to stay on Hissa with me, then I'm going to resign from the military and join you on the hunt."

"But why would you want to do that? It's dangerous, and I don't make much money," she tells him, feeling perplexed by his words.

He doesn't answer but voices a concern of his own. "I want to know why you do it. Hunting raiders is dangerous, and out here you could die. You could die with not one ever knowing what happened."

She's silent for a moment, studying his face, looking for condemnation or censure, but finding only honest interest, so she decides to confide in him.

"My parents were planet surveyors," she explains. "It was just me and them, traveling from place to place. Mom was a geologist, and Dad was a mineralogist. Together they'd take contracts to survey. They mostly worked on mapping moons for mining. We had one of those Class H ships, the small ones that can land and act as a mobile living quarters and lab. We would land somewhere, spend a few months or years surveying the planet, then pick up and move on to the next job."

"Were you a lonely child?" he asks when she pauses.

"No, absolutely not. Mom and Dad took me with them if they left the ship to take samples and always carved time out to spend with me. By the time I was ten, I could process samples and help create a mining map. I thought it was fabulous."

"But no brothers or sisters?"

"My parents couldn't have kids," she explains with a small, sad smile.

She turns her head and pulls her right ear forward to show him a scar running the length of her ear and down the back of her neck. "This is a Decanting scar. Mom and Dad used all their savings to have me grown in a lab. I found out later most of the kids grown in those labs are sold into slavery. I was one of the lucky ones who was grown and sold to loving parents. I have no memory of the labs. I was Decanted as a baby, but most of them are matured to the biological age of six before they Decant them. Makes them more valuable as slaves."

She feels him tense against her. "Humans grow children to be slaves?"

"Yeah," she sighs. "I know Mara Lost is a Decanted child like me. That's why I knew your friend would be safe with her. She wasn't as lucky as me though. She was sold and spent many years as a slave. Her and her sister."

"What happened to her sister?"

"I don't know, probably died. I don't know her story, but most owners aren't very concerned over the health and well-being of their slaves."

He rolls them over until she's stretched out on top of him, and he hugs her fiercely to his chest. "That could have been you."

"But it wasn't," Mian soothes him.

He sits up, keeping her in his lap as he does.

"So how does this story go from an idyllic childhood to a woman who hunts raiders?" he asks.

"Raiders killed them," she answers simply. "We were heading to the Tavarian home system, and we were attacked. We didn't stand a chance. Mom and Dad shoved me into the ship's survival pod and launched me."

"On a Class H ship, the pod would have been big enough for all three of you," Halin points out, his face a mask of sadness. She has a feeling he already knows what she's going to say.

"Dad stayed behind to lead the raiders away and Mom wouldn't leave him. When I realized what they were doing, I tried to stop the launch, but I couldn't." She pauses, taking a shaky breath, proud of herself for not crying. This is only the third time she's ever told anyone about her parents, and although the wound isn't raw anymore, their loss is still an ache in her heart.

"I watched the raider make a direct hit on one of the engines. Instead of shutting down, it exploded, killing my parents and taking the raider ship with them."

"How old were you?" he asks, running his hand up and down her back. The motion's comforting and helps keep her sadness at bay.

"I was nineteen. I was found by a Tavarian civil patrol. They were very kind when they found out I was an orphan. They got me a job on one of their haulers. Then I got a job on a big gun ship. The ship had a good crew and was well outfitted. We were successful. Because everyone got a percentage of each bounty, it only took a few years before I was able to buy this beauty." She grins and smacks a wall next to her affectionately. "She's old but works well. Especially after we caught our first few bounties, and I could buy her some really good guns. We started kicking ass when I bought her the better maneuvering thrusters."

She meets his eyes and finds he's regarding her with an expression containing both pride and worry. "You're a very brave female," he tells her finally. "I'm honored to know you."

Uncomfortable with both the discussion and his words, she starts untangling herself from him. "Come on, big guy, we've got chores to do. I don't know how it works on Hissa ships, but around here we can't afford to lounge around all day."

Halin tightens his arms around her to the point where she gives a little squeak, then to her relief he lets go and gets to his own feet then hauls her up. Then he starts pulling clothes from a pile he must have dropped by the hatch.

She looks down at her own ripped and ruined clothes and frowns, she's going to need to go back to her cabin for a change. She looks up just in time to catch the bundle Halin tosses to her.

"I noticed nothing we bought for you at Wint was missing from the cabin. I took the liberty of bringing you a change of clothes."

She shakes out the garments and smiles. If it makes him so happy to have her wear the extravagant clothing, she'll do it. She shrugs into the scooped neck shirt. The shoulders and sleeves of the top are loose and flow around her. The shirt gathers just below her breasts and remains fitted down to her hips. The pants are just the opposite. They are fitted high and then loosen to billow around her legs until they gather again just below her knees, leaving her calves bare. Both the shirt and pants are a deep, rich purple color with rows of glittering beads sewn in around her waist.

The style isn't cumbersome, so it doesn't bother her, and she has to admit that the soft fabrics feel divine on her skin. She runs her hands down the front of the shirt and sighs.

"This isn't going to last long," she mutters sadly.

"It doesn't matter," Halin tells her, and she looks up to see deep satisfaction on his face. "The color looks beautiful on you, and it pleases me to see you wearing something I've provided. I couldn't care less if you destroy an outfit a day. I'll buy you more."

She gives him a wry smile. "It'll matter when the bills pile up."

"You're very concerned about money," Halin comments with a frown. "I have a feeling you operate on the edge of solvency."

She shrugs. "The bounties are good, but the ammo and repairs are murder on the credits. I usually have a little left over after buying all the necessities, but not much. I'm happy though."

"I can make you happier," Halin points out and palms a breast through her shirt. She moans a little then pulls away. The man is insatiable!

"Work first, play later," she declares and moves quickly to dodge his hands. "Or don't Hissa men know how to work?" she asks with a mock scowl. Halin laughs and crosses his arms over his chest, pointedly looking at her beaded nipples, easily seen through the soft fine fabric of the shirt.

"Depends on the work."

With a groan, she hurries out of the room to start working on the guns.

CHAPTER 8

Halin's just finishing putting ammunition into an automatic loader when a klaxon sounds, echoing through the ship. Mian, who's standing just a few feet away, straightens up with a gasp. Before he can ask her anything, she's sprinting to the cockpit. He follows, catching up with her easily and ducking through the cockpit hatch right behind her. Then he watches her hastily pulling on armor, a big grin on her face. Halin follows her lead and dons his armor, glad to find his chest piece clean and fully charged.

"Distress call," she declares cheerfully. "Someone close is under attack and needs help."

Forced to curl his hands into fists to keep from reaching for her, he fights his instincts to demand they turn away from danger. He wants to snatch her up, lock her in her cabin, and steer Fortune far from any raiders or battle. He wants to keep her safe. Wants to hide her away from anything that could hurt her.

Take her away from the job she's been doing for years. He stands immobile for a moment, watching her drop into the pilot's chair and start the warm-up procedures for some of the bigger guns. She's a practiced and skilled warrior. He has no right to stop her from going into battle.

But she's mine, part of his brain screams out. She's mine and precious. I must keep her safe and secure.

His mind divides into two, and those two parts war with each other.

Protect Mian from all things dangerous.

Follow Mian into battle.

Finally, one thought flows through his mind, and he knows there is no choice but to let Mian go after the raiders. If he tries to stop her, their relationship will be over.

She'll take him to Bicoma, but that will be it. She'll never trust him again, and she'll certainly want him off her ship. He might protect her from danger this once, but she'll never let him do it again.

Letting them face a potentially deadly situation together sits far better with him than her ending their partnership and her going off to face untold dangers by herself.

Halin focuses on Mian as she runs her hands over the control console, checking data and gathering as much information as possible. He finishes securing his armor and moves to stand next to her, looking down at the display on the console in front of her.

"It looks like a small Fozin cargo hauler was captured by two raider ships working together. One of the ships has already disabled the hauler and pulled it into a hanger."

"One of the raider ships is a Defense series," he says grimly as he studies the two ships on the display. The much larger Defense ship is four times the size of Fortune and carries double the guns. It wouldn't be as fast or maneuverable as Fortune, but its guns are far more powerful.

Under normal circumstances, he would never engage in a battle with such poor odds.

"I know, but look at the dead spots," she brings up a magnetic mapping display and points out several large dark spots on the ship. "I doubt half those guns even work and Fortune has some great plating."

He can see from the display that one of the engines on the Defense ship isn't running and there are electrical dead spots all over the hull, denoting a lack of power to those sections. He remembers how skillfully she handled the two raiders chasing him down and realizes she's already calculated the odds.

"Strategy?" Halin asks, knowing she must have a battle plan.

"We hit the Defense first until it's either destroyed, incapacitated, or runs. Then we board the smaller ship and hunt down the raiders. I can only hope the Fozin are all being kept in the same place." Mian catches his scowling expression. "What?"

It takes effort, but he forces the scowl off his face. The first part is dangerous enough but boarding the second craft will force them into close-quarters combat. He and all other Hissa warriors train for such things, but everyone knows it's some of the most dangerous fighting to engage in. It's clear that this isn't the first time she's utilized this strategy. If he refuses, she'll just go alone.

How many times has she put herself in this kind of extreme situation?

"The captives are probably already dead," he points out, and Mian turns to glare at him. "If they're all dead, you'll be risking your life for no reason."

"That's not true," she argues. "They tend to keep prisoners alive for ransom or to use as slaves." Mian pauses, then tilts her head consideringly. "If you're scared, you don't need to board with me. You can stay on Fortune and monitor the situation."

"Scared?" Halin roars out, insulted down to his bones. "I'm a Hissa warrior. I fear no battle!"

Instead of yelling back at him, her face breaks out into a happy smile. "Excellent. Having someone at my back for this kind of fight will be good. Last time I boarded a vessel, they had a damn energy thrower stationed at the end of the corridor. I almost got turned into a crispy critter." She reaches over and touches a panel on the wall. A chair slides out. "Take a seat. You can run the guns while I pilot."

Trying his best to ignore the images of Mian facing down an energy thrower, he drops down in the chair and looks over the section of the control panel in front of him. He remembers the battle Mian engaged in to save him. "You controlled weapons and piloted when you rescued me," he murmurs thoughtfully, once again struck by her skill level. "That's a lot to do for one person."

"Eh," she says with a dismissive wave of her hand. "I have some good programming on the auto-targeters and a few pre-programmed flight maneuvers." Her causal attitude belies the difficulty of what she's accomplished. Auto-targeting is notoriously problematic and using pre-programmed flight maneuvers can be hazardous also. Much like a skilled musician, he can imagine her moving delicate hands between the two sets of controllers as she engages the enemy.

"This looks very standard," he grunts as he brings up several displays showing gun locations, range, ammunition amounts, and heat cycles. He can be useful there. If there's anything he knows, it's weapons. Not only has he trained extensively with hand weapons, but he also took tours on battleships and trained with all the different gunners on board. All the controls are familiar and well within his capabilities.

"Everything is pretty standard except for two things," she agrees and points to a panel off to his right. "That controls the large tail gun I added not too long ago. The thing heats up quickly so don't set the cycle any faster than a round every ten seconds."

He nods and makes a mental note. "And the second item?"

She points to another panel just over the tail gun display. "This might look like a gun control, but it controls the worm hatch."

Halin vaguely remembers the tight tube he had to crawl through to get from the dying Hope onto Fortune. "Is this how we'll board the raider ship?"

"If we want to have the advantage, then yes," she answers with a smirk. "If we hook up to the regular docking hatch, they just blow us up. If we clear off a gun and leach ourselves onto another place, they'll have to hunt to find us."

"Clever."

"Necessary," Mian counters gleefully. He's not sure anyone should be this gleeful on the cusp of battle. "Are you ready? I'm going to start a strafing run. Don't hit the smaller ship on this run, concentrate on the Defense. We might take a few hits, but Fortune is well built, and I'm good at dodging."

Halin's eyes sweep the controls in front of him, verifying that all the guns are warm, loaded, and ready to fire. "Confirmed. Guns are ready to engage," he announces, feeling the familiar cold calm of battle fill him.

Battle is no place for rage, hesitation, or doubt. If he lets those emotions in, he runs the risk of not only getting himself hurt or killed but also Mian. He refuses to be the reason they aren't successful.

He almost smiles when another thought strikes him. This battle will be the perfect opportunity to prove to Mian that he's a capable warrior and a worthy male. Suddenly the idea of going into danger with Mian at his side doesn't sound like such a bad idea.

"Starting strafing run. Use the medium size projectiles. They won't be affected by the short-range defense system," she tells him.

"I know," he mutters, and she gives a small laugh.

"Sorry," she says, pulling her attention away from the ship's controls just long enough to give him a big grin. "I should've guessed you'd be knowledgeable. At my signal, have at them with whatever you want to fire."

He feels the ship vibrate around him and the tug of artificial gravity, which fights against the ship's engines. "We might lose gravity here and there," she warns him. In response, he belts himself in. Once secured, he places his hands back on the control console, poised and waiting. Mian's capable hands glide over the maneuvering controls, her focus absolute.

"Fire at will," Mian shouts out, and Halin starts pouring rounds into the Defense. Fortune bucks violently, and Mian curses as she hits buttons. "We're good. Hull integrity is holding," she announces, but he doesn't spare her a glance, his concentration on his displays.

He sets the auto-targeting on the largest active guns, then manually fires several of the other guns that require longer reload or cooling times. He finds his aim is as good or better than the auto-targeting because he can see Mian manipulating the controls out of the corner of his eye and shifts his aim accordingly.

At first, she calls out where she's going, but soon she doesn't bother. She's far too engrossed in maneuvering around the ships, trying to keep the Fortune undamaged and the Defense from accidentally firing on its companion ship.

"These fuckers are too dumb to live," she mutters as a stray round from the Defense hits the smaller raider ship near an engine. Halin doesn't answer her comment, just focuses on keeping the guns loading, firing, and reloading.

He notices she's taking longer to come around this time and rushes to punch in commands to the large tail cannon. His fingers move fast, and he just manages to get the order entered before Mian starts another turn. The tail cannon is so large it causes a gyroscopic effect and shifts the Fortune a little as it turns, which keeps it from being hit by a round from the Defense.

The round from the cannon hits and a massive control arm on the underside of the Defense disintegrates. Mian crows out a laugh and smacks his arm with her fist. "Nice shot!"

He acknowledges her with a grunt. Mian finishes the turn only to find the Defense has started its laborious turn and is pushing the engines into a hard burn.

"They're running," Halin announces unnecessarily. He stills his hands on the gun controls. No point in wasting rounds until Mian can get them close again.

"Forget 'em," Mian orders and steers Fortune toward the smaller ship. "Be ready to deploy the worm hatch."

Halin turns his attention to Mian's set of controls and watches as she pilots the craft next to a section of the raider's hull. It's not the most skillful piloting he's ever seen, but her movements are efficient and effective, and soon she smacks the side of Fortune against the other ship. He hears the shriek of metal as the Fortune sinks claws into the other ship's hull.

"Deploy the worm hatch," she commands, and Halin smacks down on the worm hatch launch control. He can hear more grinding and shrieking metal. He can picture in his mind's eye the end of the worm hatch cutting through the other ship.

Without another word, he stands and looks around for weapons. Mian is on her feet right behind him and rushes to a cabinet. She looks over her shoulder and gives him a saucy grin as she pulls it open to reveal the contents.

Halin gapes at what he sees.

Inside hangs an assortment of weapons, including the two new plasma rifles he bought them. He eagerly hurries over and reaches over her head to start pulling weapons out and storing them on various parts of his armor, along with spare energy cartridges, charges, and ammunition magazines. Finally, he pulls out one of the rifles and slings it across his back.

He steps back and looks over to see Mian similarly armed. "I feel heavy," he complains with a mock frown.

Shooting him a puzzled look, Mian closes the cabinet and starts of the cockpit and down the hall to the room with the worm hatch. "Heavy?"

"I feel like I'm carrying far too many rounds. Do you think the raiders might be persuaded to carry a few of them for me?" he asks, following her down the corridor. She laughs at his morbid humor but doesn't stop moving until he puts a hand on her shoulder just as she's about to drop into the worm hatch.

"They might all be dead," he feels obliged to point out. "The captives. They might all be dead already."

"I know that," she says, shrugging off his hand.

"I just don't want you to get your hopes up," he explains quickly.

She shakes her head. "It's happened before," she assures him, her face grim. "If they're dead, then all I can do is avenge them."

Just like you're avenging your parents every time you take down a raider, he thinks.

"Let me go first," he requests. She's about to argue but he presses forward. "I'm sure you've always gone first," he points out. "Let me give it a try." Reluctantly, she steps back, and he wiggles himself down the worm hatch. Landing in a crouch, he sweeps the room as he moves sideways to make room for Mian to land next to him.

The worm tunnel drops them into an empty area. He's not sure how she knew there wouldn't be anyone there, but it's obvious she knew exactly what she was doing. The attack and then the docking all happened so fast that Halin wonders how many small intricacies he missed. He'll need to interview Mian later to better understand, but for now he concentrates on his mission.

"Standard one by one," she whispers. He nods, recognizing the basic maneuver she names. He stands at the door to the room they dropped into, weapons ready, and senses attuned to the ship around them.

She moves forward until she finds a defensible spot, sweeping the corridor with her smaller hand weapon as she moves. The place is too tight to use the plasma rifles, so he also keeps his slung across his back. Once she's standing against the wall with a support beam offering a bit of cover, Halin moves. He doesn't stop where she's standing. Swiftly, he moves past her, finding a position similar to hers further down the corridor and braces against the wall ready to provide cover fire if necessary. Now it's her turn to move past him, weapons still at the ready.

They don't need to speak or even look at each other as they move. They work seamlessly as if they've been training together for years. Halin only experienced this after rigorous training and drills with fellow warriors. This little human is proving to be one of the most competent soldiers he's ever worked with.

Halfway to a secure spot, a group of raiders appear from around a corner. Mian stops moving forward, drops to one knee, and opens fire. She has no cover close enough to get behind, but at least she's wearing armor.

Halin curses as he aims his weapon and starts firing. Several raiders drop, but the others duck back, finding shelter behind a bulkhead support. Mian falls back until she can squeeze herself in next to Halin.

"Did you see hostages?" she asks, peeking her head around and hissing as a shot sounds down the corridor.

"No," he answers as he returns fire.

"Good," Mian grunts, and he watches her pull something off the leg of her armor. She taps it a few times, then tosses it down the corridor. "Helmet up!" she orders, and her suit deploys the helmet over her head. Halin hastily does the same. Just as his helmet finishes deploying, a shock wave shakes the wall at their back and the plating under their feet.

Anticipating her next move, Halin is already on his feet the moment the shock wave passes, moving in sync with her down the corridor. They find only one of the raiders still alive and on his feet. The single shot he's able to get off misses both Halin and

Mian. They fire back simultaneously. They both hit, their shots making the raider jerk violently as he falls back.

Neither of them lowers their weapons as they check the other raiders to make sure they are all dead, not just unconscious or pretending.

"Regarian," Halin grumbles with disgust. "I should have known."

Regarians are a large species, almost as big as Halin's people. They're covered in fur with long snouts and protruding fangs. Although there are Regarian that run reputable businesses, the species is generally known for its tendencies to resort to raiding, stealing, or any other criminal activity.

"A good deal of the raiders around here are Regarian or Diniki," Mian explains absently as she studies the gear on a few of the bodies. "There are other species that turn to raiding, but I seem to run into these guys most often. These six are well armed. I'll bet they were sent to take care of us. The ship never fired while we dealt with the Defense, so no one's manning any of the controls. My guess is that the rest of the raiders on board are in the hangar bay looking for trade goods. Probably only another twelve or so."

"Twelve?" Halin casts her a shocked look. "That would make a total of twenty on the whole ship. Running a ship this size should require double that."

Mian shrugs. "Raiders don't even know how to run these things properly, so it wouldn't matter if they had enough bodies to do it. They capture and discard ships pretty often. It's not like they can just pull into a port and have maintenance done."

"I hadn't thought of that," Halin admits.

"Fighting raiders isn't like going to war with a regular opponent," Mian assures him. "You have to toss a lot of the rules and expectations out the window."

"So now we head to the hangar bay?" Halin asks, willing to be led by her superior knowledge of raider tactics.

"You guessed it, same one by one formation," she tells him.

Halin nods and checks his blaster's charge. Satisfied, he pulls a small energy weapon out with his non-dominant hand, noticing Mian doing the same thing. Without another word, they start making their way down the corridor again.

Soon he hears voices, and Mian ducks down, waving him forward to her side. He crouches and runs until he's next to her. She points and he can just see into a large room full of activity.

A group of about a dozen Fozin huddle together, making small noises of distress. The raiders, all of them large Regarian, are opening boxes and tossing things around. One of the Regarians stomps over to the quaking pile of Fozin.

"Where are the valuables!" he shouts, and the Fozin cry out in fear, trying to huddle even closer to each other. The Regarian grabs one of the Fozin, pulling him away from the rest. Holding him high, the raider shakes the small furry creature violently. "Where is the dimmerion? Your kind always trades dimmerion! Where is it!"

The Fozin screams in fear and tries to wiggle out of the Regarian's hold. The raider tosses the small creature down and puts a large foot on its back when it tries to crawl away. "Answer me or I start playing with the young ones. I wonder how your kind tastes. I'll make sure to start with the arms and legs. That way they can watch me as I eat them. And the screams will be nice. Fear and pain make the meat taste so much better."

"We don't trade in dimmerion," the Fozin under his foot cries out. "We trade in cloth and hides. Nothing else, I swear."

"You lie!" the raider roars and without lifting his foot, reaches out to grab one of the smallest Fozin out of the pile, obviously a child.

"I'm going to make my way around," Mian whispers through their helm comms. "Stay here. When I open fire, kill the raiders closest to the captives first."

"I'll go, you stay," Halin counters, but Mian makes a sound of disagreement.

"You're too big." She points to a ramp used to load cargo into a multi story ship.

If she wants to get to the ramp undetected, she'll have to run from one tight hiding space to another. Even with the bulky armor on, she's much smaller than he is. Considering the odds, surprise is a weapon too dear to give up. That means it needs to be her taking position on the ramp if they want to keep their presence a secret until they start firing.

"I'm going to climb up there from the back," she tells him. "Be ready to lay down cover fire if they see me before I'm in position."

Halin wants to argue but clamps his mouth shut and lets her go. Pulling his plasma rifle off his back, he double checks the charge on the weapon. Then he braces on a convenient rail, ready to lay down fire if she needs him. She moves quickly and efficiently, not bothering to try and sprint. The corridor and bay are much too crowded for her to effectively run full out. Instead, she moves from hiding spot to hiding spot, using the terrorized screams of the Fozin to mask the sounds of her movement.

He watches, almost unable to breathe, as she makes her way to the ramp and disappears behind it. Soon she reappears at the top of the loading structure. She kneels and pulls her plasma rifle from her back. She sights down and fires. One of the raiders near the captured ship gives a stifled scream and falls. There is a moment of stunned silence as the rest of the raiders look at their fallen comrade. Both Mian and Halin take full advantage.

The Regarian terrorizing the group of Fozin is now holding a child. He's looking away from Halin, holding the child high in the air, mouth open as if he's about to eat the little guy. Halin aims carefully and fires, hitting the Regarian with a clean shot through the head and watches with satisfaction as the creature falls lifeless to the ground. The little Fozin lands hard, but many hands reach out to pull the wailing youngster into the safety of the group.

Fearful the other raiders might try and use the hostages, Halin sprints to the group and crouches down in front of them, using his armored body to shield them from raider fire. He can't see Mian any longer, but he can hear her rifle firing with a measured beat. Each shot is followed by the sound of a scream or falling body. The woman has skills.

He's almost thrown back when a round hits his chest. His armor holds, and he manages to stay on his feet and return fire. It takes him several rounds to drop a raider running toward him, and then only one round to kill a raider who stops to take aim.

Sweeping his gaze over the area, he sees a Regarian holding something massive. It takes him a moment to identify the weapon, but once he does, he feels his blood run cold. The bulky weapon in the raider's grip is a modified ship's cannon. He can see where the support arm the cannon is usually mounted on has been torn away and a poorly wired control panel has been put in its place. Wires dangle haphazardly, and there's a small spark coming off the metering rod at the front of the cannon's mouth.

The thing was never meant to be fired inside a ship or be held by hand, and he knows if the Regarian succeeds in firing the badly modified weapon, it won't just fry the Regarian holding it, but it will probably explode. It'll tear the ship apart, probably killing everyone including himself and Mian.

He can't fire on the raider. Even a round fired too close could set the old cannon off. Fueled by fear and the need to protect Mian, Halin launches himself at the raider, tossing his plasma rifle aside as he sprints. He puts all his energy into covering ground. He needs to get to the raider before the idiot can figure out how to make the weapon work.

Halin's only vaguely aware of one of the raiders rushing at him from the side. The sound of a plasma rifle shot echoes above him. A scream. Then the body disappears from his view.

Another body dashes at him, but he doesn't try to dodge or deviate from his course. That raider falls away also. He makes it to the raider with the cannon just as the creature's fingers find the ignition switch. With a roar, Halin rams his large body into the equally large Regarian, and they both go down in a tangle of limbs. The cannon slides down the corridor, away from the fighting, stopping when it bumps gently against a wall.

Halin only has a moment to note the weapon didn't accidentally go off and kill them all before the Regarian is clawing at his armor. He can feel it shredding under the Regarian's steel-like claws as he brings his legs up to try and kick the thing off him. The blow is ineffective, but it gives him just enough room to pull his side arm and fire off several rounds into the Regarian's chest.

The thing gives a high-pitched scream of pain and crumples back, twitching as it dies. Halin scrambles to his feet and looks around. There are still a handful of raiders up and moving. They're firing and closing in on Mian's position, but she's no longer returning fire. He refuses to believe she is wounded or dead, so instead, he decides she must be pinned down and unable to move enough to fire back.

He can see his plasma rifle too far away and in several pieces. He has two single-hand weapons and plenty of ammunition for them. He pulls the second weapon out and starts walking toward the raiders, firing one right after another and refusing to flinch as the Regarian turn their weapons on him.

No sooner have they turned to fire on his position than plasma rifle rounds start picking them off. Halin drops behind a convenient pile of boxes. The rounds rip right through the boxes, but at least they offer him visual coverage. He reloads both guns and rolls onto his belly, firing from his prone position. He's thankful for the Range Master who drilled him until he felt like he could confidently and accurately fire in any position.

Between him on the ground and Mian firing from an elevated position, the raiders soon realize that they might not be outnumbered, but they are outmatched. They try to retreat into the captured Fozin ship, but Halin gets a lucky shot in and destroys the control panel to the ship's hatch, making it impossible for the raiders to get the hatch open. When the last two raiders throw down their weapons and drop to their knees in surrender, Halin is tempted to just shoot them rather than go to the trouble of capturing them.

"Get down on your bellies, arms and legs spread out," Mian commands from her position at the top of the ramp.

Halin stands up and keeps one of his weapons trained on the prisoners. He hopes they will try something desperate, and then he'll get to shoot them.

"Halin, secure them, both hands and legs," she orders. He looks up just in time to see her toss down some flexicuffs. She only took one hand off her weapon as she tosses them down and never moved her eyes off the remaining raiders.

Halin puts his weapons away, gathers up the cheap restraints, and slaps them on the raiders, watching with satisfaction as they tighten around the raider's limbs and then harden. Only a special enzyme will dissolve the flexicuffs. Until then the raiders are bound hand and foot.

The Regarians glare at the restraints, but to his disappointment, none of them attack. When he's finished applying the flexicuffs to wrists and ankles, he digs a toe into one and then the other, listening with satisfaction as they curse and try to move away from him. They're unable to get far because the restraints hold against their immense strength.

"Hissa mongrel," one of them grunts. "All of you will die out. Then when you're all gone, we Regarians will take your territory as our own."

"You're too dumb to even find my homeworld," he retorts, then looks up to Mian.

"They're secured," he calls out, lowering his helm and looking up to Mian's position. That's when Mian finally lowers her weapon.

Standing up, she lowers her helm and smiles broadly down at him.

"Good job," she yells as she turns to make her way down the ramp. "You're hired!"

Chuckling, he turns to walk around the ramp so he can meet her at the bottom, when suddenly he's surrounded by anxious, chattering Fozin.

"What repayment do you want from us?" one of them demands, tugging at the leg piece of his armor. "We are not a rich family. It shouldn't be more than the worth of a length of solian cloth."

"Half a length," another one argues, slapping the first one's hand away from his armor. "They have damaged our ship. It will be expensive to repair."

"I'm not," he starts to say when yet another Fozin slaps at his leg to get his attention.

"You can't have any of the expensive colors," she tells him. "Only brown or yellow. I see you are a male Hissa. You'll want the brown anyway."

Halin hears a laugh and looks up to see Mian striding toward them. "Help," he demands as a Fozin child tries to climb up his leg. Mian swoops in and plucks the child off him.

"I'm Mian Sorrow, Captain and owner of the gunship Fortune," she announces formally.

"We are the Clan Gyris," a female says, stepping forward. She was the one who told him he could only have brown or yellow.

"Greetings, Clan Gyris. For the rescue of your clan, you will give us an entire length of blue solian," she tells them sternly. "You will not argue or bargain. In exchange, we will stay with you until you safely reach Wint Station. Your ship is damaged, but it looks like there are enough of you to operate this raider ship. We'll help you lock the remaining raiders in a room. Then all of you will pilot this ship back to Wint. When you get there, the money for the bounty on the pirates is mine."

"You take the bounty. We'll take the ship," one of Fozin agrees. "We will take this ship to pay for the damage to our goods and our ship."

"It's yours," Mian agrees as she swings the child around until it starts squealing with delight. "Now find me my fabric."

With the Fozin no longer pressed together, Halin can see there are at least thirty of them. He thought there were a lot fewer because they were so small and huddled so tightly together when he first entered the hangar. After what looks like an intense discussion, they turn to face Mian. One of them speaks while several others scurry off.

"We agree to your terms," she tells Mian, and Halin watches as the two Fozin emerge from their ship carrying a large bolt of bright blue fabric. Mian hands the giggling child to one of the adults and accepts the cloth.

"Your payment is accepted," Mian replies with a small bow. "We had to punch a hole in the hull to gain access. We'll repair it before we disengage from this ship but be aware you can't do a full burn until it's properly seen to."

"We will put the ship into dry dock when we reach Wint and have better repairs done," the Fozin assures her. "Thank you for your assistance."

Without another word, the Fozin all turn away from Mian and Halin and start chattering excitedly among themselves. Mian grins and jerks her head, then starts walking away. Halin follows and as soon as they're out of earshot, he stops her and points at the cloth.

"Did you want that?"

Mian shrugs, "It's pretty. I guess I'll use it to decorate, but I didn't need it. I saw a box of it, so I knew they had it."

"If you didn't want it, why did you ask for it?"

"If I didn't ask for it, they'd never leave us alone or stop trying to bargain," Mian explains with a chuckle. "You haven't dealt with Fozin much, have you? The first time I rescued a ship of Fozin, I kept telling them they didn't need to pay me because they kept saying how poor they were. We stood there arguing over a payment I told them I didn't need until I walked away with a dimmerion component and three sets of hull patches. I didn't understand until Moriv explained to me later that most Fozin are honorable, but don't understand the idea of not arguing a price. Their tactic is to always claim to be poor and then try to out poor each other while bargaining. By telling them I didn't want anything, they thought I was driving up the price."

Halin laughs at her wry expression. "That seems complicated."

"It's just easier to demand something you know they have plenty of," she agrees. "Otherwise, they'll stand around for hours arguing with you about how poor they are." She holds up the blue cloth and grins. "I'm not sure what I'll do with this, but at least it's pretty."

"It is," Halin agrees, leaning in to give her a quick kiss. "What was that about bounty for the raiders' bodies?"

"The different species in this system set up a fund that pays out every time someone brings them a raider, dead or alive. It's a pretty standard system set up anywhere raiders become an issue. The money is what keeps Fortune in ammunition and me in food rations."

"That's logical, especially if none of the species around here have large militaries."

"They don't," Mian assures him. "Speaking of the military, you did pretty well today. Your training is excellent."

"You're well practiced yourself. Your accuracy with the plasma rifle is laudable," he replies. "Have you ever fired one before?"

"Only once. Moriv let me test one that was returned," she says with a small smile of pleasure. "It's a nice weapon. What happened to yours?"

"I think a Regarian landed on it," he grumbles, pointing back to where his rifle is scattered on the floor in several pieces. She follows his gaze and frowns in commiseration.

"Oh well, I'm sure your government will buy you a new one."

He brightens. "Good point."

"We need to head back to the Fortune," she murmurs and leads him unerringly through the maze of corridors back to where the worm hatch still connects the ship to Fortune.

As they walk, Mian tells him a little more about the current alliance of planets that pay the bounties, but he's only listening with half an ear.

Mostly he's thinking about the recent battle. Two of them just took down over twenty raiders. It's true, none of the raiders were as well armed as either he or Mian, but they still held plenty of weapons. Surprise played a large factor in their success, but even with better weapons and the element of surprise, the entire battle could've gone against them.

What are these battles like for Mian when she's alone?

They are just entering the room to the worm hatch when he breaks the silence. "You do this by yourself, with no backup?"

She waves off his concern with a careless swipe of her hand in the air. "I rarely have to board ships, but yes, I've done this alone."

"You're an exceptional warrior, but even one as skilled as you needs backup. What would you have done if I hadn't been there to distract the raiders when they had you pinned down on the ramp?"

"I had another shock grenade," she tells him. "I didn't want to throw it down because it might have killed some of the Fozin. They're pretty tiny and there were children. But if you hadn't been here, I'd have tossed it and then changed position and started picking them off again. I've handled more raiders than this by myself. They aren't organized, and they tend to be shit fighters when things get chaotic. As long as I keep my head and stay methodical, I win."

"You're very brave and determined," he says finally, making Mian bark out a laugh.

"Is that your diplomatic way of saying stupid and stubborn?"

Halin grins back at her. "Maybe."

With a shake of her head, she wiggles herself into the worm hatch and across to the Fortune. He follows right behind her. It doesn't take long to apply a temporary patch to the other ship's hull. Then they close the iris, retract the worm hatch, and unlatch the ship.

The moment they're floating free from the other ship, he grabs Mian and starts stripping her out of her armor. She doesn't fight him and once the armor's gone, he runs his hands up and down her body, making sure she's whole and unharmed. Assured she isn't wounded in the slightest, he strips out of his armor and drags her into a crushing hug.

"You're a warrior of skill," he murmurs to her.

"You're pretty good yourself," she whispers back, wrapping her arms around his neck. "I still can't believe you bum rushed a raider holding a modified ship cannon." He gives a coughing laugh at the memory.

"It's a good thing the controls were poorly wired, or he might have been able to fire before I got there. Were you keeping the others from getting to me while I ran?" he asks.

"It seemed like the least I could do for you."

"Do you find me an acceptable warrior?" He knows she can't possibly understand the significance of his question, but he finds himself holding his breath anyway.

"You're not just an acceptable warrior," she states in a husky whisper. "But the finest damn partner a bounty hunter could dream of."

It's not the formal words a female Hissa might say to a male when she's ready to cohabitate with him in preparation for potentially forming a Family Pact, but the meaning is there. She finds him worthy.

"Let's get underway," he urges. "The sooner we are traveling, the sooner we can pay attention to other things."

She laughs as he drops her back down to her feet and grabs her hand, pulling her down the corridors of Fortune to the cockpit.

"And what other things might those be?"

He gives her a wicked grin. "Very pleasurable things."

Her response is to shove him aside and sprint to the cockpit.

CHAPTER

9

The moment the ship piloted by the Fozin is within the protective range of Wint's defensive satellites, Mian turns Fortune around and starts back toward Bicoma. The trip back to Wint only added two full days of travel time. He should be concerned about the further delay to his mission. But instead, he considers that the extra time means more time he has to convince Mian to come back to Hissa with him after the Bicoma mission is complete.

"Course locked," she sings out and then jumps up and starts stripping out of her armor. He watches with interest as she pulls the chest piece off, then rips off the arms and legs, leaving the armor in a messy pile right next to the pilot's chair. Once she's down to a set of the soft clothes he bought for her, she turns to him. Striding over, she doesn't say anything, just starts pulling off his armor. The moment his groin isn't protected anymore, she reaches a hand down and cups his cock through his pants, making him groan. Apparently, she's eager.

Could this female be any more perfect?

"I've been thinking about what you said, the first time we had sex."

He tilts his head, trying to think of what he said that would make her ruminate for so long. "I like how you taste?"

"That's good," she chuckles. "But not that. You said I could fight with you a bit. You know, struggle against you if I wanted to. I've been thinking a lot about that."

His eyes widen a little at her words, remembering that conversation now. She enjoys being restrained and the bite of pain with sex. He has no issue with that. Some species need those things to even become aroused. The few times he's played with the females of those species, he enjoyed himself a great deal.

"I'm willing to do anything you want," he tells her, trying to keep himself still as she rubs him.

"I like the sound of that. Anyway, after thinking about it, a lot, I've decided on some ground rules," she announces softly in his ear. He nods quickly. Rules are fine. Everyone has rules.

"Of course," he murmurs back as he closes his eyes and enjoys the feel of her hands on him. "Tell me the rules."

"No permanent damage," she tells him, and her words make his eyes fly open with confusion.

"Damage?"

"Right, no permanent damage to my person, and I'll extend the same to you. I'm assuming we are both going to end up with some bruises, so that's fine. It all stops if I yell "raiderbait" or pass out." He's not sure about giving her bruises, but her next words drive out any concerns he might have harbored. "You can put your dick anywhere as long as I'm enjoying it. I promise not to bite."

He gives a little groan at the thought of her warm mouth on his throbbing cock, making her laugh. "I think I want it rough," she confesses after giving him another kiss. "I'm pretty sure I'd enjoy it if I could put up a fight."

He remembers her reaction when he pushed her against the wall of the cleansing unit. The smell of her arousal when he smacked her backside. Her climax when he covered her body with his, holding her head still with his hands tangled in her hair.

All thoughts of gentle lovemaking fly out of his head. He succumbs to all the impulses he's been fighting for days. With a growl, he reaches out to grab her, only to find empty air.

"I'm not making it easy for you!" she calls out as she dashes out of the cockpit. With a roar, he jumps up to give chase, almost tripping to the floor as his feet tangle in the armor scattered around the cockpit.

She's out the door and down the hall by the time he's recovered. She's fast, but his longer legs catch up with her quickly. Just as she's about to leap over a box of ammunition, he grabs her around the waist and lifts her off her feet. She brings her legs up and pushes hard against the wall of the corridor, flinging them both backward.

He grunts as he hits the opposite wall, and his hold eases slightly. It's just enough for her to fling an elbow back into his gut.

She's able to break away from him, but he manages to catch an ankle and trip her.

She lands with a startled sound, and he moves quickly to cover her with his body. He uses his weight to keep her down, grabs both of her hands, and drags them behind her back. She struggles under him, but he has all the leverage and strength.

He looks around for something to use to bind her but doesn't see anything. Then, looking down at her shirt, he grins. He lets go of her wrists, and she stops struggling.

"Giving up already," she says with disappointment. "I thought you'd—" Her sentence ends with a gasp when he rips her shirt down her back and pulls it off her.

She starts struggling, but he keeps her pinned with his weight on her lower back. Held belly down like she is, there isn't much she can do. That makes it easy to tear the soft scarlet fabric into several strips and use it to secure her arms behind her back.

He shifts his body and ties her ankles together. Standing, he hauls her up and throws her over his shoulder, careful to keep her head clear of the corridor walls. She wiggles and bucks on his shoulder, trying to unbalance him and he clamps one hand around her thighs, bringing the other one down hard against her ass. She gasps and goes still. For a moment he's afraid she's "gone limp," one of the indicators that she's objecting to what he's doing. Did he take things too far?

To his relief, she gives a little moan, and he can smell her arousal.

"Struggle and you will be punished," he tells her and loves the little sound of excitement she makes. The threat of punishment makes her start struggling again.

This time he spanks his hand down twice in rapid succession, and she squirms against him. "I'll behave," she gasps out and stops struggling.

"Good little human," he says and rubs the spot he just struck. He makes quick work of the journey to her cabin and enjoys the squeal she makes when he tosses her onto the bed. Once she's done bouncing, she looks up at him with anticipation. He forces his face into a scowl.

"You're mine. You know this and yet you still ran from me. This is unacceptable," he tells her, and her eyes darken with lust, but when he kneels on the foot of the bed, she brings her bound legs up to kick him in the chest. He catches them easily and uses that opportunity to rip her pants to shreds.

"And now you've forced me to ruin perfectly good clothing," he admonishes her. She tries to struggle, but he just lies down on top of her.

She gives a little gasp. "Damn, you're heavy."

He lifts himself a little then puts his face to one of her breasts and sucks the hard peak of her nipple into his mouth. She makes a strangled noise and strains against him.

His erection is pushing against his pants, demanding to be free. He pulls his legs up under him to give his straining cock a little relief and brings his hand up to cup her other breast, tugging at the nipple.

When he lifts his head away from her, she protests. "More," she demands.

"I'll do as I wish," he tells her coldly, enjoying the way her face spikes with both need and annoyance.

He glances over his shoulder at her legs and gives himself a moment to ponder his next action. He wants her bound, but not with her legs together. He looks around the room but is loath to rip any of her fine decorative fabrics to tie her to the bed.

Struck with an idea, he gets up and peels his pants off, easily hauling her back to the center of the bed when she tries to roll away. Tearing the pants in two, he unties her legs and then uses his ripped pants as restraints. He reties her legs spread open, using the heavy wooden frame of the bed as anchor points.

She bucks and kicks, trying to get loose, but he just uses his bulk to hold her down until he's done. Then he settles down between her legs, desperate to taste her again. She struggles violently against the bonds as he nuzzles her clit, and then she gives a small, strangled cry when he sucks it into his mouth.

He stops before she can climax, enjoying her growls of frustration.

"You're a poorly behaved slave," he tells her. "I think you need some training."

"Training?" she gasps out.

"I'm going to put my cock in your mouth, but I want you to beg me for it."

"Never," she declares even while she licks her lips and glances down at his erection.

"Are you sure about that?" he asks and then dives between her legs again. He's careful to only tease her with his mouth, drawing away just as he senses she's about to climax, and then starting over again. When she screams with frustration, he raises his head to look her in the eyes.

"Beg," he demands.

"Please," she whimpers, tugging restlessly against the bonds. "Please put yourself in my mouth."

"All you needed to do was ask, little pet," he tells her with an evil smile. He pulls her upper body up and double checks that her wrists are still securely bound behind her, only to find she's managed to loosen the knot. "Oh no you don't," he murmurs and reties the knot a little tighter.

She's panting now, and the way he's kneeling gives her access to his face. She brings her mouth to his, demanding a kiss. He gives in for a moment then pulls away.

"No, no, little pet, that's not what I want you to kiss," he admonishes her. He rises up on his knees, drawing her head forward until she can access his pulsing cock. He hisses when her sweet warm mouth closes over him. He tangles his hand in her hair and grips her head, forcing himself further into her. She moans around him and sucks harder.

Using his hold on her hair, he pulls her mouth away from him. It's one of the hardest things he's ever done, especially when she gives a small sound of distress.

"I'm not done," she protests, and he roughly pushes her back down on the bed.

"I think you keep forgetting this isn't about what you want," he reminds her and spears his fingers between her legs. He pinches her clit until she bucks under him and then starts stroking her. Soon she's screaming, her body bowing off the bed with the intensity of her climax. He doesn't stop until she's jerking with discomfort, her sex swollen and oversensitive. He withdraws his hand, enjoying the way she's panting and sweating, and then settles himself between her legs.

"Beg," he demands, putting himself at the entrance of her vagina.

"Flush yourself out an airlock," she growls back, and he barks out a laugh.

He grabs her hips in a bruising grip, enjoying their interaction much more than he ever expected. "Beg," he demands again. Suddenly, it doesn't feel like a game anymore. He needs her to give in to him.

She gives a little gasp and shakes her head. "Go fuck a minari!" she screams at him. He bares his teeth and does something he's never done in his entire life: he leans forward and bites her shoulder. She gives a strangled gasp, and he pulls back, appalled at his behavior until he sees her face.

All lust and need.

He can't wait any longer. He shoves himself in and feels her body tense. "More," she moans.

With barely suppressed violence, he thrusts his hips back and forth, taking her harder than he's ever done with anyone else. He feels primal. He can't think past how good she feels. When she tightens around him and climaxes again, he's right behind her, roaring as he spills his seed into her.

Shaking from the aftermath, he manages to untie her legs. When he turns to untie her hands, she's already freed herself. She tugs at him, urging him to settle down next to her.

"That was fabulous," she pants as she snuggles against him, throwing an arm over his chest and a leg over his hips.

"Go fuck a minari?" he asks.

She laughs and then reaches up to rub her shoulder. He sees the bite he left and winces a little. He didn't break the skin, but she will be bruised. She catches his wince and winks at him. "You can bite me anytime. It felt amazing. The whole thing wasn't like anything I've ever felt before."

"It's never been like this for me either," he confesses. His heart is finally starting to slow down, and the sweat is cooling on their bodies. He hooks the rumpled covers with his foot and kicks them up until he can reach them with his hand and draws the warm blankets over both of them. She gives a small sigh of contentment and burrows her head into his shoulder.

He drifts to sleep with the taste of her on his lips, the smell of her in his nose, and the profound desire to never let her go.

CHAPTER

10

Mian tugs at the neck of her armor for the hundredth time as they stand waiting for the Bicoma delegation to show up. The rest of the trip through Raider Alley was uneventful, so they got to spend a lot of time just enjoying each other.

Once they reached Bicoma, Halin turned all business. He asked her to don full armor and weapons and escort him planetside. He explained that now that he's the only one left of his crew to participate, he has to go without armor or weapons and act as a diplomat. She would need to be his protection, an assignment she takes very seriously.

She's currently wearing almost every piece of gear she owns, including the plasma rifle slung across her back. She knows he's nervous but doing an excellent job of not showing it. She, however, seems unable to keep from fidgeting with her gear and glancing around, wondering what's keeping the damn Bicoma.

"Nice place," she mumbles sarcastically as she sweeps her eyes over the area. The planet the Bicoma first evolved on looks like a desert wasteland to her. She doesn't see anything but rocks, gravel, and sand around them. Except for the perfect circle of stonework floor they are standing on, the place looks uninhabited by any kind of advanced species. Or anything alive for that matter.

"At least we didn't just disappear the moment we entered their system," Halin points out, also eyeing the barren landscape.

"You make a good point," she agrees. "But I don't understand why they're keeping us waiting. We've done everything exactly as they requested."

"It's probably about showing dominance," he answers with a small grimace. "We're at their mercy because they might have the knowledge we desperately need, and we probably don't have anything they're particularly interested in. This is just a little reminder about who's in charge."

"It's stupid," she grumbles and is surprised when he chuckles.

"If anyone should understand power dynamics, it's you," he taunts her.

"I'll show you power dynamics," she warns him playfully. "Maybe next time I'll tie you up."

"You can try," he invites her. He looks over, catching her gaze with his. The lust in his eyes makes her breath catch. He gives her a little growl, pulling his lip up just far enough to show a hint of fang. She feels moisture pool between her legs, and she can't take her eyes off him. She's locked in his gaze until he breaks eye contact to look at something in the distance. She follows his gaze and sees movement.

They both watch, only to be disappointed when it turns out to be one of the many small lizard-like animals that roam the planet.

"Still," she continues. "They could've at least provided shade. It's hot as a recoil chamber down here."

"Have you hung out in many recoil chambers?" he asks idly.

"I've had to reach my hand in enough of them to know how uncomfortably hot they are," she retorts.

She reaches up to wipe the sweat away from her face and pull the high neck of her insulation garment away for a moment to let some air get to her neck and chest. If she'd known they'd be standing under an unforgiving sun with no shade in sight, she would have worn something more comfortable under the armor.

Out of habit and to comfort herself, she runs her hands over her weapons again, checking they are in place, on, and loaded. She looks up to find Halin watching her.

"I wish I could do that too," he mutters.

"Wear weapons?"

"No, run my hands all over you."

She flushes and makes a show of frowning at him. "Stay focused. I don't know what these Bicoma look like or might do. Keep your mind off your dick."

"Could I put your mouth on it instead?" he asks with an innocent expression, and she laughs.

Movement again catches her attention. "I think someone's finally showing up."

He turns in the direction she indicated, his face becoming expressionless. "I think you might be correct."

Three figures are walking toward them. As they draw closer, Mian finally gets to see what the elusive and mysterious Bicoma look like. They're a tall species, towering over her and perhaps even a few inches taller than Halin, but they are thin with long limbs.

They aren't wearing any clothes, but she can't see any discernible sex organs. Their skin appears to be a rust red except for their lower legs where the red darkens to black. They walk bipedally with two legs that end in small round feet with no toes. They might have only two legs, but they appear to have numerous arm appendages, not all the same length or shape. Even more interesting is the fact that none of the three have the same pattern or number of appendages. The one in the middle of the trio seems to have an appendage so short it couldn't possibly be useful for anything, so she wonders if he's growing it out. Could these creatures shed and grow arms?

They have recognizable faces, with small mouths, slits for a nose, and two large luminous eyes. She can't see any hair or fur but out of the back of their heads are spiny protrusions that gradually change color over their length, going from deep red, to purple, to blue, then back to red on the very tips.

Once they are close enough to enter the circle of stone, she can see they are covered in very fine scales, and their eyes seem to have multiple pupils that can move independently of each other.

That freaks her out more than anything else.

Halin stands stiff and still, holding his box full of samples. Mian rests one hand on the blaster on her hip and the other on the knife strapped to her thigh. She checks the charge on her armor and then orders the helmet up. There is no way she's going to wait for a first attack before she lets herself armor up. She's Halin's only protection, and if she's taken out by a head shot, there's no way he'll survive.

Of course, considering they're meeting with a species that can make whole armadas disappear, she knows she doesn't have a realistic chance to protect either of them if anything goes wrong.

"Welcome," the one in the middle speaks first. They are using voice boxes so they must not communicate with each other using verbalization through their mouths.

"Greetings," Halin replies. "Thank you for agreeing to meet with me. I apologize for my delay."

"You were attacked," the one on the right says. "You almost didn't survive."

"This one rescued you," the one on the left points to Mian with an appendage. She notices it only has two fingers on the hand pointing at her. The fingers don't seem to have any joints, they just bend like plastic, rolling and unrolling. Weird, but still not as freaky as the eyes.

She wonders how much Halin told them when he contacted them to request the meeting be postponed. She looks away from the Bicoma and over to Halin. He's barely repressing a frown.

"Yes, Captain Mian Sorrow saved me from a raider attack," he agrees cautiously, which tells her he didn't share that information in his messages to them. "You requested only three of us travel to Bicoma on a ship with no weapons. This left us vulnerable. If it hadn't been for Captain Sorrow, I wouldn't be alive and here."

"We wish to meet this Captain," the third one with the fewest limbs announces as he focuses several of his pupils on her. She knows with the helmet up, they can't see her face, but it feels like their strange eyes can see right through her armor. She experiences an odd constriction in her chest. She's not sure what's going on, but her finely tuned sense of danger isn't sounding alarms in her head. Still, a strong trepidation fills her. These creatures might not mean her harm, but she doesn't like their focus on her.

She takes a small step forward but doesn't take her hands off her weapons or retract her helm. She gives them a small bow at the waist. "Greetings." They keep staring at her even after she straightens up. None of them talk, and she wonders why they are so interested in her when it's Halin who's come to see them.

Finally, the one in the middle puts one leg forward and the entire limb bows forward slightly, lowering the thing's body a little. This must be the Bicoma version of a bow.

"We do not have names as your species does, but you may refer to me as Leader," he tells her, then gestures to his right. "You may call this one Follower." Follower also bends its leg to give a Bicoma bow. Leader points to his left. "And this one would like to be known as Advocate."

Advocate doesn't bow. He walks toward her until he's right in front of her, towering over her. Hands tightening on her weapon, she stifles the urge to step back.

"Retract your helm," Advocate demands, and Mian glances over to Halin. He's frowning, studying first the Bicoma in front of her, then her.

"I'm the one who is here to see you," he reminds them. His voice has an edge to it. She can hear the frustration and worry.

"We will get to your matter," Leader assures him. "But we want our curiosity appeased first." Leader turns his attention back to her. "Do as Advocate asks. Or you both may leave now with no answers."

Knowing how important this mission is for Halin and all the Hissa, Mian orders her armor to retract the helmet. The first thing she notices is the smell. The Bicoma smell familiar, like the hot, sweet tea her mother used to drink in the morning. She takes a deep breath through her nose and feels comforted. Advocate doesn't move or react. He seems to be studying her.

"I want to touch your skin," he tells her, making her start after such a long silence.

"This is unnecessary," Halin barks out, turning all their attention to him. "She's not Hissa. She's here due to unforeseen circumstances. She's inconsequential to this meeting." He holds the box a little higher. "I have samples of male and female Hissa here. I brought it for you to examine and help us find a way to continue our species."

She'd be insulted by his dismissal if she didn't know he was trying to protect her. Mian shifts her gaze between him and the Bicoma, standing silently and calm in front of her.

"Advocate just wishes to touch her, just a wrist will be fine," Leader assures him. "We will see to your matter afterward."

Mian quickly unlatches and then strips off one of her gloves. "It's fine," she states quickly before Halin can say anything more. She doesn't want him to jeopardize his mission just to keep a Bicoma from touching her wrist.

Keeping her fingers in a fist, she holds up her arm. Advocate steps closer, and the smell of warm, sweet tea fills her nose to the point she can't smell anything else. Three long fingers wrap around her wrist. Advocate's skin feels cold, but soft and silky too. She expected it to be rough, considering the harsh environment they live in.

The fingers holding her wrist have claws, unlike all the other digits on his many appendages. His fingers start to warm and at first, she thinks her skin must be warming him up. But his skin doesn't stop warming after matching her body temperature. The sensation of heat continues until the Bicoma's skin feels downright hot against hers. It doesn't hurt yet, it's just uncomfortable. His grip is firm, but not harsh. She wonders if Advocate would let go if she tugged her wrist away.

Then his fingers seem to get hotter. Her skin feels like it's burning, but when she looks down there's no discoloration or any other indication that she's suffering physical damage.

She grits her teeth and stands still as her other hand curls around the grip of her blaster, pulling it a little out of the holster. She might be willing to go along with this request, but only so far. If he starts burning her for real, she's going to make him stop.

Suddenly those claws pierce her skin. The heat turns to fire and spreads through her veins. The arm Advocate is holding goes limp, her muscles no longer able to work. The Bicoma's grip is the only thing keeping her arm in the air. She moves to pull her weapon, but Advocate's voice stops her.

"I'm not doing damage," it says simply. "Be still. Don't make me incapacitate you. I just need to taste you to be sure."

She's not sure what it means to 'taste' her, but when she opens her mouth to protest, she finds she can't talk. The Bicoma's sweet smell is heavy in her nose, and suddenly her brain feels sluggish, and her heartbeat slows. The hand on her weapon relaxes and her arm falls to her side. Somewhere in her brain, she thinks she should be pulling her weapon and demanding Advocate let go of her. But it's a distant thought, like a voice calling from a half-formed dream.

"Yes," Advocate says, his voice box quieter, the voice coming out of it taking on a soft musical quality. "Calm is good."

She tries to move again, even to just step back. But now her entire body is starting to go limp. She's never lost control of her body like this. A feeling of helplessness and fear clears a little of the fog in her brain. Then the strange feeling in her mind increases, and the fog covers any concerns she might have. Her legs start to buckle.

"Lock your legs," Advocate orders. She should be terrified that her body obeys the Bicoma, but the odd feeling in her brain makes it impossible for her to be concerned. It's like she's watching everything happening to her at a distance.

"Let your eyes close," Advocate orders and her lids sweep shut. "Think of something pleasant." Images of Halin flood her mind. "That's very good," Advocate tells her.

She can't tell how long they stand there before Advocate finally pulls away from her and she has control of her body again. The fog clears. Intense pain rockets through her, dropping her to her knees. Grasping the wrist the Bicoma had been holding, she pants as the momentary agony dissipates quickly.

Examining the skin of her wrist, she finds no burns and only two small holes, one of them welling with just one drop of blood before it stops. She watches with wide eyes as the tiny wounds heal and disappear in a matter of seconds.

"You are well," Advocate assures her, still towering over her. "Stand when you are ready."

The Bicoma turns to rejoin its two fellows standing on the other side of Halin. Looking up, she sees Follower has a hold of Halin's forearm. The grip doesn't seem tight, but Halin is standing perfectly still, his eyes wide and focused on her. She can see fury on his face and knows he's being held still by Follower just as she was held immobile by Advocate. A small trickle of blood is rolling down his arm from where Follower's claws have pierced his skin.

"As you can see, she is unharmed," Leader points out. "Follower will let go if you can remain calm. We are ready to have a discussion with you."

Mian stumbles to her feet and takes a few deep breaths, trying to get the spots floating in her vision to clear. "I'm not hurt," she croaks out. "I'm not thrilled, but I'm not hurt."

Halin turns his gaze back to Follower, and some kind of communication must have happened because the Bicoma releases Halin's arm and steps back. Mian watches Halin sway on his feet, but he doesn't fall. He shakes his head violently and absently rubs the spot on his forearm where Follower was gripping him.

She looks around and finds the box of biological samples on its side just past Leader. Halin must have thrown it and tried to get to her.

"She's human," Leader comments, pointing at Mian. She almost rolls her eyes at his statement of the obvious.

"She is," Halin agrees through gritted teeth. "And I'm Hissa. I don't see how Mian is related to my reason for being here."

"Yet, you would treat her as a Hissa female," Follower continues. "You would keep her as your own. You see her as your female. The future mother of your offspring."

Mian's jaw drops, and Halin glances over at her. For a moment, the anger disappears, and she sees a combination of lust and hope; then it's gone, and his gaze focuses back on Leader.

"But she isn't truly human," Leader continues. "She is a false human."

Mian opens her mouth to snap at Leader for the insult, but Halin speaks first. "There is nothing false about her. She is human and an honorable soldier."

"Bounty hunter," Follower clarifies.

"She protects those who are vulnerable, no matter her title," Halin growls out, and she's surprised he doesn't show them angry fang.

"Still, it doesn't change the fact that she is a false human. She wasn't born. She was manufactured. Her DNA isn't pure," Leader points out.

Mian thinks she knows what the Bicoma are getting at. "It's true. I'm Decanted," she speaks finally. "But the Hissa can't grow children like me. If that's what you're trying to say. Halin told me it failed. The tech that produced me can't help the Hissa."

Follower turns his gaze to her. "You're correct. The Hissa can't grow themselves. But you were grown."

Mian exchanges a puzzled glance with Halin.

Leader speaks again. "I can see you don't understand." He focuses his gaze on Follower. They stare at each other for a time, silently communicating, then both turn back to Mian.

"We aren't going to hurt you," Leader tells her, and before she can react to his words, her armor is gone. It's not pulled off her. It doesn't fall off. It just disappears, making her jolt. She gasps and looks wildly around for her armor and weapons, feeling immensely vulnerable without them.

Everyone knows the Bicoma are formidable, but this little demonstration makes her understand how truly powerful they are. After that first interaction with Advocate, she assumed they had to touch her to incapacitate her. Now she knows that they don't even need to be near her.

At least they left her wearing the high-necked insulation suit. She'd rather have her armor and weapons, but at least she's not standing naked under the harsh Bicoma sun.

No one is dead—yet.

Stop that, she tells herself. She needs to stay focused on the positives because if these Bicoma wanted to, they could easily snap their long fingers and make the two of them disappear, just like that Anavac armada.

"That suit is brand new," she grouses. Halin's shocked face breaks into a half-smile at her outrage.

"We have left you clothing for modesty. Pull the neck of your garment down or we can remove your clothing as well," Follower orders. She can't imagine what is going on, but she's not about to obey without a demand of her own.

"Give me back my armor and weapons," she demands. "I won't touch it, but I want it back." The three are silent for a moment, exchanging glances. Then her armor and weapons appear in a pile at her feet.

"You are doing well, Captain Sorrow," Leader comments. "Now let Commander Halin see your neck."

All of them are now watching her, including Halin. With a grunt of annoyance, she hooks a finger in the neck of her suit and drags it down. It's tight but elastic, so she's able to get it down to her collar bone. To her bewilderment, Halin goes pale and sways.

She lets go of the neck of her suit and runs to him, grabbing him by his arms in an attempt to steady him. Even with her assistance, he falls to his knees, never taking his eyes off her neck. She follows him down, going to one knee next to him.

"Easy, big guy," she tells him anxiously. "What's wrong?"

He just stares at her, then reaches up and rips open the neck of her shirt. Gasping, she rears back, but she doesn't get far. Without getting up, he clamps a hand down on her upper arm, using enough force to bruise as he keeps her from moving away. He brings his other hand to her neck, running his finger along something he sees there.

"It can't be," he mumbles. He almost sounds drunk. "It's impossible."

"She is a false human," Follower repeats. "She is more than human. She is many others. The Decanted humans can be the savior to the Hissa."

Still confused, Mian looks around at the Bicoma and then back to Halin. "What's going on?" She tries to look down at her neck but can't see anything. Advocate steps forward and holds up an appendage, three fingers spread wide. The air shimmers in front of her and solidifies into a disk that reflects her image. She tugs at her ripped insulation garment and leans toward the disk. There's something dark red on her neck. She studies it, confused. Slapping Halin's hand away so she can see better, she frowns at her reflection.

"When did I get a tattoo?" she murmurs as she realizes that's exactly what it looks like. A strange geometric pattern circles the base of her neck and continues down. She can only pull the torn garment down one shoulder but sees the pattern gets looser and vaguer until it becomes just a warm red color as it gets to the edge of her shoulder.

Flummoxed, she looks down at Halin. "What's going on here? Do you think the new armor did this? Maybe I need to wear a thicker insulation shirt?"

He still looks pale, but his eyes are blazing with possessiveness. "It's not the armor." His voice is deep and raspy. "You have mating marks." He goes silent again, his gaze fixed on the marks.

Advocate drops his appendage, and the reflecting disk disappears.

Mian throws up her hands in frustration. "How about you give me a little more to go on here?" she growls out, ready to start smacking all of them around until someone explains what's going on. "It's one thing for those guys to be all mysterious and taciturn, but I need you to be way more forthcoming. What the hell is going on?"

Halin surges to his feet and pulls her tightly against him. "When two Hissa want to see if they are compatible, they'll live together for several weeks. They live in the same house, share the same bed, and become known to each other. If the female develops mating marks, then they know the two can have young together," he explains in a shaking voice. He's holding her so tightly she's surprised her ribs don't give audible cracks.

"These marks around your neck mean you and I are compatible," he continues. He bends his knees a little, tightens his hold, and picks her up against his chest. She gives a little gasp as her feet dangle, and he buries his face against the skin of her neck. "I knew you smelled good. I just thought it was lust, but now I know it's more."

"The Hissa would do well to find the other Decanted females. Many were sold. They could be rescued and provided care and homes," Leader says, reminding both of them that they aren't alone on this desolate planet. The three Bicoma stand together, watching Halin and Mian interact. They remind Mian a little of an audience. Observing but not interacting.

Or maybe puppeteer is more accurate. Setting things in motion, then standing back to see how everything will turn out. She doesn't like the feeling of being manipulated. And something tells her these Bicoma know a lot more than they're letting on. For some reason, she gets the feeling they knew about her before she even got near the Bicoma territory.

"Put me down," she orders with a halfhearted smack to the side of Halin's head. Slowly, he lowers her to the ground and lets her turn to face the Bicoma. He's not done touching her, he wraps his arms possessively around her and draws her back tightly against him.

"I humbly thank you for this gift." His voice chokes as he addresses the Bicoma. "How can the Hissa repay you?"

All three study them silently, and Mian gets a feeling they're considering Halin's words.

"Payment seems supercilious considering the female gave you the gift, not us," Leader says finally. "But if you will, we would like to keep the box of samples you've brought. Perhaps, in the future, we will be able to trade you for what we want from the Hissa. You do not have it yet, but you will. When you have what we need, we will speak again. We can only hope you truly are the honorable species you appear to be."

Those words don't sit comfortably with Mian, and she opens her mouth to demand further explanation when Leader meets her eyes. "It's not for you to understand," he states, and she feels a strange shiver of foreboding go through her.

"You may leave now," Advocate tells them, and all three link appendages. The next moment, the world goes black.

CHAPTER

11

Mian wakes slowly and gives a little groan. Her head is killing her, making her wonder how much she had to drink to cause this kind of headache. She cracks open her eyes and sees a lovely expanse of muscled chest in front of her. How drunk did she get to let someone onto her ship and into her bed?

The muscled chest expands with a breath, and a familiar snore hits her ears.

Halin.

Memories come flooding back, and she bolts up in bed. Dark spots dance in her vision, and she almost falls back down. Next to her, Halin gives a little groan and brings his hands to his head. Apparently, she's not the only one suffering.

She looks down to see she's still wearing her ripped insulation suit. Why is she dressed and Halin's naked?

Actually, how did the two of them get back to the ship? She staggers to her feet and searches out some painkillers and water. She uses the drug gun on herself, then calibrates it for Halin's weight and gives him a dose. While it's taking effect, she finds a water container and drinks all of it. She's feeling better by the time she refills the container and brings it to Halin, who's now sitting up and rubbing his head.

He looks up at her blearily. "Why do I feel like my head was stepped on by a Pienter?"

"I don't know, but the last thing I remember is being in that stone circle with the Bicoma, and now we are here on Fortune." She looks at her wrists, relieved to find her data bracelet is still there. She activates the holo function and interfaces with Fortune's computer. She gives a little relieved sigh and shoots him a grin that's more grimace than anything else. "We're floating just outside of Bicoma space. At least they didn't disappear us."

He nods his head, then winces. Did she give him a big enough dose of painkillers? "Here, drink this." She offers him the container, and he drinks greedily. "You hit the cleanser unit. I'll meet you in the cockpit. I want to check all the systems on the ship before we head anywhere."

"Join me?" he asks, and despite his pain he manages to leer at her. She sees the exact moment when his gaze falls on the marks on her neck. He reaches up to run a finger over them again, his expression turning reverent. Uncomfortable, she shoves him away with a forced grin.

"Get moving!" she orders and then enjoys the view as he strides unabashedly naked across the room. She should be getting up herself but gets distracted as she watches his beautiful, tight ass walk away until he finally disappears into the cleansing unit.

Giving herself a mental shake, she pulls off the soiled insulation garments and pulls on some of the soft, comfortable clothing Halin purchased for her. She's gotten to enjoy the feel of the fabrics against her skin, and the bright colors make her smile. After a lifetime spent in dull but practical outfits or biosuits, she's growing to love the things Halin wants her to wear.

She uses the small facility in the cockpit to clean her face. Then she tames her short hair by pulling it into a small, tight ponytail at the back of her head. Cleaned up, she drops into the pilot seat and starts going over the ship's systems, finding nothing out of the ordinary. She's surprised when she notices one of her port guns that registered a jam the day before, seems to be operating fine. Searching, she discovers all the recurring issues she has with the Fortune are fixed, and the ship's fully fueled.

Well, that's a hell of a parting gift, she thinks. All of it almost makes up for the highhanded way they treated her and Halin.

Footsteps in the corridor bring her eyes up in time to watch Halin walk in. Looking refreshed, he carries in a tray of food.

"You didn't eat," he grumbles as he walks to the gunner's chair and sits. He places the tray in his lap. The smell of food makes Mian realize she's very hungry, so she reaches for one of the plates. Halin grabs her hand and brings it to his mouth, pressing her palm against his lips, kissing her before letting go of her hand. She smiles and grabs the plate before he can get any ideas.

"Food first," she demands, and he chuckles.

"Agreed," he says. "Food first."

They eat in silence for a moment, then the ship's engines fire and Fortune vibrates as it starts moving. The navigation system must have finally finished calculations and put Fortune in motion.

"All systems working?" Halin asks, popping a morsel of food into his mouth.

"Not only is Fortune working, but everything is fixed. Everything. Even the stuff that I've been putting off because I knew it was going to cost me a lot to repair. The faulty heating unit in gun bay three is working, and I thought I was going to need to replace the whole unit." She pulls out a drawer next to her. "This broke a while back and now it doesn't even squeak! I don't know how they do it, but those guys are scary powerful. It reminds me of stories my mom used to tell me, back when humans didn't understand science. They thought natural phenomena was caused by things like gods fighting. The Bicoma are so advanced, they remind me of those stories. Their tech seems like magic." She sits back, thoughtful. "It surprises me they didn't wander the universe enslaving everyone or at least telling everyone they're gods."

"It was a shock when they made your armor disappear," Halin agrees and then gives her a salacious grin. "But I wouldn't mind being able to make your clothes disappear whenever I feel like it."

Chuckling, she rolls her eyes at him, "You and every other horny male out there. Still, that whole speech about wanting something from the Hissa in the future worries me. What do you think that's all about? It gave me a bad feeling."

Halin shrugs, obviously unconcerned. "I have no idea, but I don't find myself particularly disturbed." His gaze becomes intense, and he reaches up to touch her neck again. "You're with me, and that's all that matters."

Mian forces a small laugh, trying to lighten the mood. She sets her empty plate down and pats his knee. "Let me check a few more things, and we can have some play time."

He gives her a severe look. "We won't be doing any more of the sex-fighting like before," he declares, making her knit her brows in confusion.

"Why not? I thought you had fun too?"

"I did," he assures her quickly, his expression softening. He leans over and gives her a quick kiss, and when his fangs brush against her lips, she shivers.

Grabbing him by the back of his head, she holds him still so she can lock her lips to his. An aroused sound comes from deep in his chest. *Oh yeah,* she thinks, *you love the rough stuff too.*

"If you liked it, and I liked it, there's no reason not to do it again."

He pulls her hand away from his head and sits back. He keeps her hand captured in his. She can see his erection pressing against his pants, but he's not making any more advances, and that worries her. Halin's acting odd.

"It's too dangerous," he explains, his face worried. "You might already be carrying my young, and I have no wish to risk damage to you or our offspring."

Annoyed that he's just now thinking about the possibility of getting her pregnant, she rolls her eyes. "Well, you don't need to worry," she assures him, tugging her hand out of his grip. "I had a sterilization shot a couple of years ago."

The change in Halin is abrupt and terrifying. He violently throws the tray with the remanent of their food against a nearby wall. Grabbing her upper arms in a bruising grip, he stands up, hauling her into the air with him.

"Sterilization shot?" he roars. "Why would you do such a thing?"

Truly fearful of him for the first time, Mian lets her instincts take over. She brings her legs up and kicks out, both feet connecting with his stomach. Unprepared for the blow, Halin staggers and releases her. She lands in an ungraceful heap just behind the pilot's chair.

On hands and knees, she scrambles for the weapons cabinet, but Halin's on her before she even gets halfway there. He tackles her, pushing his weight against her.

"Don't fight me!" he roars, the playful lover gone, replaced by a raging beast.

Mian punches him, feeling his nose give under her fist. He rears back from the pain, and she tries to wiggle out from under him. He grabs her wrists, trying to pull them behind her. She never used her full strength when they were playing, but now that she feels like she's fighting for survival, she doesn't hold back.

Getting one hand free, she reaches down and grabs his cock through his pants. Her hands are strong from years of wielding weapons and doing her maintenance. She uses that strength to squeeze and twist one of the more vulnerable parts of his anatomy. Crying out, he's forced to release her other hand to attempt to wrestle himself out of her grasp. He grabs her hand, but she just tightens down. If he pulls at her hand, he'll just hurt himself.

Realizing she won't let go, he picks her up to knee height and slams her back down. She ends up flat on her back, the wind knocked out of her. She tastes blood in her mouth. She bit her tongue. His actions managed to loosen her hands and he's able to rip her fingers off him.

"Stop fighting," he demands. She doesn't talk. Without thinking, she spits bloody saliva into his face. Shocked, he freezes, allowing her to head butt his already damaged nose. She feels the top of her head makes a solid impact with his face. Letting go of her, he rears back from the pain, allowing her to scramble out from under him. He doesn't follow her. He stays on his knees, looking at the blood from his nose on his hands and then up at her face. His eyes are round with shock and confusion.

"I'm bleeding. And you're bleeding," he says in a voice full of disbelief. "I hit you. I made you bleed. And I'm bleeding too. How did this happen?" Although he sounds more like the Halin she knows, she doesn't stop moving.

She abandons trying to get to the weapons cabinet. She rolls herself under the pilot's chair and reaches for the small compartment hidden in the base of the chair. It pops open at her touch, and she pulls a small blaster out. She's on her feet and pointing it at Halin just as he's reaching for her again. The sight of the weapon makes him freeze.

"I don't want to shoot you, but I won't hesitate to put a hole in you if you try to touch me again," she warns him. Her voice is distorted from her rapidly swelling lips and jaw, but there's no mistaking the deadly intent in her tone.

"I'm sorry," he says quickly. His face is a bloody mess. She doesn't think his nose is broken, but there is blood seeping from his mouth, nose, and one of his eyes is swelling, the green skin around it getting darker from the damage.

"I don't know what's wrong with me," he tells her, his face full of fear and shame. He's holding his hands up, palms out to show he means her no harm. "I seem to be having a hard time controlling my emotions since I saw the mating marks on your neck. I didn't mean to be violent."

"If wishes were fishes, we could walk the oceans," Mian grumbles out. That's one of her mother's favorite sayings. He gives her a confused look.

"I don't care what you say. Your actions speak loud and clear," she declares. "I can't claim to understand what's going on, but you don't get to make me afraid. When we played the other day, it was about having fun and giving each other pleasure. What you did just now was anger and domination. No one gets to do that to me."

"Your lip is cut. Let me tend to you," he begs. Her face throbs and she can feel blood trickling down her chin. She ignores all of it, her eyes hard and focused on Halin.

"You're done touching me." She's relieved her voice sounds strong, and her hand isn't shaking. She manages to hold it together even though all she wants to do is curl up in a ball and cry. The last few weeks with Halin have been the best she's known since her parent's death. How could everything go so wrong, so quickly? How could she have misjudged this male?

"I don't know how to explain it, but I'd never hurt you," he tries to say, and she lets out a short, humorless laugh.

"I think my face says differently," she shoots back.

"You can hurt me back. My actions were unpardonable, and I still don't understand how I let myself do that. It's the marks on your neck," Halin continues. "The marks mean you can bear my child." His shoulders slump a little, and she watches him take a few deep breaths, probably trying to calm all those raging emotions.

"After the death of my mother and sisters, I assumed I would never find a female to bear my young. I just assumed I'd never have a child. I'd never know the joys of having a family of my own. And then the mark appears on you, and I find there isn't just hope for my species, but specifically for myself."

"You know I get a say in all this, right?" she asks him sarcastically. "I'm not just some Minari pet you can breed or smack around when you aren't happy with me."

He seems taken aback by her words, as if it never occurred to him that she would object to his plans. "I never thought of you as a pet," he says quickly. "I just felt betrayed when you so casually mentioned you altered yourself. It felt like you ripped my hopes and dreams out of me. I didn't think. I just reacted. Then you started fighting me. I don't know why, but it just triggered something in me."

"Fine, I get that," Mian says and realizes she does understand him. She wonders what she would do if she was given the hope of having her parents back only to have the hope brutally ripped away. "But I think you need to spend the rest of the trip in the cabin."

He opens his mouth to protest, but she violently shakes her head and moves out of the way so he can walk to the door. "Don't make me drug you," she warns him. "I don't trust you right now.

That means either you let me lock you in my cabin, or I put you under for the rest of the trip. I don't have any sleep pods, so it would have to be sedation, and that's dangerous to do for more than two cycles in a row."

She watches his face closely, braced to shoot him if he tries to attack her again. She'll make sure to aim for his shoulder and feels thankful she made Halin buy her several tubes of nanos. The nanos will heal him if she's forced to wound him.

Still, she doesn't want to wound him in the first place, even after what he's done.

"I'll allow you to lock me in the cabin," he finally agrees, and she lets out the breath she didn't know she'd been holding.

"After you," she says and waits for him to walk past her before she moves. He's quiet for the trip to the cabin and only turns to face her once he's inside. He looks strangely resigned and determined at the same time.

"It's going to be a long trip," he points out. He gives her a small smile, showing a bit of fang. She tamps down her instinctive reaction to his familiar, mischievous grin. "If I agree to be good, will you visit me? We could talk and do other things."

She shakes her head, feeling depressed at the idea of facing the next week without getting to interact with him. "Afraid not, handsome." She steps to the door controls and starts tapping them while keeping her weapon aimed at him. "You're in lockdown until we get to Wint."

"No, we are going to Hissa," he states, stepping toward the hatch. She brings her gaze back to him. He stops, his hands curling into fists at his side. "You agreed to take me to Hissa."

"That was before. Now I'm dropping you at Wint," she announces, proud of the strength of her voice. "I consider our contract finished, and I will not require any further payment from you. I'll drop you at Wint, and you can find your own way back to Hissa."

Rage contorts his face as she slams her hand down on the control panel. The hatch slides shut and locks in place. She hears his body thud against the hatch, and then she hears him pounding on it with his fists.

"Yeah," she says with deep sorrow, finally letting the tears start to fall. "That's how I thought you might react."

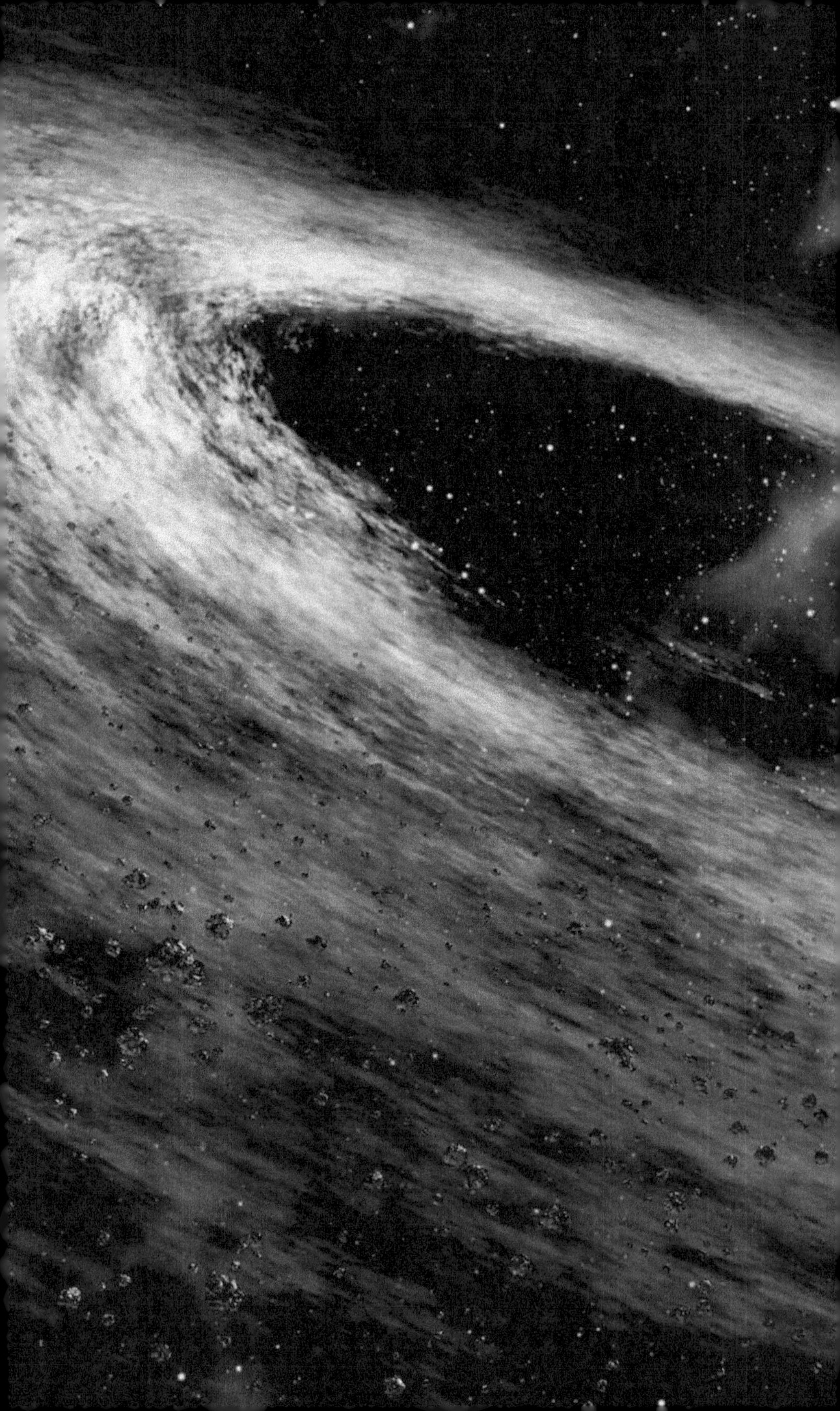

CHAPTER 12

Halin pounds on the door until both his hands are bloody messes and his throat is raw from roaring. His entire body is shaking when he takes a step back.

Control, he thinks to himself. I need to get myself back under control. This isn't like him. This isn't the Hissa warrior and Commander that spent so many years in service to his people. If anyone who served under him could see him now, they'd be shocked at his actions.

He struck Mian.

Looking down at his large hands makes him wince. How could he have done such a thing? He hurt her. A deep and profound shame rolls through him.

He wishes he could understand why he did it, but he doesn't even remember striking her. It's almost as if he woke up suddenly and realized she was hurt. He must have hit her to cause those injuries.

The sight of blood dripping from her chin will haunt him.

She doesn't even want to talk to me, he realizes as he looks over to the coms next to the door. They're dark, shut off. Mian's a professional. She'll have made sure he can't contact anyone, on the ship or off. He doesn't even try opening the hatch. He knows it's locked. She wouldn't overlook that. She's a smart and skilled female who's done nothing but help him, and he just terrorized her.

Slumping down in a padded chair, he lets his head fall back and gives a little groan of agony. His head still hurts a little from what the Bicoma did to them, and his stomach feels like it's tied in knots. His fists are throbbing, and his shoulder aches from where he hit the door when he rushed at her. His nose isn't broken, but it's so swollen he can't breathe through it, and one eye doesn't want to focus.

But all the damage Mian did to him pales in comparison to the fact that he hit her. That makes him want to violently void the contents of his stomach. How could he have done that?

The look on her face just before the door closed was the most damning part. It hadn't been fear.

The look on her face was one of pure betrayal.

How could he explain to her what he's feeling? The moment he woke and realized the marks on her were real, that it hadn't all been a dream, all he wanted to do was pick her up and cradle her in his arms. He wanted to mate with her, make her gasp with pleasure, and plant his seed in her. He wanted to watch his young grow in her belly.

He wanted to hold their child in his arms.

He wanted it so badly he could almost feel a small, fragile body in his hands. Somehow, he knows their young would have her beautiful eyes. And their child would be brilliant and fierce like her.

As images of his future young filled his head, the instinct to protect overwhelmed him. He would protect both mother and unborn child with his life.

Then she told him with calm dispassion that she had deliberately chosen to sterilize herself. Her words ripped him in two. He'd acted without thought, and now he's paying for his barbaric behavior.

If he could get her to talk to him, he might be able to smooth things over, win her to his side. Now that his brain is working again, he remembers it was a chemical sterilization, perhaps it can be reversed. She might still be able to bear his young. They just need to talk. He can reason with her.

She isn't alone anymore.

Her human parents might be dead, but now she'll have all of Hissa ready to be her family. All of Hissa will love her. She doesn't have anything to fear for herself or her young. He just needs to explain all that to her.

Unfortunately, he hadn't quite gotten himself under control when she told him she was going to drop him at Wint Station. That was too close. Leaving him at Wint means they'll be parted too soon. He needs more time. He needs a chance to woo her back.

But no gentle words of persuasion came out of his mouth. The same emotional maelstrom that hit him in the cockpit came over him again. He'd rushed her, his only thought to get his hands on her. He knows it was wrong, but he felt the need to force her to obey him. If he could just make her listen to him, he's sure he can make her understand. Make her realize that he is hers, and she is his.

Then he roared and pounded on the door. How likely is it that she'll listen to him now? He's never made so many mistakes in such a short period of time.

He needs to be calm and controlled again. He needs to be the male who commands fleets. He needs to remember how to use his natural negotiation and manipulation skills, the very reason he was sent on this mission to meet the Bicoma in the first place.

If he can just talk to her, he knows she can be convinced to go with him. But he needs time and access.

Opening his eyes, he lifts his head and looks over to the locked hatch. But first, before he can make anything happen, he needs to get out of this room.

With renewed determination, he gets up and starts searching the room, going through every nook and cranny looking for something useful. He wants to curse when he doesn't find anything he can utilize to get the hatch open. Taking a break from his search, he enters the cleansing unit. His hands are covered in his dried blood. Holding them under the spray, he watches the blood slowly wash off. That's when he realizes how to get out of the room.

Quickly drying his hands off, he looks around the floor of the cleansing unit until he finds the panel he needs. He pushes his fingers through the plate. Gripping it as best he can, he braces his legs and pulls. The steel gives a small screech as it gives. He can feel the grates cutting into his hands, but he ignores the pain. Finally, he's pulled it open enough to reach the components inside. He starts feeling around until he finds the capacitor. With a sigh of relief, he gently tugs it out. Then he breaks off a piece of the metal grate.

He hurries to the hatch control panel and uses the jagged bit of metal grate to crack the edges of the control panel open. He has to be careful. If he cracks the whole plate, it will set off an alarm. His hands are steady as he works, but it takes more concentration than it should. Halfway through, he wants to pound the plate with his fists instead of this tedious delicate work. He's fighting his violent instincts every step of the way.

Once all the edges are cracked, he wedges the piece of metal grate under the panel cover and lifts. Holding his breath, he goes slowly, listening for the telltale click that would indicate he set off the alarm.

He's able to open it far enough to reach inside and pull a few wires out. They're incredibly small in his big hands, and he has a tense moment when he thinks he might have pulled one out too far. Once they're out far enough, he pulls the wires apart, exposing ends to hook to the capacitor. The moment the wires are attached to the capacitor, it releases its small charge. That is enough to make the hatch panel light up, and the door slide open.

Moving quickly, he leaves the room, letting the hatch close behind him. He stands in the corridor for a moment, thinking about what to do next. He needs Mian to listen to him, but he's got a bad feeling there is no way she will sit quietly and let him explain if he just walks into the cockpit. He needs to be able to capture and secure her. He'll make it so she has no choice but to let him make his case.

He thinks about the contents of her ship and remembers the box of prison restraints he ran across when they'd been trying to find space for all the items that he purchased at Wint. Unlike the flexicuffs, these restraints are gentle, meant to be worn for long periods without doing damage.

He finds the box quickly and upends the thing, dumping its contents on the floor, sifting through until he finds restraints that look like they'll fit Mian's small wrists and ankles. He experiences a moment of doubt as he holds the restraints in his big hands. These have been used to hold raiders and murderers. They are meant to keep individuals who've done horrible things from getting loose before they face justice. Mian doesn't deserve to wear such devices.

Maybe he should just use fabric to restrain her. Then he remembers how easily she untied herself. There is no way the method they used when playing would keep her restrained if she didn't want it to stay that way. No, it'll need to be the prisoner restraints, or he might as well just hand her the blaster again.

With restraints in hand, he jogs soundlessly to the cockpit. Soon he's standing to the side of the open hatch, listening to her inside. It takes a few moments before he realizes she's crying. His grip tightens on the sharp metal of the restraints as he listens to her sobs. He did that. He caused that.

And he's about to cause even more distress.

I'll make her understand, he tells himself. *Everything will be fine. I just need her to listen to me. Everything will be better once she agrees with me. When we're done fighting and she understands I'm right, I'll make her joyful. It will be difficult for a while, but in the end, she'll be happy.*

He peeks his head around the hatch frame to see her curled up in the pilot chair, legs drawn up, arms tightly wrapped around her shins, and her forehead resting on her knees. He wonders how long she's been like that. Maybe if he lets her shoot him, it will make her feel better. He's ready to take a couple of blaster hits if that means she'd stop crying.

But he knows it's not that simple and steels himself for what he needs to do next. He glances around her, seeing the small blaster resting on the control console in front of her. Her armor and other weapons are still neatly piled in the far corner where the Bicoma left them when they transported the two of them back to Fortune. The blaster is the only close weapon, but the way she's curled up in the chair means she won't be able to reach it if he's fast.

After taking a couple of deep breaths, he launches himself through the hatch.

Before she can even look up, he's on her. Grabbing both her wrists, he clamps on the restraints. Belatedly, she tries to fight, but by then he has control. He pulls her out of the seat and shoves her to the floor, using his weight to hold her still as he secures her ankles.

He growls when he turns back, and she punches him with one fist wrapped around another. She doesn't have room to maneuver, so the blow doesn't do anything but tap his cheek. He flips her onto her belly and sits on her, dragging her hands out from under her body and over her head. He releases the restraints then twists her arms around so he can secure her hands behind her back.

"Raiderbait!" she screams under him. "Get off me, you piece of Pienter shit!"

"I'm sorry, Mian," he whispers regretfully. "This isn't for play. This is for keeps."

As he stands, he hauls her up and throws her over his shoulder. He ignores her as she rages at him, struggling against the bonds. "Please don't fight," he says, holding her legs steady as he walks. "You're only going to hurt yourself." She doesn't listen to him, and he can't say he's surprised. It's not long until her breathing is ragged, and she's soaked in sweat from her struggles.

When they reach the cabin, he opens the door and then spends a few moments programming the hatch to stay open. There's no one else on the ship, and he doesn't want to run the risk of getting trapped in the cabin. The trick he used to open it from the inside ruined the panel. It will need to be entirely replaced before the hatch will work from the inside again.

Once he's satisfied they won't get caught on the wrong side of the hatch, he strides to the bed. He tries to lay her down gently, but she's thrashing so hard he has to concentrate on keeping her head from hitting the headboard. Her cursing and screaming hasn't abated since leaving the cockpit. His female has impressive endurance.

"Stop," he growls. He grows fearful she'll damage herself. He lays on top of her, using his body weight to force her to be still. When she goes rigid, he rises just enough to see her face. Her expression is one of total hate.

"Let me loose," she demands. He notices the bruises forming on her face and her swollen lip from the earlier fight. He needs to tend to her injuries. But first, he needs to make sure she's secured.

"You know I can't do that. I don't think I can even trust you enough to let you have your hands secured in front of you." He sits back, using his hips to keep her pinned under him. He can't keep her hands bound behind her back. It will become uncomfortable quickly, and potentially even dangerous if she ends up in a position that reduces the circulation in her arms. He eyes her headboard for a moment and then looks back at her.

"I need you to be still," he says. She glowers at him.

"I need you to stop being a piece of Pienter shit," she replies. His female isn't one to be subdued easily. He might have bruised her, but it will take more than his thoughtless attack to break her spirit.

He carefully gets off her. "I'll be right back." He hurries to where he dumped out the box of prisoner restrains and digs around until he finds a set of cuffs with a long chain between them. He's just getting back to the cabin when he hears a muffled thump and a small cry of pain.

Heart in his throat, he rushes in to find Mian on the floor next to the bed trying to get her knees under her. She's so intensely focused on her goal she doesn't notice he's back. He follows her line of sight and sees a small compartment in the wall he didn't notice before.

Striding over, he ignores her baleful look and taps the door to the compartment. The door slides open to reveal a small blaster and a knife. He looks back at her, and her expression doesn't waver. At this moment, he has no doubt she'd use the blaster on him and not just to wound.

With a sigh, he leaves the compartment and picks her up, easily carrying her back to the bed despite her struggles. Once on the bed she stops moving, but he sits on her anyway. She's probably hoping if she's quiet he'll leave again. He secures one end of the restraint to the sturdy headboard and then reaches for her hands. He unlatches her wrists, and she moves with the speed of a well-practiced fighter. Evading his grip, she manages to get a jab in. He hisses in pain when her fist connects with his swelling eye.

Grabbing her loose hand, he secures her wrists back together in front of her. Then he attaches the other end of the headboard restraint to the small length of chain between her wrists. He gives it a couple of good yanks. That satisfies him that it will hold her, but still allow her enough room to be comfortable. Confident she can't escape, he moves off her, careful to steer clear of her kicking feet.

But once she's free of his weight, she stops fighting and rolls onto her side, curling her legs up against her body. She suddenly looks small and fragile, and he feels ashamed again. When she speaks in a calm, monotone voice, it makes his heart hurt. His female, so full of life, should never sound so dull or flat.

"I've done nothing but help you." her voice is hoarse from screaming, making him wince.

"I'll care for you," he promises and hurries to find the med kit and bring it back to the bed. She remains unmoving as he cleans the blood off her face and holds a cooling pack to her bruised cheek. Trying to comfort them both, he touches her hair, stroking her head.

He stops when he sees her eyes. They're dull and full of pain.

"I need you to listen to me," he pleads.

"Go ahead and talk then," she says in a flat voice, the betrayal seeping out of her face to be replaced with a look of despair. That look tells him it's useless to talk to her at the moment. She won't hear anything he has to say.

He tosses the cooling pack aside and crawls onto the bed, thankful she doesn't fight him when he pulls her to him, cradling her body against his. He buries his face in her neck.

"I'm just going to hold you," he whispers, feeling despair rising up. "We can talk later. But I just need to feel you against me for now."

"It's not like I can stop you," she points out harshly. She shivers, and he notices her skin is cold against his. Reaching down, he draws the soft cover over both of them.

She doesn't smell as she should, he realizes. Instead of her normal sweet smell, she stinks of anguish, pain, and fear. He knows he's the cause, and agony fills his chest. He curses himself for being an undisciplined fool.

I'll convince her to stay with me tomorrow, he thinks and closes his eyes. He's exhausted from the riot of emotions he's felt in a short time, and the intense amount of effort it's taking to control his anger. *This can't be how it ends for us. She has my mating marks around her neck. She felt great affection for me. I can make her want me again. We just need a little time.*

He lets himself fall into sleep once he feels her body relax against his and her breathing even out. He falls asleep almost believing the lies he's telling himself.

CHAPTER

13

Mian doesn't fight when Halin carries her through the connecting hatch from Fortune to the small shuttle that arrived a few minutes ago to take them down to Hissa. He has her hands manacled behind her back and her ankles restrained with only a foot of chain between them, reducing her to a hobbling gait. Halin carrying her seems a better alternative than stumbling every other step. He sets her down just inside the shuttle, and they face the Hissa pilot waiting for them.

The pilot stands at attention, grinning at Halin. Then he frowns when he notices her standing bound next to him. The man's eyes almost seem to pop out of his head when he notices the mating marks around her neck. Straightening up, he taps his finger over his heart, staring hard at her throat.

"Eyes on me, Pilot Garin," Halin growls, and the man's attention snaps back to his superior. "I appreciate the formal greeting gesture, but she doesn't know it. Besides, can't return it even if she understood." Halin taps two fingers between his eyes, and the Pilot returns the gesture, but his eyes keep wavering over to her.

"Sir, she's, uh, she has..." Garin's voice trails off, and he points to her neck.

"I'm aware," Halin notes wryly. "Those mating marks are why we're going before the Council the moment we are planet side."

"Right." Garin's attention snaps back to his assignment. "The doors are being held open for you sir. I'll have you there in twenty."

"Make it ten," Halin orders. Despite his cool, commanding demeanor, she can tell he's anxious. He's worried about this Council. That could work in her favor.

Yesterday, he explained the Council is the highest ruling body on Hissa. That means they have power over Halin and could be her avenue for escape. At the very least, she can make a case for being let out of the restraints. Garin's just as big as Halin. If these two are the standard size of a Hissa male, she might be able to convince these Council guys that her small stature offers no threat. Once she's no longer bound hand and foot, she's got a chance at freedom. Just one blaster will make all the difference.

It's the mating marks that worry her the most. If this Council decides these mating marks mean Halin owns her, then she's screwed. If she's forced to stay with him, she'll never get free. He knows better than to relax around her.

"I'm sorry, sir, but maybe we should release the female. Those restraints will be pretty uncomfortable during free fall," Garin protests, eyeing her. "If you want me to get you down that fast, I'll have to free fall most of the way down. Can her body even handle that? She seems rather small."

Mian almost snorts. Under normal circumstances she'd assure the pilot she's not fragile and she likes the occasional free fall through the atmosphere. But for the last two weeks, she hasn't spoken a single word.

Halin tried all types of things to get her to talk. Begging, cajoling, deliberately trying to make her angry. He even faked a raider attack, but she refused to interact. Hurt by his betrayal, she retreated into herself, unwilling to interact with him except to request the basic necessities.

He left her secured to the bed most days, forced to add a bolt in the wall after she managed to work part of her beautiful headboard loose and get free. Her freedom didn't last. Halin caught her before she even made it to a weapon.

After that, he didn't leave her alone. If he was in the cockpit, he secured her to the bunk there. If he needed to do maintenance, he'd find a place to secure her in the corridor. He searched her cabin for more weapons but realized quickly he'd never find all her hiding places on the ship. It was easier to keep her at his side as he took over Fortune.

She never reacted as he dragged her, bound and helpless, around the ship, or brought her back to the cabin to secure her on the bed. She remained passive, unresponsive, and alert. Always on the lookout for an opportunity.

However, she wished her traitorous body got the message too. During their sleep cycle, Halin curled himself around her. She might be furious with him, but in those quiet moments, she luxuriated in his warmth. The smell of him made her want to rub herself against him, and her body ached for his touch. He never forced himself on her, but he would stroke her, and sometimes put his mouth on her. He'd wait until she was panting and writhing, then he'd stop and try to get her to talk to him. She never did, but there were a few times she came very close to giving in.

The fact that she still wants him is what hurts the most. Even after what he did.

She looks over to find the pilot giving her a meaningful glance, and Halin just shaking his head. "A violent free fall won't bother her. I'm not sure there's much that does," he assures Garin. "I'll make sure she doesn't suffer any ill effects from the restraints."

"But she's female, sir, and so small," the pilot protests again.

Halin barks at him. "Get this ship on the ground in ten minutes or you're relieved of duty."

Intimidated, the pilot rushes to the front of the shuttle, and Halin roughly pulls her toward a seat. He settles her down and latches her in. She just stares straight ahead, even when he nuzzles her neck.

"You'll like this," he promises. "It's a wild ride when they do it this way, and Garin's a good pilot."

She doesn't look at him or respond, and he sighs. He settles into the seat next to her, and after he's secured himself, he reaches over to rest a hand on her thigh. He does that all the time, touching her as if they are a loving couple. It isn't sexual. It's a comfort thing. He'll rest his hand on her shoulder, back, leg, or arm. She wishes she could enjoy all his touches instead of spending her time fighting her feelings for him, forcing herself to remember his betrayal.

Then she goes to move and remembers that she can't touch him back. Her wrists are cuffed together and chained to her waist. Then she doesn't have to work to be angry anymore.

The hatch to Fortune closes, and Garin maneuvers the shuttle away. No sooner are they clear than Garin is hitting Hissa's atmosphere at a rapid pace. She feels her stomach quiver as they start to free fall. She represses a shout of excitement at the feeling of it. She keeps her expression shut down. Looking over, she catches Halin watching her closely for any reaction. She gives him a blank look and turns to gaze straight ahead.

They're landing much sooner than she expects, and the shuttle doors open with a soft hiss. Warm, damp air invades the cabin. Halin unlatches her and walks her out of the shuttle. Her first sight of Hissa is almost nonexistent as over a dozen large men surround the two of them. They all look angry and fierce, and for the first time, she starts feeling real fear.

All these men are as tall as Halin or taller, broad, muscular, and many of them are wearing armor and weapons. She's never felt intimidated in her life. Until now.

As the men loom over her, she presses back against Halin, the only comfort she has in this new place. Better the devil you know and all that.

"Back up," Halin barks out.

"We are here to escort you to the Council." One of the men with a nasty scar running down his face and across his nose steps forward. He looks down at Mian with open curiosity. "I'd never even heard of Decanted humans, but now within a month we have two show up with mating marks."

"Two?" Halin asks with obvious shock.

"Tiran arrived a week ago with a Decanted female named Mara," a man in full armor explains. "She developed his marks just as they arrived here. They are off planet now, searching for her sister Lara. There's much hope they can find her and bring her back."

The scarred man runs his hand over his chest, right over his heart. "It's assumed the sister is compatible to our species also. They're twins. I'm sure we can convince her to pick one of us."

"I'm sure," Halin echoes as he takes in the men around them. "There are many honorable males on Hissa to choose from." Mian manages not to snort derisively at his words. "But that is a discussion for later. Although it seems you know some of my news already, I'd like to present my findings to the Council."

"I'm assuming that's when you'll explain why this one is bound?" the scarred man replies with biting sarcasm. "Although she does appear rather deadly, I'm not sure the restraints are necessary with such a force to guard you, Commander Halin."

She feels Halin stiffen next to her, but he ignores the man's barbed comment. "She's my concern, not yours," he growls. "Move out." The scarred man nods and turns, yelling out orders to the men around them.

Mian moves slowly, hampered by the leg shackles. When she stumbles for a third time, he picks her up and throws her over his shoulder. This new view of Hissa is even worse than trying to see around the men. She hears faint growls from the men surrounding them, but none of them verbally object to her treatment. Or perhaps they wished she was dangling over their shoulders.

She could be freed from Halin only to end up caged by a different Hissa.

Soon they are walking into a large, single-chambered stone building. She can hear the voices of many men, and she's able to raise her head enough to watch most of the guards struggle to shut a set of massive stone doors. An ominous feeling creeps up when she hears those heavy doors behind them thump closed. She can't see much until Halin finally stops and sets her down on her feet. She blinks, letting her vision clear and the dizziness subside from being rapidly stood up right after having her head dangle upside down. When she can see, she draws in a sharp breath.

There's an impressive stone dais directly in front of her with thirteen men seated at it, but they aren't the only ones in the room. All around her Hissa men are seated, silent with intense eyes focused on her. Only Halin and she are standing in a clear area just in front of the raised dais.

Every single face in the entire place is frowning.

"Why is the female restrained?" one of the Council members asks with a hint of outrage. He's speaking in Space Standard, probably for her benefit. "Is she a criminal?"

"Councilor Salis, she's a bounty hunter, not a criminal, but I fear she will hurt herself if I turn her loose," Halin answers quickly, and she almost breaks her silence to say something caustic. His tone is deferential. It seems even Halin is intimidated by the Council.

"We're willing to take that risk," another Council member says dryly. "Release her restraints."

Halin undoes the shackles on her ankles first, then releases her hands. Rubbing her wrists, she rolls her shoulders, turns to him, and punches him in the throat. When he bends over gasping for air and grabbing at his neck, she knees him in the face. Then she steps back quickly as he staggers from her blows.

Several men stand to move toward her, and she looks around for a handy weapon. But instead of grabbing her, they continue past her towards Halin. She was so worried about the men going after her that she didn't notice Halin's recovery and attempt to grab her. They pull him back and he curses and fights to get loose.

"Enough!" a voice from the dais roars out. She looks up to see an angry face peering down at her. "Don't hit him again."

She looks the man in the eyes, trying very hard not to be intimidated. "I can't promise that," she answers honestly.

The Council member's eyes widen. "Why not?"

"If he tries to restrain me again, I'll fight him," she explains, and to her relief, the man nods.

"That is a valid reason. Can I assume your attack on him was reprisal for being restrained?" When she nods her head, the Council member grunts and sits back.

"He's kept me restrained for the last two weeks," she elaborates, hoping to garner sympathy. "I didn't deserve that treatment."

"You were going to leave me on Wint," Halin roars. "I couldn't let you just leave me." She flinches a little at his words, and the Council members look over at him with surprise.

"It's my ship and my right to drop a passenger off at a reputable station. You could have easily found passage to Hissa from there."

"I don't care about that," he bellows at her. "You're mine. You're not allowed to just leave me behind." She feels herself tremble a little at the violence in his voice.

"Calm down, Commander Halin, or you'll be sedated," one of the Council members warns, and Halin stills.

The Council member turns his attention back to Mian. "We are shocked to see that it's Halin who needs to be restrained. We'll keep him away from you for now. Can I assume he's the reason behind those mating marks?"

She nods mutely, unable to look away from Halin's enraged face.

"Did he rape you?"

The question makes her gasp, and her eyes fly up to fix on the Council member who spoke.

"No," she shakes her head quickly. "What we shared was mutual and pleasurable. He became irrational after Bicoma. After the marks on my neck appeared. I don't know what happened."

"You said he kept you restrained on your ship?" asks another Council member.

She nods. "He acted violently, and I locked him in my cabin. He escaped and subdued me. I've been in restraints for the entire journey here." She hears a buzz of murmurs go through the gathered men. It's all in Hissa so she can't understand what they're saying, but many sound upset.

"Did he rape you after leaving Bicoma? While he was keeping you restrained?" The entire building grows quiet with that question. Mian finds she needs to clear her throat before she can talk.

"No, we shared a bed and he held me, but he didn't force himself on me." The look of relief on the Councils' faces are easy to read, and she realizes these men are very worried they'll need to do something drastic to Halin.

One of the Council members looks at Halin. He isn't struggling but watching the exchange with barely repressed hostility. She can't tell if it's directed at her or the Council for asking about rape.

"We've all read the report you submitted about what happened to your ship and how you reached Bicoma," another member speaks to Halin, silencing the grumbles. "Is this female you brought before us in chains the same Captain Sorrow that rescued you?"

Instead of answering the question, Halin snarls at the man. "No one is to touch her. Those are my mating marks. I demand to join in a Family Pact with her. She's my female."

"Considering the way that she was brought before us, I have doubts about that claim," another Council member mutters, and she can hear grumbling from the men around the room. From the sound of it, they don't approve of her treatment, and she feels a small ray of hope.

"I'm Captain Sorrow of the independent gunship Fortune," Mian says quickly. That draws all their attention back to her. "I've been kept a prisoner on my ship and brought here against my will. I demand to be released and taken back to my ship."

"Captain Sorrow, do you know what those marks around your neck mean?" a Council member on the far right of the dais asks.

Self-consciously Mian rubs the marks.

"Halin told me it means he can get me pregnant," she tries to say offhandedly. "I'm Decanted. The Bicoma said it has something to do with the DNA used to create me."

"Do you know why that's important to us?" he presses.

"Because you lost all your females to the Great Death," she answers reluctantly. "But I'm sure there are other Decanted women out there that would love to be here."

"That may be so, but we can't just let you leave without giving our men a chance to court you. I'm sorry Halin treated you so poorly. His conduct will be reviewed. For now, however, we ask you to enjoy our hospitality."

"Even if I want to leave?" Mian demands, taking an aggressive step toward the Council. "I'm not a slave. I was born free. I was bought and raised by loving parents. What you're doing isn't honorable."

She feels a little gasp go through the room at her words, and a buzz of conversation starts. One of the council members seated toward the center eyes her thoughtfully.

"You're not wrong," he finally states. "We'll need to discuss your official status and create laws to govern how the Decanted females will be treated, especially for cases like yours, where the females aren't slaves that we can buy and set free here on Hissa. It could take some time to develop protocols. Until then, I suggest you make the best of it. Enjoy our planet and meet our males. The marks on your neck will fade in a few weeks if you and Halin don't have sex again. Even before that happens, you're free to entertain other males if you're so inclined. Let's see if any of them can make marks appear and woo you into a Family Pact."

She opens her mouth to object when another Council member speaks up. "We won't force you to bed males. We only ask that you spend time interacting with them. Talk to them. Let us show you the best that Hissa has to offer. We're a rich people. We can provide you with many gifts and diversions while you stay here."

She has no idea what that means, but at least they aren't saying she has to stay permanently. They aren't letting her go either. They need time to determine what to do with her. That gives her no clue as to what they might eventually decide.

She's not interested in dating any other Hissa men, but she knows how to bide her time. She'll wait to do something desperate if they vote against giving her liberty.

Besides, hasn't she been telling herself she needs a vacation?

"Very well," she concedes and gives a startled gasp when a roar of rage sounds next to her.

"She's mine!" Halin bellows. "No one touches her. No one goes near her." He struggles and several more men are forced to help the first two to hold him. The Council members lean their heads together and speak in low tones before they straighten up and regard Halin.

"Halin, this Council deems you unstable. You're to be taken to medical," the Council member at the very center of the dais declares. "I've known you my entire life, Halin, but I don't know this male acting so irrationally before me."

A look of shame crosses Halin's face at those words. He stops struggling. Mian meets his gaze. His eyes beg her to let him stay, to speak up for him. She opens her mouth, but no words come out.

The Council member continues, addressing the men holding him. "Assign guards. Take him to medical and have the menders examine him. Sedate him if you have to." At those words, Halin renews his struggles, and Mian watches with tears in her eyes as he's dragged away. She wanted to get away from him, but not like this.

"Revin," a Council member calls out and the man with the scarred face steps forward. "You will be in charge of her safety. Draw as many men as you need. She can stay in the housing we use for diplomats."

"Understood, Councilman Hitan," Revin replies and steps to stand next to her.

Hitan looks up to the rest of the Hissa in the room. They had all fallen silent as the drama in front of the dais unfolded. "We have a great deal to discuss. Laws and protocols will need to be developed to deal with Decanted females. We will abstain from Council meetings for the next month as we deliberate over the issue. If anyone has input, you can submit it through the normal channels." He looks over to his fellow Council members who all nod their heads.

With that, all thirteen Council members stand up. This must be the cue for everyone in the room to stand because they are all on their feet only a second later. Then the Council member in the very center of the dais speaks loudly to the crowd.

"We declare this Council session over. We will open the doors now and bid everyone a good day and bright night. May Brimming bring you love and life and may Diminish keep you safe from strife."

All the men in the cavernous room speak in unison, their voices filling the space. "Thank you for your service, Council. We give the Moons thanks and hope their bright light will guide you to the best decisions for all of Hissa."

"Thank you for your service, men and women of Hissa. We will endeavor to deserve your trust," the Council reply in unison and step off the dais. No one else moves as the Council members all make their way to the massive double doors and together push them both open. The whole thing has the feel of a very old ceremony. What makes Mian's heart hurt for the Hissa is that they still include "women" in the verbiage despite their civilization's devastating loss.

Although they're being urged to leave, many of the Hissa are reluctant, casting longing looks at her as they file out. Then she sees several men carrying out an unconscious Halin, and a small sound of distress comes out of her throat.

"He's fine," Revin assures her. "They sedated him. If they hadn't, someone might have gotten hurt. I've never seen the Commander act this way."

"You and me both," Mian mutters. How did her loving and fun Halin turn into that violent, possessive person?

"Medical will sort it out," Revin assures her. "Perhaps he'll get his senses back in time to court you himself. Although for my own selfish reasons, I hope you might look to me for comfort while he's gone."

Mian looks up at the large man. Why does she bother thinking of him as large? All these Hissa tower over her. Using the word large and Hissa together is redundant. If the hundred Hissa who just filed out of the room are anything to go by, there's no such thing as a reasonably sized Hissa. As long as she's on this planet, no one's going to be standing eye to eye with her.

"I'd like a shower and a change of clothes. He didn't trust me enough to let me bathe or change, and I wouldn't let him do it for me."

Revin leans over and sniffs, then grins. "You smell lovely," he assures her, and Mian realizes the man is a flirt. She gives him a small smile and shakes her head.

"Stow the charm for now. Shower and clothes," she demands, and he nods and turns. It's then she notices the other man who also stayed behind.

Revin addresses the man just behind him. "Selan, do you know where we might find clothes small enough to fit her?"

"On my own damn ship," Mian says with barely suppressed annoyance. "Just take me up to my ship, and I can pack enough for an extended stay."

Both men grin at her, but Revin shakes his head. "I'm sorry, Captain," he explains. "But you're not allowed off planet until the Council reconvenes. Not even for a quick trip to an orbiting ship and back. Just tell us what to get, and we will send someone."

Mian sighs, knowing it was too much to hope for that they would let her on Fortune. If she could get aboard her ship, there's a slim chance she could figure out a way to escape. But these men are too cautious. She gives them instructions, and Selan pulls out a data pad to record what she wants and where to find it.

"And whatever you do, don't touch anything unless I've specifically said to!" she warns him. "You might not survive the consequences." That gets Selan's attention, and he double checks her instructions before sending the message off.

"Your things will be planet side soon. We'll escort you to your lodging now," Revin tells her. She expects to see some of the planet on the journey to her temporary housing. But between being hurried along and packed tightly between not just Revin and Selan, but four other warriors, she doesn't even get a glimpse of much except the tops of some stone buildings and a little greenery.

She wonders if she'll ever see what the planet looks like.

In short order, she's inside her new, and hopefully interim, home. Revin shows her how to work everything and then warns her there will be guards posted and she's not to go anywhere without them. After that he leaves, and she suddenly finds herself alone.

That could have gone better, she thinks to herself. She couldn't get access to Fortune, and she has round-the-clock guards. Escape is going to be tough when she decides she's had enough.

Then she remembers Halin raging and trying to get his hands on her. *But then again, it could have gone a lot worse.*

CHAPTER

14

Mian wakes suddenly when a large hand covers her mouth. She throws a punch before she's even opened her eyes and hears a chuckle as her assailant captures her fist.

She goes still and blinks, staring hard. A face finally takes shape in the dim light of the room. Halin is grinning as he looks down at her. "I'd rather you didn't scream. That could get uncomfortable fast."

He pulls his hand away from her mouth and releases her wrist. To her surprise, he scoots back on her bed until he's crouching near her feet. She sits up and tries to get her sleep fogged brain to work.

"What are you doing here?"

"I would think that's obvious," he replies with a shrug. "I needed to see you."

"They took you to medical."

He makes a little scoffing sound at her words. "If they wanted to keep me there then they should've used better restraints. Or kept me drugged." Suddenly, he drops his head, and she can just make out the expression on his face. It's shame.

"I don't know what's wrong with me," he admits. "I don't feel right." He rubs his chest absently. "I can't seem to control myself around you. I have a strong impulse to grab you and take you somewhere secluded. Some place where no one could find us. It's hard to fight."

"And even with that, you thought it would be a good idea to break out of medical and come visit?" she asks, voice heavy with sarcasm.

He shakes his head. "I know I'm dangerous right now. I don't know what's going on. But looking back, I can tell I haven't felt right since we left Bicoma." He takes a deep shaky breath. "I needed to see you so I could explain that I'm not going to fight with the menders. I want to get better. I don't want these violent thoughts constantly swirling around in my mind. But I need to be able to see you while they test different things on me. I don't think I could keep my sanity if I can't see you."

Mian regards him thoughtfully. "It looks like I'm not going anywhere any time soon," she points out, not sure why she feels the need to reassure him. This version of Halin, sitting at the foot of her bed, flashing fangs as he grins, and speaking with articulation makes her hope that whatever is wrong with him can be fixed. She wants the violent Halin to be the aberration.

"This is one of the finer dwellings close to the port," he tells her, glancing around the dark room. "It appears they're treating you well."

"They got my things from Fortune and fed me a massive dinner. The guys guarding me kept telling me to eat more and shoved food under my nose. I feel like a strange combination of honored guest and captive. And the way they keep pushing food makes me feel a little like a prized animal being fattened for slaughter."

"They didn't let you on your ship, did they?" he asks with a knowing grin. She raises an eyebrow and gives him a sour expression, making him chuckle.

"No, they didn't let me on Fortune," she says regretfully. "But I've been told I get to tour a couple of places tomorrow. Meet lots of people and see lots of nice things. I was wondering—" she starts to say, but a low growl ticks out of his throat, making Mian stiffen.

"Don't let any of them touch you. If any of them get too close you need to tell them you're mine." She moves slowly away from him and to her relief, he stays where he is.

She feels better when she's standing in the doorway to the bedroom. It's not so much that she thinks she can get away now. Halin could easily cover the distance between them in two strides. But the fact that he's letting her create space between them indicates he's somewhat in control.

"Easy there," she says in a soothing voice. "That growly possessive thing isn't helping your case. If you want to see me in the future, tone it down." She watches him close his eyes and draw in a deep breath. When he opens them, he appears calm again.

"That was harder than it should have been," he admits. "Can I hold you? I find I need to feel you in my arms and fill my nose with your scent. I wouldn't ask, but my head hurts, and being close to you makes the pain go away."

Mian hesitates, unsure if she can trust him. In the short time she's known him, he's been both a lover and a jailer. "You growl or roar at me again, and I scream for the guards. I'm pretty sure if they have to haul your ass back to medical, they'll chain you down this time," she warns him. When his familiar mischievous smile curls his lips, a small warmth unfurls in her chest. She loves that smile.

"If I do anything that makes you scream, I'd rather it wasn't from fear."

Huffing out a chuckle, Mian steps back to the bed. Sliding in, she pats the empty space next to her. "Come on over."

Halin stretches his body out next to her, but despite her earlier bravery, she stiffens.

With a look of sadness, he gathers her close to him. "I hate that I've put that look on your face," he whispers. He runs a hand up and down her back. Soon she starts to relax in his arms. "There," he murmurs. "That's better."

"Your species seems advanced," she says. "I'm sure your menders can figure out what's going on with you."

"Speaking of menders," he starts, and she tenses up again. "No, don't get upset," he tells her quickly. "I'm not going to say anything about your sterilization. I'd like you to be seen by the menders for your general well-being. I've seen how stingy you are with anything, well anything except spending credits on Fortune. I'm sure you never go to a medical suite except for dire emergencies. I'd like our menders to make sure you're healthy."

She can hear his concern and nods. "Sure, I guess I can let them poke and prod me to keep you happy."

He hugs her to him just a little tighter. "Thank you, my heart."

The endearment makes her flush with pleasure, and suddenly his hand is slipping between her legs. She doesn't protest as he finds his way under her night clothes. Soon he's stroking her sex with those skilled fingers.

She gives a little sigh. "Oh, that feels good." She moves against him, wanting more. He hasn't touched her intimately since leaving Bicoma and she aches for him.

"I need you," he states. She stretches her face up for a kiss and then realizes that's not what he meant. She hesitates for a second, and his face transforms from need to despair.

"No, not yet," he says and starts to pull his hand away. "I'm sorry I broke your trust. I deserve your refusal."

"Give a girl a moment to think," she growls out, grabbing his hand to hold between her own. "You can be overwhelming. It's not fair."

He gives her a questioning look and doesn't try to pull his hand out from hers. She feels him tremble against her and understands he's fighting his need and aggression with everything in him to give her the time to decide. She knows he'll leave if she demands it, even though it might cost him dearly.

She's never been this important to anyone but her parents. Never had anyone wanted her so badly. Never felt so needed.

She pushes lets his hands and sits up. He rolls away, disappointment clear on his face. She pulls her top off. "Get those clothes off," she demands and shimmies out of her sleep pants.

He freezes and turns his head to look at her, his eyes going wide when he sees she's already naked. "Are you sure?"

She puts her hands on her hips and juts her breasts out. "Do I look like I'm not sure?"

He grins and practically rips his clothes off. Before she can say another word, he's on her, pushing her back on the bed and settling his hips between her legs. She gives a little sigh as his weight covers her, only realizing at that moment how much she was missing the feeling of him on top of her.

He kisses her, taking his time. She runs her tongue along one of his fangs, enjoying the way it makes him shudder. "Did it hurt very bad?" he asks.

"When you hit me or when you kept me restrained?" she asks, confused.

"No, I know those were hurtful things, and I expect some day for you to hurt me so I can forgive myself," he tells her with brutal honestly. "But do you think you will ever be able to forgive my betrayal? I paid back your kindness with brutality and force. I should have let you take me to Wint. I could've spent my time convincing you to come home with me." He draws back, and she sees regret on his face. "It shouldn't even have been an issue. There is no reason I should've acted so badly when you told me about sterilizing yourself. That was your decision and your right, done long before you met me."

"That's all true," she agrees, deciding to ask something that she'd kept buried, fearful of his answer. "Why does it matter that I can't have children? Is that my only value? You seemed to like me well enough before Bicoma and all the revelations about the Decanted. What changed?"

Dropping his head, he buries his face in her neck. She feels his hot breath against her skin. She waits, her ardor cooled by the conversation. He rolls them to the side, tucking her tightly against him.

"It felt like you betrayed me. When you told me so casually that you'd ended any chance of us having young it was…" He takes a deep breath, and she feels him shudder against her. "I felt like my heart was being ripped out of my chest. After I saw the mating marks, I pictured you getting round with our child. I saw our young in my mind. It would be a girl, and she would have your eyes, and I would care for you both. I could almost feel her little body in my hands." He stops talking, overcome with the memory.

She feels like she wants to cry. "Then it felt like I took that all away?"

"I know it's not rational."

"Emotions rarely are," she sighs. "I remember my mom once saying love is impossible to quantify but easy to be overwhelmed by."

"Your mother was a wise parent," Halin says after a moment. "I miss my mother and sisters. I was so young when they were taken that I have few memories. Each is precious to me."

She wraps her arms and legs around him, hugging him tightly. They hold each other like that until the first moon is high in the sky, casting a warm light through the window.

Finally, Mian speaks. "I'm not sure I've forgiven you yet," she starts and feels him tense against her. "But I'm willing to let you woo me, that is if you still want me." She feels his cock harden against her and almost laughs.

"Is there any doubt I still want you?"

"Even if I probably can't have children?" she asks and holds her breath for the answer.

"There will be other Decanted females found, Hissa doesn't need to rely on you to repopulate the species," he assures her. "If there are no children, I'll be sad. But my love for you wouldn't diminish."

She grins from relief. "You guys do realize that we humans usually only have one baby at a time, max maybe two. We don't give birth to litters."

He gives a little laugh. "I'm sure one of the menders has figured that out. After Tiran presented Mara with mating marks, the menders were eager for samples and started researching human females. Requests have been made to Earth for information on Decanting technology, and preparations are being made for a diplomatic mission. Already we have found information that led us to several Decanted females sold into slavery. Ships have been dispatched to find them and bring them back."

"That's fast. You guys don't mess around."

"Not with something this important."

They both fall silent, and Mian moves against him, enjoying the feel of his erection pressing against her; then she remembers the question that sparked the whole conversation.

"What were you asking me?" When he gives her a confused look, she elaborates. "When you asked if it hurt? What were you referring to?"

Suddenly he grins, playful and passionate. "Did it hurt when I bit you? Because I find I want to do it again." The idea of him biting her makes her insides warm. His nostrils flare and his grin is wide enough to show off fang. "You did like it!"

"Maybe," she responds with a sly smile. "Might just need to try it one or two more times before I decide if I liked it."

"I'd be happy to help you test this theory," he tells her and nuzzles her neck, running his fangs along her skin. Her breath hitches and she moves her hips against him.

Bracing himself on one arm, he runs a hand down her shoulder, collar bone, and then cups her breast, moving his callused thumb over the tip. The rough skin of his thumb feels good against her nipple, and she tries to push forward to increase the pressure. He rolls them back over, using his bigger body to pin her. He keeps his touch light and tormenting until she finally makes a small sound of frustration.

"You're killing me," she growls at him. "If you don't give me more, I'm going to tie you down and take what I want!"

He kisses her neck, then moves down her body, kissing and scraping fang as he goes. "I think I might like to be your prisoner. Being used by you would be more than any captive could hope for."

"Perverted Hissa," she grumbles, trying to get her arms out from under him so she can touch and torment him.

Instead, the moment he's not pinning her arms down anymore, he pushes her legs apart with his wide shoulders, ducking away from her searching fingers. He gently bites the inside of her thigh, eliciting a little moan from her. He works his mouth closer to her sex, and she can tell he's deliberately pushing his fangs against her flesh. There's enough pressure that he is almost at the point of breaking the skin.

She stills as he runs his fangs up her leg, nibbling, and threatening, but not piercing. She's panting by the time he reaches her sex and nuzzles his face between the folds there. He licks his tongue across her clit. She pushes her hips up, desperate for the feel of his mouth on her.

"Please," she begs.

"I like the sound of your voice when it's so breathless and needy," he murmurs, pulling her labia apart so he can blow a little breath of air across her needy flesh. She moans and tries to thrash under him, cursing when he holds her hips down. She whimpers and struggles more.

"Beg me again," he demands, and his commanding voice sends a delicious shiver through her.

"What if I don't?" she challenges, looking down her body to see his eyes lift enough to meet hers. His gaze is hot and promising, and just the look on his face is almost enough to make her climax.

"Then I leave," he growls out. "I leave you desperate and wanting. Do you want me to leave?" He runs a finger over her clit, and she draws in a sharp breath.

"Please stay," she begs.

"That's not enough, I think you know what I want to hear," he tells her. She feels two of his fingers slip inside her, making her shudder with need.

"I'm yours," she whispers, staring into his eyes and realizing she means what she says. "Stay and enjoy what belongs to you."

"Mine," he declares.

"Yours," she agrees and then gasps when he swoops down and sucks her clit into his mouth. She wants to scream, but all the air seems to have left the room, and her climax sweeps through her with enough power to make her vision hazy.

When she's finally done thrashing under him, he draws back, grabs her hips, and flips her over onto her stomach. She feels a moment of unease, but he lets go of her the moment she's turned over.

"On your hands and knees," he commands. Her movements are clumsy. The intense orgasm left her loose limbed and boneless. With his help she manages to get on all fours and widens her legs to steady herself, looking forward to feeling him penetrate her from behind. His hands are on her hips, but he doesn't move against her.

She looks over her shoulder to see him poised behind her. His expression looks like he's fighting with something.

"Halin?"

He looks up to meet her eyes, and she sees fear.

"I don't want to hurt you," he blurts out. "I feel out of control. I'm scared I will hurt you again, and you will never forgive me."

She relaxes at his words, pushing herself back against him. "You won't hurt me," she promises him. "I need you inside me, please."

"Promise me you'll kill me if I hurt you," he demands, and she almost laughs.

"I think that's a bit extreme," she gasps out as he starts pushing himself inside her.

"No," he grinds out, his voice barely above a gravelly whisper. "If I hurt you again, I don't want to live anymore. You're the most precious thing in my world, and my life should be forfeit if I ever cause you fear or pain again."

Unwilling to engage in this conversation any longer, Mian pushes her body hard against him, forcing his erection deep inside of her and making them both gasp with pleasure.

"If you stop, I'll kill you right now!" she threatens. He chokes out a gasping laugh.

"As my love demands." He starts moving and brings one hand around to start rubbing her sensitive clit. It's not long before she's gasping and moving against him, desperate for the next orgasm.

As her climax hits, she can feel herself squeezing his cock and a deep sense of satisfaction swells through her when he goes stiff, finding his release.

He moves for just a little longer, then pulls her tight against him. He maneuvers them down onto the bed, cradling her in his arms. He manages all these movements without pulling out of her and little shivers of pleasure echo through her as he slowly softens inside her.

"You'll smell like me now," he murmurs, tightening his hold around her.

"You know I'll be cleaning myself off later," she points out and prepares herself for his temper to flair. She feels him freeze.

"I want to chain you to me. I want to steal you away and keep you isolated so they can't even see you, let alone touch you. I find the impulse driving me, just as powerful as the primal need for food or water."

Not once during that little speech did he tighten his grip, or start roaring, so Mian relaxes a little. "But you know that's irrational."

"I know it. And I'm fighting that part of myself," he agrees quietly. "I must return to medical before anyone notices I'm gone. I'm willing to cooperate so they can fix me, make these thoughts controllable. I've never been like this before. I don't understand what's going on, but I promise this will be conquered."

Mian feels hope for the two of them with those words. "I trust you," she promises. "Just hold me a little longer and then you can go."

They both lapse into silence, enjoying the feel of each other. Finally, reluctantly, he starts to untangle himself and rise.

"What are your plans for tomorrow?" he asks as he draws on his clothing. She notices his shirt is ripped in several places and grins.

"I'm getting a tour," she reminds him. "I didn't get to see much yesterday. I'm scheduled to visit various places for the next week, all supervised by my guards. I think I'm being shown a place called the Citadel tomorrow."

He turns and takes a step so he's standing next to the bed, towering over her. He sounds a soft growl that makes the fine hairs on her body stand up in alarm. "You won't let them touch you. The guards or any other males."

It's an effort, but she forces her body not to react to his threat. Instead, she sighs and gives him a disappointed look. "What do you think?"

He closes his eyes, and she watches him wage a battle with himself. "You're an honorable female," he finally says. "If you felt loyal to a male, you wouldn't let any other claim you."

She nods and gets up on her knees to hug him. "I'm willing to be loyal to you if you keep working on whatever is going on in your head."

He wraps his arms around her again. "The menders took many samples from me today and tried out a few suppressants. They're hoping to find some anomaly that explains my actions. I'm sure tomorrow will be full of the same. But I'd like to return tomorrow night, if that's permissible?"

"You better," she tells him with mock severity.

He releases her and is halfway across the room to her open window when he turns back with a small, sad smile. "I wish I was the one to guard you and show you my world."

"You will," she promises. "Get better. I expect you to show me your home and tell me more about your family."

At her words, he gives her a brilliant smile. "I'd like that." With that, he jumps on the windowsill and drops out of sight. She lets out a deep breath and falls back on the bed. She feels ridiculously happy, even though the man who makes her feel that way might not be sane.

But then again, she decides, sanity can be overrated.

CHAPTER 15

Mian opens the front door of her house to find four guards waiting for her. She recognizes the scarred Revin but doesn't know any of the others.

"We'll be guarding you today," Revin explains and introduces the men around him. "These are some of our finest warriors. This is Dacon, Povin, and Veran." As he says their names, the men tap their fingers at the center of their chest and gaze at her with hungry eyes. She notices they're having a hard time keeping their eyes off her neck, and it's making her self-conscious. Maybe a tour around Hissa isn't a good idea after all.

Revin must have noticed her expression because he barks at the men. "Eyes up!"

All the men stiffen and snap their gaze up to meet hers. Revin addresses her apologetically. "My men will stop staring at your mating marks, but others will look, and I can't order men not under my command to look away. Try not to take it personally. You need to understand how desperate we are. Those marks around your neck represent something every Hissa male wishes to have."

"Right, I understand," Mian assures him. "It's just really disconcerting. I've spent a lot of years on my own. Before that, I was generally working among species that aren't breeding compatible with humans. I've never had so many males pay so much attention to me."

"If you're too uncomfortable you can stay in the house. But if you feel brave enough to venture out, it would be my honor to introduce you to Hissa," Revin tells her, and she can see a bit of anxiety in the large warrior's expression.

She decides to be bold. It's her natural inclination. "What aren't you telling me, Revin?" He looks a little surprised, then looks away for a moment as if thinking something through. Finally, he returns his gaze to her and explains.

"Halin's a good friend to me. We grew up next to each other and trained together." He suddenly stops talking and his nostrils flair. He leans close to her and breathes in deeply.

She rears back, giving him an annoyed look. "I don't like you that close."

He doesn't listen to her and leans in a little further, so she takes several steps back. When he steps forward, keeping pace with her, she's irritated enough to give him a warning shot. She taps him on the face with an open palm. She puts enough force into the blow to get his attention but doesn't even leave a light mark on his skin.

"The next one will be a fist to your throat," she warns him. "Just so you know, you're a hell of a lot bigger than me. That means if I decide I need to hit you, I'm going to make sure the first one counts and puts you out flat. The second hit will make sure you don't get back up."

His eyes widen with surprise, and a large grin curves his face. "You're fierce."

Dacon steps forward and places a restraining hand on the warrior's shoulder. "Revin." The name is a warning, and she watches Revin take a deep breath and give his head a little shake. He looks to Dacon and gives the man a small nod.

"I'm fine," he assures the other man. "She smells good, but she also smells like Halin."

"You can smell him on me?" she squeaks out. "I used the cleansing unit this morning."

"His scent is unmistakable," Revin tells her with a shrug. "He was here last night, and I can tell you both enjoyed yourselves."

"Well, this is embarrassing," she mutters.

Revin's expression twists into one of anger. "You find Halin an embarrassment?"

Puzzled by his change in tone, she tilts her head as she regards him. Where did this furious indignation come from?

"I find it embarrassing that you can smell I had sex. I'm an adventurous gal, but even I like some privacy." Revin seems to relax at her words.

"I forgot you were born free," he admits. "Slaves would have no expectation of privacy. I assumed you were embarrassed because of Halin, not because you have an odd sense of propriety."

"Hey," Mian protests feeling downright maligned. "I'm human, raised free, and whatever I think is appropriate goes. I don't ask you guys to start adopting human customs, so don't push your Hissa norms on me."

Revin is about to retort when Dacon intercedes again, addressing Revin with a forceful voice. "This isn't part of our mission today."

Revin looks at Dacon. At first, she thinks he's going to yell at the other man, but instead his features relax into a wry expression.

"You're correct, Dacon. I apologize for my improper behavior so far. First, I find myself overwhelmed by her scent, and then I became unnecessarily aggressive in defense of Halin. I'll recuse myself of this command and hand my leadership to you. You've always been the voice of reason no matter the circumstances."

Dacon nods. Revin steps back so the other man can stand before her. At this rate it won't matter if she wants to leave the house or not. They're going to spend all day talking and arguing at the front door.

Dacon taps his finger to his chest in greeting. She moves to tap her finger to the same place, but Dacon stops her.

"Men greet women by tapping our chests over our hearts. It's a way to tell you we see you as the heart of us. To greet us, you tap your fingers to your throat to show us you understand we're willing to lay down our lives to protect you. It's been a long time since we had females to greet properly, so it might seem minor to you, but I know it'll thrill many to see you perform a proper greeting," Dacon explains.

It's a simple thing, so she taps her finger to the base of her throat. "Like this?"

All the men beam. "Exactly. The men will greet each other by tapping fingers to the forehead between our eyes. It symbolizes our mutual agreement to keep watch over our females and children. When Mara and her sister get back, you should tap your belly in greeting. It's an acknowledgment of one life-giver to another."

"It's not the most complex greeting system I've ever had to learn," Mian comments thoughtfully as she runs through the various taps in her head. She'd rather be greeted as a fellow warrior but isn't going to go against custom.

She taps her throat to each of them and then addresses her question to Dacon.

"Do all of you know Halin, or just Revin?"

"We're all good friends of Halin," Dacon explains. "That's why we insisted we be given guard duty today. We hope to convince you to stay and give Halin another chance to woo you."

Now the previous conversation starts to make sense to Mian. "You guys are some loyal friends."

Nostrils flaring as he takes a deep breath, Revin growls a little. "You have no idea."

Sliding her eyes over to him, she arches an eyebrow. "I smell that good, do I?"

"You smell so good that even the scent of Halin mixed in isn't enough of a deterrent," he confesses and then looks surprised at his own admission.

Povin steps forward. "I have a temporary solution to this issue." He pulls a small bottle out of his pocket and tosses it to her. She catches it and examines the item. The liquid inside is a light red, but there are no labels on the bottle. She pops open the top and sniffs. She can't smell anything.

"I was one of the men that held Halin back from you at the Council meeting yesterday. I caught your scent and knew it would be an issue later, so I brought a powerful scent neutralizer. If you wouldn't mind taking it in the cleansing unit and using it, then put on fresh clothes, it would help us and all the other Hissa males behave."

"I've never been told I stink by so many in such a short time," she grumbles, and Povin laughs.

"You don't stink, Mian," he assures her. "If anything, you smell too good. I was in the group that greeted Mara when she first landed with Tiran, and I don't remember her smelling this good. I don't know why your scent is so much stronger, but it's powerful enough to be affecting me even when I wasn't standing close. Please use the wash and change clothes. We can wait out here for you to finish. Or you can remain inside all day if you wish."

"The choice is entirely yours. We'll be guarding you no matter the decision," Dacon adds. They all nod their heads in agreement.

Mian steps back with a small sigh. She does want to explore Hissa, not stay cooped up inside all day. Taking a shower and changing her clothes is a small price to pay to be able to go and explore a new planet. "Come on in and make yourselves comfortable. I'll be quick," she tells them and hurries upstairs.

She washes first with soap, and then the scent neutralizer, making sure to get every part of her. It leaves her skin a little dry, but she ignores the discomfort. The rest of the clothes brought down from Fortune are the ones Halin bought her. She ends up wearing a bright peacock blue in the same shirt and pants style as all the rest. She hasn't worn these clothes yet, so they should be scent-free. If Povin's red liquid does the trick, she'll be safe.

When she comes downstairs the men all stand, sniff, and then smile at her.

"That's a very nice outfit," Veran tells her. "The color is much better than the drab outfit you were wearing earlier." She had originally put on one of her standard gray ship jumpsuits.

"Yes, much better," Povin agrees.

"You guys are obsessed with clothes." She grins at them, then steps closer to where Dacon and Revin are standing. "How do I smell?" They both lean in and sniff.

"You have no scent," Revin says with approval. "Even up close, all I can smell is the cotton that makes up your clothing and a faint hint of ammunition. But I can't smell you at all."

"This will make it much easier to convince you of Halin's worthiness," Dacon mutters. "I feared I might fail because your scent compelled me to pursue you for myself."

"Well, that's good news, but damn, you guys do have a good sense of smell. This outfit was sitting on top of a box of ammunition while Halin and I were unpacking everything." She looks over to Povin. "I used up half the bottle. Do you think you could get me more?"

"That's easy," Povin tells her quickly. "I'll have more made and delivered by the end of the day." He leans in and looks closely at the skin of her forearms. "Your skin appears dry. I'll have something sent along to help with that as well. The scent neutralizer is harsh."

"That'd be great," she agrees and then gestures to the door. "So, are we going to get this tour started or just stand around talking about my smelly body and dry skin?"

All four men chuckle, and Dacon steps forward. "There will be two of us with you at all times, if not all four of us. When we walk, there will be two of us in front and two of us behind you. Please don't wander off. If you need anything, feel tired or hungry, just tell us. Today is for your pleasure so there is no need to push to see everything."

"Great, let's go exploring." Without another word the men form a protective force around her and start marching her out the door with practiced ease. It's obvious that this isn't the first time these men have worked together. "Where are we heading first?"

"Knowing you're a warrior, we thought you might like to see the Citadel. There is a batch of males halfway through their training. We thought you might like to observe," Dacon explains as they walk. She only half hears what he says because she's distracted by everything she sees. Now that she isn't surrounded by a dozen tall male bodies, being quickly moved from one indoor area to another, she has a chance to look around and admire Hissa.

The first thing she notices is how green and lush everything is. She can see dense jungle between the buildings as they walk. There are patches of colorful flowers interspersed in the green, and she catches whiffs of sweet smells in the warm, damp air. The home she's been assigned is just on the outskirts of the city, and they follow a walking path through the city. The men keeping their pace leisurely, allowing her to take in everything around her. She's thankful when they stop talking to her so she can concentrate on observing.

All the buildings are round, and she realizes the Hissa like that shape. The windows are round, the doors are round, and now that she thinks about it, even her bed is round. Now Halin's grumbling about square hatches on Fortune makes sense.

She hears a mechanized sound and notices some kind of small transport coming toward them. It's on tracks and seems to be moving only a little faster than their sedate walking pace. As it nears, she can see it's an automated tram, and although it's empty, it trundles along its tracks right past them.

"Is that a kind of public transport?" she asks.

"It is," Dacon agrees. "The trams are powered by geo-thermals. Many of the things on Hissa are powered that way, including the houses. The trams run nonstop, day or night, and have designated stopping points all along their tracks. The tracks run out like spokes from our city center. Only those Hissa that live very far into the jungle don't have easy access to the tram lines. Most Hissa like to walk, but if there is something heavy, or if someone is tired or injured, they'll use the trams."

"They were used much more when we had women and children," Revin comments quietly. "Children loved the trams." All the men fall silent at his words, and Mian quickly asks another question to draw their attention away from the painful topic.

"I've noticed you guys have top-of-the-line everything," she observes. "That armor you're wearing is the latest generation."

She points to the weapon on Dacon's hip. "I didn't even know plasma pistols existed with dual cartridge loading ports. And the boots Revin is wearing cost almost as much as my ship. Where's the money coming from?"

"I like a woman who knows her gear," Veran comments, making the other men chuckle.

"Both our moons are rich with rare minerals," Revin explains. "Several generations ago when we discovered this and started mining and trading, our wealth rapidly rose. We also realized very quickly that we are a prime target after we were attacked a few times. We focused on building a military to keep Hissa safe. Almost half the Hissa population serves in the military. The equipment we wear, that you seem so envious of, is all standard issue. We want our warriors to go into battle with the best we can offer."

"Are attacks still an issue?"

"Not much anymore," Povin assures her. "At first there were constant attacks and several full-scale invasion attempts. Now we mostly guard the haulers that take our processed minerals outside of our system to be sold."

"That explains a lot," she says.

She notices the path they're walking on has gone from hard-packed dirt to stone and the buildings are closer together. The gorgeous stonework around her is beyond distracting. Even the path under her shoes is elaborately laid down, with different colored stones creating complex geometric patterns. Most of the buildings, also made of stone, are etched with intricate geometric designs.

As they draw close to the city center, it's apparent that the Hissa take great pains to incorporate their jungle into the city. The entire sides of buildings are covered in green, flowering vines. There are spaces between buildings where jungle plants grow thick enough to create a feeling of privacy between towering stone structures. It must take an enormous amount of effort to keep the jungle from taking over the entire city and keep the greenery limited to certain areas.

Most planets she's visited stick to either the ancient part of their civilizations, living similarly to their ancestors, or they go the opposite tact, embracing advancement. The first category ends up in caves or huts, while the second group builds sterile cities full of steel and glass. But the Hissa have managed to interweave their advancements while still keeping the aesthetic beauty of their planet.

"This city is dazzling," she comments and hears all the men make sounds of pleasure at her words.

"There used to be many cities like this on Hissa," Revin explains. He's been pointing out different patterns and stones as they walk. "After the great death, there weren't enough of us to inhabit more than one city, so most of us moved here. The other cities were swallowed by the jungle. It's the hope of many that someday our population will grow enough to reclaim those cities from the jungle. For now, most live here or on the moons. A few live deep in the jungle, unwilling to mix with the rest of us."

"Lost souls," Mian murmurs to herself, but Revin hears her.

"Yes, souls lost to their grief," Revin agrees. "This way. We are almost to the Citadel."

Shuttles are landing in the distance when they turn perpendicular to the path they were originally following. Soon they crest a small rise. Mian pauses to take in the large training area stretching out before her. A low stone wall marks the edges of the training field.

Just beyond the field is a massive stone building that makes her think of a fortress or castle. There are giant cannons mounted in a tight ring around the building. Outside the ring of canons is another ring of smaller buildings with retractable roofs, probably containing guns that need to be sheltered from the weather. There are also shield generators on top of the tallest part of the castle, adding another layer of protection.

"I'm guessing that's where non-combatants go if there's an attack," she murmurs, and the men follow her gaze.

"Yes, under that building is a large area to shelter the most vulnerable," Veran explains. "It's the most heavily fortified and protected place on Hissa. We haven't had to use it in my lifetime, but we maintain it nonetheless."

Have they not had to use it because they haven't been attacked or because there are no women and children left? One reason is good; the other makes her heart hurt for this species. She turns her attention to the large open field where men, all dressed in the same dull brown outfits, are running obstacle courses, wrestling, or practicing a number of other fighting techniques. She watches them with interest for a few minutes, envying the Hissa's large, powerful bodies.

A flash of light catches her attention. When she zeros in on the cause, she smiles and points eagerly. "Is that what I think it is?" All the men look to where she's pointing.

"If you're thinking it's a weapons range, then yes, you'd be correct," Revin answers and chuckles at her expression. "You want to go there next, don't you?"

Nodding her head vigorously. "Oh yes, very much so." Amused by her eagerness, they guide her around the training field and toward the weapons range. It's set off far to the side of the training field but takes up just as much space. She's so eager to get there she ends up pushing the men into a slow jog, and they arrive just as an exercise starts.

She watches with rapt attention as a Hissa male in full armor waits behind a line, watching a light above his head. He's holding a plasma rifle just like the one Halin bought her and has several smaller blasters strapped to his person. His helmet is up, and his body is tense and poised.

The light turns off, and he sprints forward. She watches him dodge several blasts and gasps with worry. Could they be using live rounds during a training exercise?

"Calm yourself," Dacon soothes her, a hand on her shoulder keeping her from grabbing a weapon off a nearby rack and running after the man to guard his back. "This isn't real. If a round hits him, it only makes his suit show a dark spot. He's wearing training armor, and the shots are set on a harmless, low charge."

She nods but doesn't take her eyes off the warrior. He ducks behind a large stone and returns fire, targeting one of several training drones hovering in the air. He manages to hit and blow one up but misses the next one. It's obvious he's too anxious. He's letting his adrenaline interfere with his aim. Without trying to take another shot at the second drone, he leaps out from behind the boulder and sprints down range, just barely missing another blast.

As he runs, he doesn't check his periphery and a small, many-legged robot that looks like a mechanized spider rises from a hidden hole and catches his foot, tripping him to the ground. With movement almost too fast to follow, it's on top of him and tapping the armor repeatedly, making the entire suit go dark.

"Halt!" a voice calls out, and all the action stops. The small, mechanized creature hops off the warrior and disappears back down its hole. The man remains still until someone walks up and taps the armor with a small device, removing all the dark spots. When the armor darkens it must restrict movement, mimicking battle damage.

"This is impressive," she comments, her hands itching to touch the weapons. The man who yelled halt is suddenly in front of her.

"You must be Captain Sorrow," he says, tapping his fingers to his heart. "I'm Merin, the Range Master here."

Taping her fingers to her throat, she smiles. "You can call me Mian. This is an excellent training field."

"Yes," he says looking around. "We've worked hard to make it so. All the drones and attack bots run individual, random patterns so there's no way for a warrior to know when or where they'll be. The suits help us determine what we did wrong, and all the training is recorded, so it can be reviewed later in a classroom. We also change the layout of the range every week. Sometimes we'll set down an old ship on the range and have the trainees run exercises through it."

"I wish I had access to something like this when I was learning," she comments wistfully.

Merin looks visibly startled by her words. "Learning?"

"Mian is a bounty hunter. She stalks raiders," Dacon explains.

"But not anymore," Merin states with a frown. "It's much too dangerous."

That's too much for Mian.

"Were Hissa women helpless?" she asks, drawing everyone's attention to her. "I kinda get the feeling they were incapable of protecting themselves. You know that's dangerous, right? To keep women defenseless, especially if they have children to care for and protect."

The moment the words are out, she feels growls vibrate in the air around her, even her guards sound pissed.

"My mother was an exceptional marksman," Merin tells her with real anger. "She taught me how to shoot. Our females were not helpless. Many were warriors that stood side by side with our males to defend Hissa."

Mian holds up her hands, palms out. "I'm sorry. I didn't mean to upset anyone. The thing is, I've been getting a lot of flak from you guys over my job. That made me assume you treated your females as if they were helpless."

The growls stop suddenly, and she looks around to see abashed expressions on most of the men's faces. "It's just you," Dacon tells her, his scale pattern flushing a grayish color before going back to the familiar blue. "We've been without women for so long that it's hard to think of someone as rare and precious as you in battle."

"It appears we haven't been treating you with the respect due to a warrior," Merin states, drawing her attention back.

"So, if you're going to start respecting me as a warrior, how about letting me have a turn on the range?" she asks, seeing her opening and grabbing it. "I saw the hand-to-hand training in the field. You guys are too big for me to play one-on-one out there. But this," she points to the range. "This is right up my alley."

"I'm not sure that's wise," Revin starts, but Merin cuts him off.

"We either accept she's a warrior or tie her hand and foot and lock her in a home," he states flatly, and the men around him give a few snarls. She's guessing everyone knows how Halin brought her to the planet, and it's apparent they don't approve.

"If we can find training armor to fit you, then you can take a turn on the range," he tells her and turns his attention to one of the dozen trainees gathered around them. "Simin, run to the fortress and see if you can find adolescent training armor. That should just fit her." Simin sprints off and returns a short time later, out of breath and carrying a set of armor. Nearly vibrating with excitement, she slips into the armor. Except for being slightly too big in the chest and a little tight in the hips, it fits her perfectly.

"For this exercise, you can have two single-hand weapons and one rifle," Merin explains.

"I'd rather have mine," she murmurs as she plucks a gun from the rack in front of her. These blasters are a bit bigger than she normally uses, but she can make do.

The Hissa watch silently as she starts arming herself with two hand blasters and spare cartridges. She checks each weapon carefully as she loads them, then places them in the holsters built into the suit. She notices the plasma rifles are smaller than the ones Halin bought and assumes they're specifically for training. She likes the smaller weight and how it fits easily into her hands. Just like the trainee, she decides she'll enter the range with the plasma rifle in hand and then pull the smaller blasters as she needs them.

When she's done arming herself, she turns to face the men and finds they're all staring at her with various degrees of lust.

"That was arousing to watch," Dacon tells her, crossing his big arms over his chest.

Holding the plasma rifle in one hand and letting most of its weight rest on her shoulder, she gives the assembled warriors a big, sassy grin. "You haven't seen anything yet."

Several men bark out laughs at her words, but Merin just grins and gestures her to the start line. He points down to the far end of the range.

"Do you see that orange circle on the ground?" he asks, and she nods. "That's your objective for this exercise. If you reach the circle, you've accomplished your mission."

"Right, I need to step inside it?"

"Yes, but all of you needs to be inside it," he warns her. "Even a toe outside the line and you've failed. The armor has standard training shut-off settings. If you're hit in a limb, the armor will deactivate, and that spot will go dead. Two hits to the chest and your whole armor will freeze until I come and unlock you."

"Understood." She takes a couple of deep breaths, then engages the suit's helmet. She brings the plasma rifle up and rests the butt of the weapon against her shoulder, checking the sighting marks in her helm's heads-up display.

"Ready?" Merin asks.

"Ready," she replies. She doesn't look directly at the light, unlike the trainee. Instead, as Merin steps away, she keeps her eyes on the field in front of her, confident she'll see the light change out of the corner of her eye.

When the light goes off, she steps forward, keeping her knees bent as she moves and sweeps the area with her weapon. She doesn't sprint to the boulder, she knows better. The trainee she saw run was much faster than she and barely made it. If she gives into temptation and runs, she won't be able to accurately fire.

She's only three steps in when one of the first drones appears. She sights and fires. The smaller, lighter plasma rifle barely gives a kick. The round hits dead center, and the small flying device explodes. Unlike the trainee before her, there isn't a second one right behind the first drone. Three of the spider machines emerge from the ground. She picks off the first two quickly, but the third is too fast and is on her leg before she can sight the plasma rifle on it.

She drops the rifle and pulls a blaster from the holster and fires. The spider explodes next to her, but not before it makes her right leg go limp below the knee.

Damn, she just lost the use of her lower leg and she's only a third of the way to her goal. Annoyed with herself, she holsters the blaster and scoops up her rifle, checking the charge and swiftly loading another cartridge.

She takes a tentative step and finds she can still move, it's just slow and ungraceful. Her right leg below the knee feels like deadweight, but the armor keeps her dead foot from dropping with each step and getting in her way. The only thing she might point out to them later is that if she were truly wounded in that leg, she'd be in some serious pain. Learning to function through pain is a tough lesson and hard to simulate. Maybe they can install some kind of shocker unit into the suits.

Her thoughts are interrupted by three drones. As they appear in the air over her, she drops to a knee to keep her dead leg from affecting her aim. She sights and fires, ignoring the fire coming at her. With three blasts she's destroyed the drones. Movement out of the corner of her eye has her swinging to her left just in time to blast a spider.

Stumbling to her feet, she moves as rapidly as she can, while still maintaining enough balance to aim effectively. She sees a drone just lifting off and manages to get a shot in before it's very far off the ground. She gives a small triumphant laugh as she watches it crash into another drone coming out of the same spot. Two kills with one shot. Damn, she's feeling on point today.

She takes several more steps and almost falls into a hole where a spider is emerging. Quickly, she puts her already 'wounded' leg forward to protect the rest of her and sweeps the butt of her rifle down to batter at the creature. It tries to crawl on the injured leg, but she manages several blows, and it flops back, twitching slightly.

She hears the whine of a drone and reacts on instinct, ducking down and rolling. She hears a round hit the ground where she was kneeling, and she finishes the roll on her back, bringing the rifle up, aiming from the hip, and firing. To her surprise, the shot wings the drone, and it flies wildly around her. It ends up taking several hits meant for her from other drones before crashing down.

Her work is far from over, there are still two more in the air. She manages to down one, but the second one gets a round off and it hits her left arm, making the armor around that limb go dead to her shoulder. She consoles herself that at least it wasn't her dominant arm.

She drops the rifle. The two-handed weapon is useless to her now that she has a 'wounded' left arm. She grabs the dead limb and holds it to her suit front. "Attach left arm to chest," she orders. The suit locks the arm in place, making sure it won't flop around and get in her way.

She rolls to her feet, pulls the smaller weapon out of her holster, and starts moving to the orange circle again. It's only about ten feet away now, but she has a strong suspicion those ten feet will be the hardest.

She's proven correct when a line of spiders emerges right in front of her, and she quickly steps back several feet. She puts the dead leg in front again and starts firing. She picks off three before she runs out of ammunition in the gun. She doesn't have enough time to refill, so she discards the weapon and plucks the next weapon from the small of her back. She's managed to create a hole in the line of spiders and is able to gain ground when another drone appears.

Knowing the drone is a bigger threat, she sights and fires at it, ignoring the spiders for a moment. She misses with the first round. The smaller weapons aren't as accurate as the rifle, but she manages to hit it with the second round. She looks down just in time to see a spider almost at her good leg. She fires and kills it, but her gun registers empty. There's another spider almost on her. Finding her balance on her bad leg, she gives the dead spider at her feet a good kick. Her aim is slightly off, but she still manages to send the dead spider barreling into the moving one, breaking a few of its legs and slowing its progress considerably.

"Hold weapon," she orders the suit, slamming the blaster against her chest just above her secured "dead" arm. Thankful that this suit comes with the standard ability to magnetize areas on command, she lets go of the blaster. With the weapon held in place by her armor, she can use her good hand to pull the empty charge cartridge out and discard it on the ground. Without needing to look down, she retrieves a new cartridge from the holster on her thigh and slams it home.

"Release weapon," she demands as she wraps her fingers around the blaster grip. It's a near thing, but she manages to bring the weapon up and pick off three more spiders. She gets all three before they are within touching distance, but only by a scant margin. This is her last cartridge and her last weapon. That's bad enough, but then she sees three more drones pop into the sky.

With a sudden stroke of brilliance, she holsters her blaster and reaches down and grabs one of the dead spiders. She slams it against her chest.

"Hold unknown object to chest," she orders the armor, and the spider sticks to her chest. She grabs a second one and slams it to her back. "Hold unknown item to back." Grabbing a third one, she puts it to her head. "Hold unknown object to helmet." Now she has spider armor and a spider crown. She probably looks awkward as hell but looks don't matter if it works.

Dropping to her knees, she tries to aim at one of the drones but takes a blast to the chest before she has a chance to fire. It hits her spider armor, so no dead spots appear. She sights and aims. This time it takes three rounds to take out just one drone.

They are moving faster, adapting to her speed and if she takes much longer, she'll be out of rounds. It's time to give up finesse and skill and just move.

With all the strength she can muster, she pushes off, feeling her muscles strain. She ducks her head and rolls, finding she's close enough to end up with half her body in the circle. Suddenly, a spider is on her good leg and the entire limb goes dead, from hip to toes. She flips on her back and fires, finding two spiders were clinging to her dead leg.

With both legs dead and one arm dead, her movements are beyond clumsy, but the idea of just giving up doesn't even occur to her. This might be a training exercise, but that doesn't matter. She will always fight to the bitter end.

Using her good arm and her abdominal muscles, she claws and rolls the rest of herself into the circle just as a drone fires and hits the spider on her head.

Once in the circle, she stays on her back and tries to catch her breath. That was fun. She wonders if they'll let her have another go. She knows she could do better next time now that she has a good feel for the speed of those spiders.

"Release unknown from chest and helm," she orders the suit, and the spiders fall away. "Helm down." The helmet retracts, and she takes a deep breath of warm air full of the scent of flowers. Her suit legs and arm are still dead, so she waits, panting and grinning.

Soon her vision is filled with Merin, Povin, Revin, Dacon, and Veran. "Hey, guys," she greets them cheerfully. "Mind unfreezing the armor?" Merin hastily touches the armor, and she regains full use of her limbs again.

"Release arm from chest," she orders and once her arm is free, she sits up and grins at them. "That was fun!" she declares, then frowns at the faces staring down at her.

They are all regarding her with the same shocked expression. It's not flattering.

"What? Did I do it wrong? Merin told me I just had to make it to the orange circle. Was there something I missed?" She holds up a hand. "And how about helping a girl up?"

Merin recovers first and hastily reaches down to help haul her to her feet. "No one makes it to the circle on their first try," he explains. "I grew up training, and I didn't even make it the first time. I didn't make it until my third attempt."

"Oh," she says with a shrug. "I guess there's no training like actually fighting for your life in the corridors of a ship when raiders are doing their best to kill you. This was easy compared to that."

Dacon makes a strangled sound. "Easy?"

She gives him a grin and nods. "Sure, easy. No pain and I knew I wasn't going to die. That makes it easy. And fun. Did I mention I'd like to do it again?"

"No one has ever thought to use the spiders as shields," Merin mutters, shaking his head. "Why didn't I think to do that?"

"I got trapped in an engine room once," Mian explains. "I used an ambulatory stand with an engine on it as a walking shield. I had it walk forward, and I crouched behind it. I was able to poke my rifle through an exhaust port on the engine and fire. It worked great and saved my life. It's not the first time I've had to be creative in combat." She notes several of the men's blue scale patterns pale at her words, but they keep their mouths shut.

"You're a brilliant warrior," Veran tells her, his face full of awe. "When your leg was disabled, I was sure you would be taken down quickly. But you didn't falter. Merin almost called a halt to the exercise. He was worried you'd fall and hurt yourself."

Sending Merin a thankful look, Mian rolls her shoulders "Thanks for not stopping it. That was the most fun I've had in a while."

"I know you want to do it again, but would you consent to speaking to the trainees who just watched you?" Merin requests. "You can come back any time, and I will gladly let you run the course as many times as you like, but I think your input to the students might have real value."

Feeling flattered, Mian nods. "I'd love to talk, but I'm not sure how useful it would be. I'm not formally trained. I've just had a lot of real-life experience."

"I'm positive you have more to contribute than you think," Merin tells her confidently. They troop back to the staging area to find the dozen trainees in armor have been joined by another dozen trainees in sweat-soaked, dull brown shirts and pants from the training field.

Feeling a little uncomfortable at all the attention, Mian concentrates on putting the weapons away.

"You didn't run," the trainee that had gone before her states boldly. She looks up at him to see he's genuinely confused. "Why didn't you run? You would've gotten to the circle faster."

"No," she counters easily. "I would have gotten dead faster. I saw you run and get taken out despite your speed. I'm sure I'm only half as fast as you. My legs are shorter, and I've never been a great runner. If I ran, it would've been harder for me to sight and fire effectively. By walking, I could defend better.”

“You decided to sacrifice speed for accuracy,” another trainee speaks up. She looks over to him and nods.

“Yes, exactly.”

“Is that always your strategy?” another one asks.

“No. I've sprinted sometimes,” she tells him. “It depends on the circumstances. But generally, if I don't know the terrain or where the bad guys are, I'm safer if I take it slow and steady.”

“Can you tell us about a situation in which you decided to run instead of going slow and steady?” a voice in the back asks.

“Sure,” she says and starts telling them about the time she had to check a station taken over by raiders. She's not sure how long the impromptu interview lasts, but her voice starts to get tired, and she's feeling the effects of the exercise after being held almost immobile by Halin on the trip here.

“I believe Mian might be fatigued,” Revin says, cutting off yet another question from a trainee. Merin steps forward with a small frown.

“Revin is correct,” he announces. “Training is concluded for the day. I'll make the recording of Mian's run available. Study it. We will discuss it more tomorrow. Dismissed.” There is some grumbling, but everyone except for Merin and her guards starts filing out.

Once the place is empty, Merin turns to her. “You've impressed us all, Mian,” he says and taps his finger between his eyes and then taps his chest over his heart. She taps between her eyes and then at the base of her throat. Emotions well up inside of her. Merin just acknowledged her as a fellow warrior. She gets the feeling tapping two places isn’t something that’s usually done, but it appears these Hissa are creating a new custom just for her.

“Thank you for the experience,” she counters.

“I know from the information sent out by the council that you might leave us if Halin doesn't get better and no one else catches your attention,” Merin says and ignores the other men when they give him warning growls.

“That's true,” she answers honestly.

“I would beg you to consider staying,” he starts, and Dacon steps forward, trying to push Merin away from her.

“She's still wearing Halin's mating marks,” Dacon states, his voice deep with anger. “Don't act dishonorably.”

Merin steps away shaking his head violently. “No, that's not what I meant,” he tells Dacon. He turns his gaze back to Mian. “I'd like you to become an instructor here. Your skills are exemplary and although it's hard to admit, better than mine. It would be of great benefit to all Hissa if you would stay and teach."

Pleasure uncurls in her chest at Merin's praise. All the other men's faces light up at his words as they nod in agreement.

"Yes, that's an excellent idea," Revin concedes. "There is much practical knowledge you can share."

"I concur," Dacon tells her. "I'd like to take a course instructed by you. I'm impressed at your quick thinking and would like to learn to think like that on the battlefield."

"Honestly, guys," she says quickly, feeling both flattered and uncomfortable. "This is a great training environment, but my speed and skills came from real battle. Short of leading your men against raiders, I'm not sure how good a teacher I'd be."

"Raiders," Merin says thoughtfully. He gazes down range lost in some deep thought.

"Consider it at least," Dacon urges, his words bringing Merin's focus back to her.

"Yes, you should consider it," Merin pushes but still seems distracted. "I must go and do some research. It's been a pleasure to meet and learn from you." Merin taps his chest once again and turns to stride off without a backward glance.

"Well, that guy's all business," she mutters.

"Merin is very focused," Revin agrees with a last look at the retreating man. He turns his gaze back to Mian. "Are you hungry? It's well past the midday meal, and I know my belly is too empty for comfort." The other men rumble in agreement, and Mian realizes she's starving.

"Food sounds like a great idea," she says and strips out of her armor. The moment the armor's off, all the men sniff and take several steps back. "But I guess I should go home and a shower first," she says with a sigh.

"That would be advisable," Dacon agrees and turns to lead the group out of the range. Mian notices all the men are keeping their distance now that her scent is back. It's annoying but doesn't remove the smile from her face.

"We could take you on one of the footpaths into the jungle after our meal. You might enjoy the scenery," Revin suggests as they walk.

"Excellent idea," Dacon agrees.

"A hike sounds fine," Mian murmurs. She'll bug the guys to take her back to the range tomorrow.

Guns, food, and friends. It's more than she expected to find when Halin dragged her chained and unwilling to Hissa.

Perhaps hanging out on this planet won't be as horrible as she feared.

RESCUING HALIN 169

Perhaps hanging out on this planet won't be as horrible as she feared.

CHAPTER

16

Standing at the open window, Mian scans the dark ground outside for Halin. Diminish, the smaller of Hissa's two moons, casts a weak light on the landscape and helps her search. She's not sure how long she stands there, but the second moon, Brimming, is just starting to edge over the horizon when she grows too concerned to remain inside. She can't imagine Halin wouldn't show up if he promised he would. Something must have happened. She needs to slip out of the house and start looking for him.

She's debating using the cleansing unit one more time to kill her scent, but before she can decide, a loud knock at the front door interrupts her internal debate. Hurrying down the stairs she feels anxiety knot her stomach. There aren't many reasons the Hissa would disturb her at this time of night, and none of them are good. She swings open the large round door to see Revin and a man she doesn't know standing there with strained expressions. Before Revin can say a word, the stranger grabs her and starts dragging her behind him.

"We must hurry," he growls out. Mian is about to launch a fist at him when the man abruptly stops and turns to face her. He leans over, takes a deep breath, and growls low in his throat. His scale pattern flashes purple, and his expression turns lustful.

Then Revin is there, shoving the man away from her. Revin's movements mean her knee hits air instead of the stranger's groin. The move is violent enough to throw her off balance, and she almost ends up on her ass. Another set of hands grab her and steady her, and she turns to see Dacon. He lets go and quickly steps back, hugging his arms around his chest as if he's in pain.

She curses herself for deliberating too long. She should have used the cleansing unit instead of staring out the damn window like a princess in all the fairytales her parents used to tell her. She's acting like some addle-brained idiot from an old Earth romance vid.

"Why does she smell so good?" the stranger demands. His scale pattern isn't purple, but it didn't go back to blue either. Now it's hovering around a dark brown. He's irritated.

Well, welcome to the club, Mian thinks.

"I don't know, Sarin," Revin tells him. "But you need to keep your distance. I know you're concerned for Halin, but you need to calm down and keep away from her."

Revin looks at her and jerks his head to indicate where he wants her to go. "Wash and change clothes. We'll wait out here for you."

Mian ignores his order and addresses Sarin. "What's wrong with Halin?"

"He's acting feral, insane!" Sarin barks out, making Mian flinch back. "He won't talk, only roars. He's hurting himself trying to get out of medical. He screams for you. I demand you go to him and see if you can calm him down. You caused this. You need to fix it."

A jolt of fear goes through her. "I thought Halin was doing better." She looks to Revin, questioning. His expression is grim.

"What Sarin is saying is the truth," he confirms. "Halin become progressively worse throughout the day."

Her mouth twists into a frown. Halin's been suffering while she blithely hiked around the Hissa jungle? That explains why all her guards started acting distracted after the midday meal. It also explains why Revin kept disappearing to talk to people on his data bracelet.

How could they let her traipse around, unaware of Halin's pain, when they could easily have informed her? Taken her to him. Let her try and help.

Rage deepens her voice when she addresses Revin. "Why didn't you tell me this?"

"I tried to get permission to tell you, but many on the Council are against it. Some worry your presence would make it worse or he might hurt you. It took hours of arguing to get the Council's approval to simply ask you if you would visit him." Revin casts his eyes to the stranger who grabbed her. "This is Sarin, Halin's brother. He's the reason the Council relented and agreed to let us tell you about Halin."

She looks at Sarin. "Give me a few minutes to wash. It'll make it easier for everyone to be around me." The tense man nods, and she rushes back into the house. She's washed and changed in record time. Hurrying back downstairs, she finds her escort's grown by two more men she doesn't recognize. Without another word, they hustle her into a small private transport vehicle that looks a lot like one of the tram cars but with larger wheels. Before long, they are pulling in front of a large building, and they rush her inside.

The moment she walks through the door, she can hear Halin roaring, and she breaks into a run. The men don't try to stop her. They just keep up.

She skids to a halt when she gets to Halin's room. Six men are trying to subdue him. A ruined medical bed is on its side, twisted and broken. Torn restraints on his arms tell the rest of the story. He's fighting to get to her.

"Halin!" she calls out to get his attention, and his eyes lock on her. Sarin wasn't exaggerating when he said Halin was becoming feral. The expression on his face looks like it belongs to an animal too long denied something it desperately needs.

She gives a little start of fear and takes a step back. He froze when she called out, but her small movement galvanizes him back into action. Roaring loud enough to hurt her ears, he throws his body against the men trying to subdue him. Because they don't want to hurt him, she can see the men are losing ground. Tamping down on her fear, she moves forward until she can just touch his face over the shoulder of one of the straining men.

"Halin, you need to stop fighting," she tells him. At her touch he stops moving. His eyes focus on her again. He doesn't talk, just growl and rubs his face against her hand.

"I'm right here, but you need to stop fighting," she repeats. She pushes at the man holding Halin by the torso. He slowly releases his grip and steps away so she can bring her body closer to Halin.

Halin drops his head closer to her and takes a deep breath.

Then he gives another small ticking growl. "You don't smell right." His voice is guttural and raw.

"I will in a minute," she promises. Without breaking eye contact with Halin, she addresses the other men in the room. "Why doesn't everyone go ahead and move away so Halin and I can talk?"

A man rushes into the room waving his arms from distress at seeing Mian there. "No!"

Halin reacts quickly and violently. He uses the distraction to shove several of the men off of him and grab Mian to his side. The men still holding him try to regain ground, but they're worried about hurting her in the process.

"Everyone, back up!" Mian screams out. Halin's hold on her is causing enough pain to make her pant, but she doesn't struggle. He doesn't mean to hurt her, but his aggression is getting the better of him with all the other men crowding in the room. She knows he doesn't realize what he's doing.

She ignores the pain and forces her voice to remain calm and controlled. "Back up. I've got this." No one moves, so she locks eyes on Revin. "Get them out or I swear I'll hunt each of you down and cut something precious off with a dull knife."

"He's dangerous," the man who just rushed in yells out. "You need to get her away from him. He's not rational. He'll hurt her!"

Sarin grabs the new man by the arm and pushes him away. "You're going to need to move away, mender. Right now, he's got her, but if you get closer, he might do something we'll all regret."

"I told you this was a bad idea!" the mender nearly screams in Sarin's face.

"And you also told me using any stronger drugs to sedate him might stop his heart," Sarin reminds the man grimly.

Fearful they will try and drug him, Mian pushes herself hard against Halin's side. "Out!" she shouts at all of them, ignoring the painful hold Halin has around her belly. "Out, NOW!"

"But Captain Sorrow," the mender begins, and she turns her angry gaze on him.

"No! You give me a chance to calm him down or I'll get my hands on a plasma rifle and start shooting!"

"She's good. I wouldn't challenge her," Revin states with grim humor.

"We're letting go," one of the men holding Halin announces in a strained voice. "Timon, Somen, do you hear me? We're all going to let go and back up."

Halin gives a low growl but doesn't move. The moment his other arm is free, he brings it around to pick Mian up and hold her high against his chest with her legs dangling. She gives a little gasp and smacks his arm. He turns and pushes her against the wall, putting his big body between her and the other men in the room.

"Can't breathe," she pants. With a grunt, he loosens his grip a little, and she takes in a deep lungful of air while the other men all start backing toward the door.

"Lock it behind you," she calls out to them. "No one comes in without asking permission."

"I'll stand guard," Sarin assures her.

"We'll stand guard," Revin tells her, eyeing Sarin. "Both of you need to be kept safe. Do you understand, Mian?"

It's clear he's telling her he doesn't trust Sarin to make the hard choice between her safety and Halin's life. She understands impossible choices like that and vows she'll do everything in her power to keep Revin from needing to making that kind of decision.

"I'll call for help if I need it," she promises and feels Halin growl against her back, but he doesn't tighten his hold, so she relaxes a little. Revin doesn't say anything more, just nods and starts moving everyone out of the room. Once he has the men out, he gives her one last look, a torn and tormented expression on his face, then he turns and closes the door behind him with a soft click.

The moment they're gone, Halin drops her on her feet and rushes to the closed door. Grunting from the effort, he pushes several heavy pieces of furniture against it. She watches with raised eyebrows as he barricades them in. When he's finally done, he turns to her with a determined expression.

"You don't smell right," he declares and grabs her up in his arms again.

She gives a little squeak, and soon she's sitting on the floor in the corner of the room while he's ripping off her clothes. She expects him to suck on her breast or dive between her legs, but instead, he just starts rubbing his body on hers. With a small sound of frustration, he rips at his clothes until he's naked from the waist up. He pushes her back and spreads his body on top of her, rubbing and growling. After a few minutes, he sighs with satisfaction, and when he meets her gaze, she can see intelligence now.

"I was dying without your smell," he whispers. "I don't know what's wrong with me. I managed to keep my sanity yesterday, but today it was worse. About halfway through the day, I couldn't take it anymore. I decided I couldn't wait any longer to see you, but they wouldn't let me leave. They drugged me, but the drugs never lasted long. I couldn't think straight. All I could focus on was getting free and getting to you."

His body relaxes against hers and she taps his arm. "How about rolling on your side? I'll cuddle, but you're a little heavy to be on top for long." He rolls off her and gathers her to him, holding her tightly. Thankfully, it's not so bad that she can't breathe.

"You know, something's going on with me too," she confides. "The guys are telling me my scent is getting stronger. I had to bathe three times today with this scent neutralizer Povin gave me. Something strange is happening to both of us."

"My memories of today are hazy," Halin admits. "By the afternoon, I don't remember much except fighting and being in pain. I remember the menders saying they don't understand what's wrong with me. They're worried."

"Too many drugs. They could hurt or kill you," Mian states grimly. "We aren't going to let that happen. If I need to hang out with you here all day to keep you calm, we can do that, no problem."

Halin is silent for a long time. Tired from a full day of activities and an evening spent worrying, Mian is just starting to drift off to sleep when he speaks. "I fear I might hurt you."

His words make her tense up. Suddenly she's wide awake. Fear of bodily harm tends to do that to a person.

"Do you feel like you need to hit me?" she inquires cautiously.

"No, I'd never do that. But I'm not in control when you're away from me or there are all these other males present. I fear I might inadvertently damage you. I couldn't think earlier. All I could see was you. I would've killed those other men if you hadn't stopped them. I wouldn't have even thought twice about it. I didn't even recognize Sarin until you were touching me, and I could think again. Even then, if he tried to pull you away from me, I would have seriously injured him and not cared that he's my own brother."

Mian takes a deep breath. "You weren't like this before. Even when you got so angry on Wint and threw Moriv, you were more rational. It's almost like the possessive, primitive part of you is being exaggerated somehow."

Mian thinks about everything they've done. All those days spent with Halin in the close confines of Fortune. His easy charm and playful attitude. That all changed very soon after the visit to the Bicoma. Could both of them have been infected by something on that planet?

"I don't deserve you," Halin tells her, his words sudden and surprising.

"Probably not," she agrees with a grin, and he gives a tired chuckle. The sound making her heart feel lighter and loosens the ball of worry that settled in her stomach the moment Sarin knocked on her door earlier. If he can have moments of lucidity enough to laugh, then there's hope.

"Looking back, I can see I was already acting irrationally when I got back on the ship after visiting Bicoma," he says, echoing her own thoughts. "I was consumed by the idea that you might slip away from me. All I could think about was keeping you with me. Keeping you safe. Getting you back here. Then we got back here, but nothing felt right. There were too many males. Too many eyes watching you." A little growl escapes his throat. He coughs trying to stop it and then sounds a soul-weary sigh. "My people had to save you from me. I can't believe I kept you in chains." He makes a sound of pain deep in his chest. "I was a horrible, abusive male to you."

She waves off his comment with a snort. "I think you're right. I think you picked up some kind of virus or something back on Bicoma. That means you're not to blame for whatever caused you to go caveman."

"Caveman?"

"It's an Earth thing Mom said whenever Dad acted too macho and annoyed her," Mian explains. "The answer to all of this has to be on Bicoma. Something from that planet is affecting us both. I didn't smell so strong before Bicoma, and you were a perfectly rational Hissa. We need to go back there and see if they'll talk to us. They might be able to fix it if we tell them what's going on."

"It took years of diplomatic exchanges before they agreed to allow us to visit the first time," he tells her glumly. "Even if we get permission quickly, the Council won't let us both go. They won't want to risk you."

"What's our other option, watch you slowly go insane? You're doing well now, but what's to say you're not going to get worse even when I'm with you?"

"They need to put me down," he declares, his voice flat.

Mian slaps him with enough force to turn his head. Shocked, he looks at her with wide eyes. "Did you just strike me?"

"And I'll do it every time you say anything that stupid," she warns him. "I'm not going to let anyone put you down. If they won't let us go, then we don't bother asking. We'll get aboard Fortune and go to Bicoma by ourselves. I'll fire on any Hissa ship that tries to stop me."

"Our military is large and strong. They'll chase you and maybe even fire on Fortune to disable her. They could kill you trying to stop us. I won't allow it," he says, gripping her against him.

Mian gives him a steely-eyed look. "No, they won't fire on the Fortune at all. They'd never risk killing a precious female who could have Hissa young," she points out, showing him her cold, calculating side. "I haven't seen a doctor, er mender, yet. They don't know I'm sterilized. For all they know, I might already be pregnant."

"True," Halin says with a slow nod.

"That means we get on Fortune, and if they try to do anything, we just threaten them with me. If they get too close, I warn them I'll go to extreme measures to escape. I'm sure you showed them my bounty hunter records from Fortune. There were a couple of close calls where Fortune and I almost didn't make it out. They know I'm determined. They'll have to let us go. We just need to get to my ship."

"I might be able to help with that," a voice says, startling them both. Halin reacts first, jumping to his feet with Mian in his arms. He sets her down in the corner and puts his back to her, ready to use his own body as a shield.

Sarin is standing in the room, holding up both hands to show they are empty and staying as far away as he can and still be in the room with them. Peering around Halin, Mian notices an open maintenance grate and looks up to Sarin with a raised eyebrow.

"When things went quiet, I got worried," Sarin explains. "I only meant to look in and make sure you were both alive, but then I heard you talking. Halin sounded like his old self, so I thought I'd be safe to enter."

"Nice to know you care," Mian retorts. Halin says nothing, instead, he gives a low, warning growl and shows Sarin his fangs. Mian strokes his back. "Easy, Halin, that's your brother over there. He's family. He'd never hurt you or me."

There's no reaction to her words. It's as if he can't hear her. Having another male in the room has flipped a switch in his head. He's only instinct and emotion now.

Damn. Reasonable thinking Halin has disappeared, replaced by feral Halin.

"It's me," Sarin says, his face full of concern and pain. "We grew up together. Trained together. We competed in everything. We held our sisters and mother while they died. We stood together in grief after our father killed himself. You're my only family left."

Again, there's no indication that Halin understands anything Sarin is saying. If anything, the growling gets more intense. Mian sighs and looks over to the devastated man.

"You're going to need to get us to my ship," she tells him. "And you're going to need to figure out how to do it without us coming into contact with any other males."

"Do you think you can drug him?"

"Isn't that dangerous?"

"If we had to drug him consistently, then yes it would weaken his heart until he died. One more time shouldn't damage his heart. The last dose the menders gave him only lasted an hour. On most Hissa his size it should've lasted almost six. But an hour gives us enough time to get him on a shuttle and back to your ship."

"Make the plans, then get me the drug," Mian orders him. Sarin gives a sharp nod and leaves, closing the grate behind him. The moment he's out of sight, Halin relaxes and turns to wrap his arms around her. He breathes deeply, so she knows her scent must be coming back because he makes happy, soft noises. She relaxes into his arms and lets him just hold her, waiting for him to be able to think again.

"What just happened?" he asks, bringing his head up and blinking. "We were on the floor cuddling, and now we're standing." Before she can answer, he pulls in a deep breath with his nose and a beatific smile uncurls across his face. He leans over and kisses her neck and then runs his tongue over her skin. "By the moons, you smell good," he groans.

"I need you to focus," she tells him, ignoring the way his actions are making her all melty. "Sarin was just here. He's going to get us on Fortune and I'm going to take us back to Bicoma. Those guys are bizarre, but powerful. I'm sure they can figure out what's going on with the two of us."

"Two of us?" he questions, meeting her gaze with slightly unfocused eyes.

"Do you remember the conversation we had before Sarin came in?" she asks. Frustration fills her when he shakes his head. "Right, then you're just going to need to trust me."

"I trust you," he states simply. "Even when I can't think, I know you're there." His voice is raw from all the roaring, and she feels him quiver against her. "If I die, promise me you will find another male to protect you.

She rubs her hands up and down his back, trying to soothe him. "Don't be an idiot," she murmurs. "We're going to be fine."

He buries his head against her, giving off a small growl. "Promise me," he insists. "The thought of you being with another male makes me want to rip things apart, but the idea of you alone fills me with terror. Promise me you will stay on Hissa if I don't survive. Promise me you will let another comfort you." Obviously, he doesn't remember the plan to leave Hissa and seek help from the Bicoma.

Annoyed, she slaps a hand over his mouth to silence him. "Shut up. What you're talking about is a non-issue, so just shut up about it because we're going to figure out what's wrong and fix it."

He goes quiet and just holds her. A sound behind them spurs Halin into action. He grabs her up and pushes her into the corner again, shielding her body with his own. A drug gun comes skittering across the floor, stopping when it bumps against the wall next to her foot. She waits until she hears the grate close again.

"Halin?"

He takes a deep, trembling breath and his hold loosens. She pulls back just enough so she can see his eyes. "I know we were talking, but I can't remember what we were talking about," he admits, dropping his head and resting it against her shoulder. "All I feel is aggression and possessiveness. I want to bed you, but I can't. The instinct part of me is too afraid someone will sneak up on us while I'm distracted." His body is hard against hers, nothing but tense muscle ready to fight.

"I just need you to trust me," she whispers, stroking his chest and reaching up to capture his lips with hers. She gives him a chaste kiss, but he grabs the back of her head and deepens the kiss. They're both panting by the time she pulls away from him.

"Do you trust me?" she asks and draws him down until they're both sitting on the floor. He gives a little growl of disapproval. He doesn't like sitting because it's a vulnerable position. She makes soothing noises and kisses him again.

"Trust you," he growls out. She shows him the drug gun and his growls become louder, but he doesn't move. She presses it against his neck, and he doesn't flinch. "Always trust you." She triggers the gun, her eyes never leaving his.

His eyes close, and she tries to catch him as he slumps sideways. She manages to keep his head from banging on the floor. "It's going to be fine," she promises him, feeling tears prick her eyes. "I won't let anyone hurt you."

She gives herself a moment to just hold his head in her lap, running her hand over the scale pattern on his head and murmuring comforting words. Reluctantly, she moves his head off her lap, placing it gently on the ground. At best, the drugs will last an hour, but she has a strong suspicion they won't last that long. There's no time to waste.

"Sarin," she calls out. "He's unconscious."

She hears movement, and then the door to the room is being forced open, slowly pushing the barricade back. Then Sarin, Revin, Dacon, Povin, Veran, and two more men are streaming through the mangled door and upended furniture.

"We don't have permission for this," Sarin tells her as he and another man reach down to lift Halin's limp form. "We need to move quickly."

"Just get me to Fortune. I can do the rest," she assures him as she scrambles off the floor to follow. Revin grabs her shoulder, halting her progress for a moment. His nostrils flare and she watches him fight with himself before taking several hasty steps back.

"You can't take him there by yourself," he insists. "We need to go with you to keep him from hurting you."

"You try to board my ship and I'll make sure you regret it," she promises him, and his eyes widen at her threat, but then narrow.

"You wouldn't kill me," he states confidently.

"No," she agrees. "But that doesn't mean I can't incapacitate you. You saw me on the range. Do you think you'd stand a chance if I decided I didn't want you on my ship? Fortune is littered with little traps and surprises, and it won't take long before you find yourself vented into space or running afoul of a PKB."

"Halin kept you subdued," Revin points out with a cruel smile. She doesn't rise to the bait, just tilts her head and gives him a cold smile of her own.

"Halin spent almost two weeks traveling with me before that. He learned my hiding spots. You won't. Think you can keep me bound long enough to keep me from accessing a weapon? Are you that confident in your detection skills that you think you can find all my hiding spots? Are you willing to risk your dick to find out which one of us is cleverer? Or crueler? Something to think about before you answer: I love Halin and I broke his nose. I'm not sure I even like you right now."

Noting his look of apprehension, she takes a small step closer to him and lets her smile widen, showing her teeth. "My smell affects you, but your smell doesn't affect me. How long until I can make sure my smell puts you in a vulnerable position?"

Revin scowls at her. "You're being foolish."

"No," she disagrees. "I'm being a warrior. I know my limits, and I know my skills. I'll be safe with Halin, but if any of you guys try to travel with us, I know I'll spend all my time trying to keep him from going crazy. Follow in another ship if you feel you need to, but no one else is allowed aboard Fortune except Halin."

"Very well," Revin agrees with obvious irritation. "We'll follow on another ship. Don't fire on us."

She gives him a genuine grin. "You're safe as long as you don't get in my way."

"I'm now convinced you and Halin belong together," he grumbles and strides out to catch up with the others. She follows close at his heels. "You're both too stubborn and arrogant for your own good."

"It's not arrogant if it's true."

He mumbles something she doesn't catch but gives up his argument.

They catch up with the others just as they are shoving Halin into a large transport vehicle. They all manage to fit inside, but it's tight. Thankfully, the port isn't far away. Soon they're loading her and Halin into a shuttle. Povin takes the pilot seat and with more haste than grace gets them in the air.

Mian doesn't know how Sarin did it, but soon they're boarding Fortune. The men carry Halin to her bed, easing him down with care. She's surprised when they don't leave immediately. Instead, they stare at her living space, looking around with open curiosity.

"Semin told me you decorated like a Hissa," one of the men comments as he reaches out to touch a scarlet drape. "I didn't believe him, but you've made this room beautiful."

"It's a place any Hissa woman would be proud to call home," Sarin agrees. "My sister would have loved the color of the walls."

"Thanks for the compliments, but it's time to go," she says as she tries to usher the men out, worried Halin will wake up from the drugs at any moment.

She manages to shove them out the cabin door and down the hall. She almost has them all boarded on the shuttle when Sarin stops at the shuttle hatch, refusing to move. He waits for her to meet his gaze. With hands on hips, she meets his eyes with a challenge and insult ready on her lips. Neither is necessary because his expression is one of fearful hope.

"You're a warrior I'm proud to know," he states with a gentle, soft voice. He taps his fingers to his throat and then to his heart. "They might have tried to create a human, but they bred a proud, capable Hissa female warrior instead."

Touched by his words, she taps her throat and gives a little bow with her head. "Thank you for the compliment. I'll do my best to guard us and find a cure for Halin."

"I have no doubt," he replies, and she thinks she sees longing on his face as he turns. If only it were me that inspired such devotion."

She doesn't have time to respond before the hatch closes. Rushing to the cockpit to get Fortune underway, she hurries to set the navigation system, thankful to find the ship is fully fueled. Once the ship is underway, she checks the displays and sees a Hissa gunship, twice the size of Fortune, following her at a respectable distance.

"I guess I don't need to worry about any raiders trying to get revenge on me," she murmurs. She has to admit it feels good to have backup for once.

She makes her way back to her cabin to find Halin just starting to wake up from the drugs. She strips out of her clothes and settles in the bed next to him. The previous day's activities are catching up to her. She needs to run diagnostics on the ship and check their food stores, but she'll do that later.

Right now, she needs to wrap her arms around Halin.

CHAPTER

17

Halin holds her tightly as they stand in the stone circle waiting for the Bicoma to show up. He was mostly lucid for the trip from Hissa to here, having only one small meltdown when he first came fully awake after leaving Hissa. Smelling Revin and Sarin on her sent him into a primitive roaring fit. Finally, he calmed enough to allow her to lead him into the cleansing unit.

After thoroughly washing her, he grabbed her and tossed her onto the bed, rubbing himself on her until she only smelled of the two of them. After that, he remained mellow but unfocused. She tried repeatedly to engage him in conversation, but he acted almost drugged, unable to follow a train of thought for very long.

He only got worse as the days passed. Then he stopped talking altogether. Although she wasn't sure if he understood her or not, he let her lead him around. It's a good thing. If he resisted getting into Fortune's shuttle, she might have been forced to drug and drag his ass around. That wouldn't have been fun for either of them.

Thankfully, he not only let her lead him into the shuttle, but out of it once they hit the desolate desert surface of the Bicoma homeworld. He refused to let go of her the moment they exited the small shuttle, so now she stands in front of him, his arms wrapped around her like steel bands, scanning the horizon and waiting for the Bicoma to show up.

Even though the Bicoma granted Fortune passage, Revin, Sarin, and the other Hissa were forced to stay just outside Bicoma space. She feels the loss of the extra support but refuses to be deterred from her mission.

Scanning the horizon, Mian hopes they don't keep her waiting like last time. She's not sure she can keep Halin out in the open very long. He didn't want to leave the shuttle. Even after she managed to get him out of the shuttle and into the stone circle, he keeps trying to pull her back. He doesn't like to be out in the open, and every time something skitters under a rock, or a shadow moves, Halin growls and looks to the open hatch of the nearby shuttle.

Constant petting and soft, soothing words are keeping him in the stone circle, but she doesn't know how much longer he'll allow the two of them to remain in such a vulnerable spot. She's not wearing any armor or weapons because there's no point. That makes skin-to-skin contact a little easier. She's in one of the sets of clothes Halin bought for her on Wint. It's what she's been wearing the past few days. When they hug, he'll often rub the fabric between his fingers and smile. Somewhere deep inside him, he remembers the clothes.

At least the light cotton of her outfit is helping her stay cool. The planet's air is intensely hot and arid. The dry breeze means sweat doesn't have time to gather on her body. If they're forced to wait much longer, she's going to have to give in to Halin's inarticulate demands to go back in the shuttle, just so she can re-hydrate.

The sun is almost at its zenith when Halin growls, arms tightening around her. Looking up to where he's staring, she sees three Bicoma walking toward them. She can't be sure, but the three look very similar to Leader, Follower, and Advocate.

"You need to be calm," she tells him. "They're here to help." At least she hopes they are here to help. Halin tries to pull her toward the shuttle, but she digs in her heels and smacks his arm until he finally looks down and meets her eyes.

"You need to trust me," she tells him. She can see confusion on his face, but finally he grunts and nods. "I need to talk to these creatures," she explains, wondering how much is getting through. "You need to let me stay here and talk to them."

He grunts again and remains in the center of the stone circle as they approach.

"Greetings," the one in the middle addresses her. "I'm Leader. This is Follower and Advocate. We are joyful to see you Captain Mian Sorrow, false human."

She ignores the greeting and the title and levels them with a pleading look. "There's something wrong with Halin," she states. She tries to take a step forward, but he holds her back. She doesn't struggle. He isn't trying to drag her into the shuttle, so she's willing to call it a win.

"What is wrong with Commander Halin?" Leader asks.

"After we left here, he became aggressive. It's gotten worse over time. He can't seem to even talk now. It's like his brain is devolving. Becoming more instinct than thought."

"Of course it is," Advocate states. "That's as we expected."

Mian's too stunned to speak for a moment. "As you expected?" Her voice isn't much more than a croak when she finally manages to form words.

"We needed to test the Hissa, and he was the only one," Follower explains.

"Test?"

"We needed to know the Hissa could be trusted with something precious, something delicate. Something they might find delectable. We had to know they would have control."

Mian feels equal parts confused and annoyed. "Are you saying you did this to him? On purpose?"

"Of course," Leader says.

Mian would have launched herself at the Bicoma if Halin didn't have her in such a strong embrace. As it is, she can feel him picking up on her emotions and tensing up, ready to jump at the Bicoma to defend her. She can't afford for him to get agitated, so she takes a few deep breaths. She needs to stay calm and in control, so his aggression doesn't get out of hand.

"Why would you do this to him? He might have been hurt or killed." She's proud of how even her voice is. It only sounds mildly accusatory.

"Better his life ends than we trust the Hissa to find our Treasure and they fail us because they lack control."

Ignoring their blatant willingness to sacrifice Halin for their own ends, Mian latches on to the most confusing part of that statement. "Treasure?"

"There is a Decanted female that is one of us," Advocate explains. "We do not know how it was done, but she is out there. We can feel her. We cannot leave our system. We cannot leave our suns. But the Hissa already have a reason to seek out Decanted females. They can find her. We need them to bring her to us when she is found."

"There is a Decanted Bicoma?" Mian asks, feeling like the universe might have just tilted around her. She knows the scientists messed with a lot of alien DNA to create the perfect Decanted children, but how would they even get ahold of Bicoma DNA, let alone figure out how to combine it with a human?

"She is like you, a false human. We need her."

"And you need the Hissa to find her?"

"Yes. We feared the Hissa might harm her in their quest to reproduce, so we decided to use the two of you as test subjects. It was easy to tell the Hissa they couldn't have a ship with weapons. We were aware of the danger. We were also aware of you, Mian the false human, and your reputation for protecting those attacked. We set the events in motion and hoped it would be you who rescued the Hissa delegation. We asked they send only the worthiest males to meet with us, hoping you would like one of them enough to engage in mating behavior."

She's shocked and knows it shows on her face. "There are so many things that could have gone wrong," she whispers. "Halin could have died."

"He did not," Advocate points out. "You rescued him and brought him to us. We could not have hoped for a better outcome."

"What if I didn't make it to the Hope in time? What if Halin died?"

"We would have simply requested more Hissa," Follower says calmly, making Mian's blood run cold. "We would request Hissa until the situation was as we needed it with you and a Hissa male on our planet."

"You couldn't have known," she whispers. "Couldn't have known we'd have sex or that mating marks would show up."

"We can know," Advocate informs her. "Because all Hissa are breeding compatible with all Decanted humans. Mating marks would appear no matter who you had sex with, as long as you enjoyed it."

Well, that's a revelation that'll make the Council jump for joy. "Did you change my scent too?" she asks, barely keeping her anger in check.

"We did," Follower confirms. "We let his higher brain functions bleed away, leaving only instinct, and made your scent too delectable for any Hissa male to ignore. Those conditions are ripe to create violence and abuse. Now you are here with no marks of abuse on your body. He kept you safe and protected, even though he can no longer even think with language, only feelings and images."

"We had hopes for the Hissa," Advocate says. "He exceeded our expectations. We are relieved."

"I'm glad you're so happy. Now fix him," Mian demands. Halin growls at her angry tone. She pets him and coos to calm him. He doesn't relax, but the growling diminishes.

"We will need to touch both of you," Follower warns, unperturbed by either her tone or Halin's growl. Just like last time, the familiar smell of her mother's sweet tea envelopes her, and she knows it's affecting Halin too because he seems to relax slightly.

Mian wiggles until Halin allows her to move out of his arms. She turns to face him, pulling one of his arms away from his body. Holding his one arm with both hands, she steps backward and pulls him with her toward Leader.

"They're going to make you feel better," she promises. "You want this, I promise. You trust me. Just keep trusting me."

He resists, but she keeps speaking to him in a soft, calming, reassuring voice as she walks. Reluctantly, he follows until Leader can reach out to touch the arm Mian is holding. He gives a growl and tenses.

She lets go of his arm with one hand and reaches up to draw his face to hers. She kisses him, hoping her scent overwhelms him. He shudders against her and growls even as she kisses him but doesn't pull away. Leader wraps a three-digit appendage around his wrist. She feels the clawed fingers of another Bicoma wrap around her forearm. She can see it's Advocate out of the corner of her eye but ignores him in favor of keeping Halin distracted.

When the claws dig into his flesh enough to pierce his skin Halin brings his head up and roars. She can feel his body tensing, readying to strike out at Leader. Then he stiffens against her, and she knows the Bicoma has immobilized him.

She doesn't fight Advocate's grip, just braces herself for what's coming. The familiar fiery pain lances up and down her arm as his claws pierce her skin. She ignores the discomfort and fixes her gaze on Halin. She watches as intelligence seeps back into his eyes. When he blinks and rolls his eyes to meet hers, she knows he can think and reason again. She almost collapses with relief.

"You are both returned to your original markers," Advocate announces and withdraws his hand from her arm. Leader releases Halin, and she can feel the moment Halin has control of his own body again. He doesn't growl. He doesn't roar. He doesn't snatch her up and run away. He gently wraps his arms around her and heaves out a big, heartful, sigh.

"I don't know what happened," he whispers into her ear. "But I have a strong suspicion you just saved my life."

"That's two you owe me," she murmurs, throwing her arms around him and hugging him tightly with relief. They hold each other like that, forgetting about the Bicoma until Leader speaks again.

"There is one of us you must find," Leader reminds her. "When she is found, she must be brought to us."

Mian turns to face them. She wants to refuse the request. She wants to scream at them and pull out a blaster and shoot all of them for what they put her and Halin through. Instead, knowing the immense power of these creatures, she makes herself nod her head in agreement.

"The Hissa will bring her to you, but how will they know? If she's Decanted, then she'll just look like a normal human."

"She'll be unmistakable," Advocate assures her. "You'll know she is of us, even though her appearance is human."

"She'll help guide you," Follower explains. "You must trust her as you trust each other."

"She is delicate. You must not let the Hissa be forceful with her," Leader warns.

Mian gives him a hard look. "I think Halin has proved the Hissa ability to care and protect females." Her voice comes out even and she doesn't give in to the impulse to take a swing at the Bicoma. She's proud of her restraint.

"Just so," Advocate says. "We wish you to be compassionate with the female. She'll be conflicted and in pain. You must understand this wasn't our wish. We didn't manipulate her into existence. We don't know how it came to pass, but we must rectify and preserve. She is our new start."

Mian isn't sure she completely understands what the Bicoma are saying but nods her head anyway. Something occurs to her, and she cocks her head, regarding them shrewdly.

"You're powerless outside the Bicoma system, aren't you?" she asks. "You have all this tech, all this power, but you can't leave here. There's something you desperately want, but no one you trust enough to get it for you without holding it for ransom."

"Not until now," Advocate agrees. "We trust you and the Hissa now. We will see you again, Captain Sorrow, when you deliver her to us."

"Sure," she mutters, but decides she's not going to be the one bringing this precious "treasure" back to Bicoma. She's not getting within a light-year of this place ever again. Someone else can have the dubious pleasure of delivering that poor decanted woman into the hands of these powerful and manipulative beings. That is, assuming, they ever find the Decanted woman with Bicoma DNA mixed in. Considering the size of the universe, it's a daunting task.

Halin makes a puzzled sound, his hold on her loosening as he looks around them.

"We left here," he states slowly, as if waking up from a dream. "We left Bicoma. We were on our way back to Hissa. Why are we back here? What happened?"

The Bicoma begin to withdraw, and Mian urges Halin toward the shuttle. "We need to leave. I'll explain it all when we are outside Bicoma space," she promises. "But for right now, we really, really need to get out of here before I do something stupid and deck a creature that can make me disappear with a thought."

CHAPTER

18

"You're not hunting raiders anymore," Halin practically shouts.

Far from being intimidated by his volume, Mian cocks an eyebrow at him and crosses her arms over her chest. "Aren't you tired of having this argument yet? I'll hunt if I want to. Besides, how are you going to stop me? Put me in restraints again?"

An expression of shame crosses his face for a moment, and she feels guilty for using that tactic. "Come on," she cajoles. "Going after raiders is what I do. It's part of who I am. I wouldn't know what to do if I wasn't hunting."

"We just need to find you something else," he declares stubbornly. In a flash, his expression goes sultry, and his scale pattern flashes purple. "I can think of ways to distract you," he points out and reaches for her. She dances away from him with a laugh.

"Keep those hands to yourself, I'm still sore from last night! Give a girl a chance to recover."

"You loved last night," he says with a laugh and lunges at her, easily catching her because she isn't putting much effort into getting away. "Tell me where you hurt and I will make it feel better," he promises.

She reaches out to him but pulls back when she feels a wave of nausea go through her. Clamping a hand over her mouth, she just manages to pull a trash receptacle out of the wall before she vomits up her breakfast. She feels Halin behind her, trying to comfort her as she retches.

Once she's done, he draws her to the bed and insists she rests. "The shuttle to Hissa will be here soon, and you're going straight to the menders once we are planetside," he insists. She pushes his hands away and sits up.

"I'm fine," she promises, surprised to find she's telling him the truth. No sooner had she finished emptying the contents of her stomach than she felt fine again. "It's probably just a minor thing. Maybe one or two of those ration packs were bad."

"I hate that you eat those things," Halin grumbles as he stands to gather a wet cloth and cylinder of water. He helps her drink and then bathes her face with gentle hands.

She shrugs. "It takes too long to fix food, and those things are effortless. I like food well enough, but it's never been that big a deal to me. I'd much rather just eat what's fast and handy."

"It only takes minutes to prepare food and those ration packets are tasteless and make you sick," Halin retorts, gathering her into his arms.

A series of sounds echo through the ship, telling them the shuttle has docked with Fortune. He stands, then picks her up, cuddling her to his chest. "Let's head down to the surface. The menders will want to check on me as well anyway. Once we are both cleared from medical, I can show you my home. I think you'll like to examine my bed. I spent a lot of credits on it."

She snuggles against him with a chuckle. "But does it have weapons hidden in it?"

"Maybe," he responds. "You'll have to do a thorough search to find out."

She doesn't object as he carries her to the shuttle. It feels too nice to be held, and her weight doesn't seem to be a burden to him. The shuttle pilot looks back and grins when he sees Halin sit down and settle Mian onto his lap.

"Take your time," Halin tells the pilot. "I'd like the ride to be smooth."

"This time," Mian quips.

"Very good, sir," the pilot calls out as the hatch clangs shut. The shuttle vibrates slightly, but neither Halin nor Mian pay much attention. They're too busy touching and nuzzling each other to care. It comes as a bit of a surprise to both of them when the shuttle sets down.

Halin tries to carry her out of the shuttle, but she wiggles in protest. "It's one thing to carry me around like a kid when no one's around, but there's no way I'm letting you do that on Hissa proper. Not when I'm sure there'll be a ton of guys waiting to greet and escort us."

"Why not? You're not a burden, and you feel good in my arms," he murmurs and gives her shoulder a little nip. She laughs and pushes until he reluctantly lets her slide down his body to stand on her own two feet.

"Warriors don't get carried around and snuggled," she retorts, and he barks out a laugh.

"Maybe they do," he counters.

She eyes him and grins. "When I see Sarin carrying around and cuddling Revin, you can carry me around as much as you want," she challenges and hears the pilot chortle, making both of them laugh.

"How about a compromise? Let me hold your hand?" he asks, and she grabs one of his hands in hers.

"I would enjoy that," she tells him, so they link hands to walk down the shuttle ramp.

She stumbles to a stop as a small crowd breaks out in happy shouts and greetings. Revin, Sarin, and Dacon stride over from another shuttle to join the cheering crowd.

"I feel like one of those entertainers on the fiction vids," she mutters, and Halin gives her hand a small squeeze.

"You're much better than one of them," Halin assures her.

Veran hurries up to meet them with a grin. "It's good to see both of you looking so well." Leaning forward, he takes a deep breath; then his grin gets even wider. "And smelling so normal also."

"Are you saying I don't smell good anymore?" Mian jokes, relieved to get confirmation that her smell isn't overpowering any longer.

"I'm stating you smell good, but not irresistible," Veran assures her.

Halin gives him a mock scowl. "Keep your distance, Veran. This one's mine. Go find your own bounty hunter." Veran pretends to pull away in fear, making them all laugh.

"You'll never know how much the sound of your laughter fills me with relief," Sarin comments as he catches the last part of the conversation. The brothers tap between the eyes in greeting, then Sarin grabs Halin in a fierce hug.

"You scared me, you idiot," Sarin says, choking on the words a little.

"I wasn't thrilled with the situation either," Halin points out dryly and pulls away from the embrace. "At least the parts I can remember."

Mian notices several medical personnel rapidly making their way to them, and she tugs at Halin and points them out. He sighs and nods. "It looks like we get to spend time at medical."

The crowd parts, and the medical personnel usher Mian and Halin into a waiting transport. Soon they're sitting on chairs in an exam room waiting for the menders to poke and prod them. Well, Halin is in a chair. Mian is settled in his lap and so comfortable that she's almost asleep when someone comes bustling in through the door. Instead of a mender or med tech, it's Range Master Merin.

"You're back!" he declares with a startling amount of enthusiasm. Mian watches as the staid Merin seems to vibrate with excitement. "I thought I might send a missive to you but decided to wait to tell you in person. Then I find out you were brought here, not taken to Halin's home. I had to call my cousin on the third floor to come down and distract the monitors so I could sneak in here, but I couldn't wait any longer. I really couldn't."

Smiling with amusement, Mian looks over to Halin and then back to Merin. "What's so exciting, Range Master?"

"Raiders!" he crows eagerly. "Hunting raiders!"

Halin frowns and shakes his head, holding Mian just a little tighter against his chest. "Mian shouldn't hunt raiders anymore," he starts to say, but before she can argue with him, Merin interrupts them both.

"We hunt the raiders!" he announces with too much volume. At Halin's wince, he speaks a little softer, but with no less animation. "We use them as practice! It's perfect! Real-world examples for training. We have seasoned soldiers lead trainees and hunt down raiders. It'll keep the experienced warriors on their toes and provide skills to our young recruits."

Wide eyed, Mian stares at him for a few moments as she digests his words. "You're suggesting the Hissa declare war on raiders?"

Merin almost dances with glee. "Not suggesting, doing. The Council has already agreed. Our forces will rotate through Raider Alley. We're currently working on permission from the nearby systems and stations, so no one thinks we are trying to invade. Domin, the Council member in charge of the diplomatic exchange, thinks we should have everything settled within a few months."

"That's brilliant," Halin compliments Merin who shakes his head and points to Mian.

"She gave me the idea. When she ran the range exercise and won the first time with no formal training, but plenty of real-world lessons, she made us realize how important that kind of experience is."

"You ran the range?" Halin asks, and Mian grins when she sees his astonished expression.

"She ran a third-tier program with a circle entry goal," Merin elaborates.

"I got to the circle on my first go," she brags.

Halin chuckles and hugs her. "I have a feeling you'll never stop surprising me. And now you have no reason to go back to hunting raiders. It looks like we Hissa are going to take care of that for you."

She gives a little non-committal shrug. "Perhaps."

"I'll leave the two of you," Merin tells them. "I have so much to plan and arrange. The range is running at night now so trainees can practice in low light conditions. I need to go. The next group is scheduled to start soon."

"Thank you for bringing us this news," Halin shouts out as Merin disappears.

A small frown wrinkles Mian's forehead. "It sounds like they are going to be utilizing the range all day and night. I hope I'll still be able to get range time."

"I'm sure they will let you play with them any time you want," Halin assures her. "But you don't need to stay battle ready. The fight is no longer yours."

"Perhaps," she says again, and Halin drops the subject, talking instead about his house and the surrounding area.

"I have exciting news," Canil, one of the many menders taking care of them, sweeps into the room.

"More exciting news," Mian laughs. "I didn't think this day could get any better. Are you here to tell us Halin is all better?"

Canil looks momentarily nonplussed but recovers. "I haven't bothered to look at any of Halin's tests. I assumed by his ability to walk and converse without trying to drag you away in chains or hit me means he's cured," Canil points out sourly. Mian raises an eyebrow at his tone, and the mender has the grace to look mildly embarrassed. "Sorry, that was uncalled for. Let me start again." He focuses on Mian, pulling a seat close so he can sit and look her in the eye.

"You have young inside you," he states, his eyes gleaming with happiness.

Mian freezes. "No."

Canil looks up to Halin with a puzzled expression, but Halin looks too poleaxed to respond. Canil returns his gaze to Mian. "Yes, there is a child growing in you. I'm guessing you've been pregnant for three weeks."

"No," she says again. "I had myself sterilized. I can't get pregnant."

Canil eyes her suspiciously. "How were you sterilized?"

"Chemical," Mian explains. "I had it done years ago on Gleem Station."

Canil looks relieved. "Those kinds of sterilizations are easy to reverse," he assures her.

"But I didn't reverse it," Mian points out. "It must be someone else's results you looked at. It can't be mine."

Looking insulted, Canil sits back and regards Mian with exasperation. "You're the only female on the entire planet at the moment so unless Halin is pregnant, I'm not sure how I could have gotten someone else's results mixed up with yours."

"I'm pregnant?" she whispers and suddenly feels lightheaded.

"Easy, my little warrior," Halin murmurs to her, drawing her back against his chest. "This is good news," he assures her. She looks at his delighted, smiling face.

"You did this!" she accuses, and he shakes his head.

"I would never betray your trust," he assures her quickly.

"Except when you were under the influence of the Bicoma," she retorts, and then a realization hits her. "They did it," she whispers, looking down at her belly. If they could mess with Halin's body enough to make him shed his intellect, it would be easy for them to reverse her sterilization.

For the first time in a long time, she feels like crying even though no one is bleeding or dying. She's not in chains, and she isn't on a ship ready to explode.

"I'm going to be a mother," she mumbles in a shaky voice.

"We would like to send home a medical technician to monitor you and the child day and night," Canil tells them, totally unaware of Mian's emotional distress. "And we'll want to run tests daily. And—"

Halin cuts him off with a harsh voice. "I think Mian needs time alone to digest this news."

Canil looks up from his data pad and blanches when he sees Halin glaring at him. Remembering that it was only four weeks ago that Halin was able to pull restraints apart and it took six men to hold the warrior down, the mender hastily stands up and backs away. "Of course, you both may go home. I'll arrange your schedule and for help to be assigned to you."

"No help," Halin orders. "Mian is strong and a warrior. We'll come in for testing when necessary. But she'll want privacy in our home."

"But I really," Canil starts to protest but snaps his mouth shut when Halin growls. "Yes, very well then." He hurries out of the room.

Mian doesn't watch him leave, she's too busy staring uncomprehendingly down at her belly.

Halin reaches out and places his hand on her stomach. "This child will know nothing but safety and love," he vows. "We'll all take good care of both of you."

"You can't know that," Mian protests. "There are so many dangers out there. You can't make a promise like that."

Halin doesn't talk until she finally looks up and meets his gaze. She feels lost and knows the emotion must show on her face. But instead of bullying her, Halin's familiar, mischievous smile forms on his face.

"You might be right, or I might be right," he murmurs to her. "But if you want to know for sure, you're just going to have to bear this child and watch it grow surrounded by love. Protected not only by the two of us, but all of Hissa. I think the odds are in my favor."

She relaxes against him, and for the first time since the death of her parents feels like she has a home. A real home. A place where she belongs and people who would miss her if she died.

"I love you, Halin."

"I love you too, my little warrior," he whispers. "Welcome home."

CHAPTER

19

Mian absently rubs her swollen belly as she examines the holo star chart in front of her. Leaning forward, she pokes a finger into it and taps a small solar system. "That one looks promising." Admiral Vorin leans in to see what she's pointing to. "Why that one?"

Mian taps the air three times so that the solar system is enlarged, and the planets are tagged with names, sizes, and other important statistics. "It's got everything hiding raiders might want."

"Please explain," Lieutenant Diven requests as he and several other men crowd her against the table producing the holo star chart to get a better look. Mian gives a little grunt, and Admiral Vorin quickly pushes the men back with a small growl of warning.

"Sorry." Diven looks aghast as he gazes down at her eight-month pregnant stomach. "Are you well? Should we escort you to medical?"

"Let's not go overboard," Mian grumbles. "Just give me a little room here." The dozen men standing at the holo chart all take a large step back, and she just barely keeps herself from snickering.

The entire ship keeps an eagle eye on her. At first, the men tried to take her in hand themselves, escorting her from place to place when Halin wasn't around, and trying to drag her to medical any time she sneezed. It only took a few incidents and one man being sent to medical himself to convince the men to keep their distance. Now, whenever any of them feel she's being too stubborn, they call Halin.

She learned quickly to hide any discomfort the baby causes, only showing fatigue, irritation, or pain when she's alone with Halin. She doesn't want the entire ship to rebel out of fear for her health and send her back to Hissa, not when there were so many raiders to hunt down.

Merin might have convinced the Council hunting raiders was the best way to train their warriors in real combat without having to declare war on an entire civilization, but the Council fought tooth and nail to keep Mian away.

As if she'd let them. It took months and a few massive arguments to convince not only Halin, but the Council as well, to let her accompany the Hissa armada sent to Raider Alley. Merin argued on her behalf also, pointing out her skills and superior knowledge of raider tactics. The Council finally agreed as long as she remained on the flagship, safely away from combat. And did everything the menders on board told her to do. She obeyed, but it was getting to the point where she felt like she spent at least half her time in medical getting scanned, poked, prodded, and questioned about all her bodily functions.

If even one more medical technician or mender pats her on the head and tells her to be still, she might have to start shooting people. Or she would if Halin hadn't locked all her guns away where she can't get to them.

"Perhaps I should contact Halin," Diven says, drawing Mian's attention back to the meeting.

She glares at him. "No, you won't. At least, not if you know what's good for you."

Diven grins at her, unaffected by the threat. He's been her escort often and is used to her dire warnings by now. "You promised you'd go back to bed after twenty minutes on the bridge. Your time's almost up."

Sighing with annoyance, Mian points at the system and addresses the admiral. "None of these planets are viable to build on. Most of them are gas giants and unsuitable for life anyway. No minerals so there's no mining, and the sun is too weak and unstable to set up ion farms. In short, no one goes there for any reason. It's about the only solar system around here that doesn't even have an outpost. It's the perfect place for raiders to hang out and wait, hoping all of you will get bored and go away."

"You think they're deliberately avoiding us?" Lieutenant Sahin asks. The Hissa aren't used to fighting an enemy that won't meet them head on.

"Without a doubt," Mian assures him. "They avoided Fortune, and she was just one little gunship. You guys have been blazing around Raider Alley, taking out ships left and right. Then, all of a sudden, Raider Alley doesn't have a single raider in it."

"Could they have moved to another sector?" the admiral asks with a frown.

"Not yet," Mian says with a shake of her head. She brings both hands down to rub her distended belly and realizes her discomfort's been growing as she stood there. As much as she hates to admit it, she's ready to rest again.

"Raiders are opportunistic, and this sector is very ripe. I'm sure they're willing to hole up and wait, hoping you'll just go away. If you guys stay, they'll eventually leave and set up a new Raider Alley somewhere else. But for now, I can guarantee you they're playing the wait-and-see game."

"And you think this is the most likely place they'll wait?" Lieutenant Sahin asks, eyeing the holo chart with interest.

"Not necessarily all of them, but I'm sure a lot of them are there," Mian explains. "Remember, they aren't a unified force. They're all independent. Sometimes one or two ships will join together for mutual benefits, but the ties are tenuous and easily broken during combat." The men around her nod. They've heard this before from attending her lectures about hunting raiders.

"What do you think you're doing?" a voice roars out, making all the men in the meeting room turn and flash fang. Mian doesn't even jump at either the voice or the men forming a protective barrier around her. She's gotten accustomed to the way Hissa men instinctively move to defend her. They all relax and move away from her when they see it's Halin striding toward them instead of a threat.

Her eyes go to his neck where an exact copy of her mating marks are tattooed as part of their Family Pact ceremony many months earlier. She loves to run her fingers over those tattoos and think about the fact that she's got a family again.

A family that tends to be bossy and overly protective, but perfect in every other way.

"I was looking at a holo chart," she says quickly, putting on her best innocent face. "And now I'm done. We were just about to leave. Right, Diven?" The lieutenant casts her a sideways glance and shakes his head.

"Don't get me in trouble," he mutters to her and steps away as if she's contaminated. Halin strides up to her and sweeps her into his arms.

"Foolish female," he grumbles and then eyes Diven. "Was she about to leave?"

"She's uncomfortable and should rest," Diven tells him, and Mian flashes him a surprised glance. And here she thought she'd been doing such a good job of hiding her discomfort. Diven looks at her and gives a little snort. "You're not as clever as you think you are."

"I'll take her. I'm done training for the day. You're dismissed from duty," Halin tells the Lieutenant. Diven looks downright relieved.

"Thank you, sir," he says. "She's being difficult today. I think your young is making her irritable." The other men in the room chuckle, and Mian opens her mouth to tell all of them what she thinks of their humor. Halin turns and strides out with her in tow before she can get a word out.

"No one is to contact her for the next full cycle," he calls back.

Mian remains quiet for the journey, knowing better than to ask Halin to set her down. He tends to carry her everywhere now, treating her like she could break if she took a single misstep. Mostly, she deals with his overprotective attitude with humor, but occasionally she's gotten so annoyed that she's resorted to desperate measures.

Including restraining Halin to their bed so she could have her wicked way with him after being refused sex for several weeks in a row. Halin was outraged at first, but it didn't take long to make him see the error of his ways. Especially when the menders backed her up by confirming it's a safe activity to engage in.

Back in their quarters, Halin carefully puts her down on the bed. It's the same one she had on Fortune. She was shocked to find her familiar bed instead of the standard issue ship bunks when he first showed her to their quarters. When she questioned him, Halin admitted that he wanted to do something special for her, and knowing her affection for the piece of furniture, he was determined to keep it with them even on board a Hissa military ship. Turns out that it wasn't hard for Halin to convince everyone to let Mian have the bed. They all want her to be happy and content.

Then she found out the men who helped move it from Fortune to the battleship liked it so much they had copies commissioned. Now her square, wooden bed is all the rage on Hissa. The Tavarian artisans who make them are so busy the beds are on backorder.

With a sigh of relief, Mian rolls on her side, enjoying the feel of the plush comforter. Halin carefully climbs in next to her, curling his body around her and placing a large, gentle hand on the swell of her belly.

"Isn't it time for our young to join us yet?" he asks with a small, frustrated sigh of his own. Halin's both eager to hold their child and also have her comfortable again.

He was very upset last week when he found her sobbing in the cleansing unit because she couldn't see her feet when standing anymore. That emotional outburst ended up with a trip to medical. After the menders and medical technicians confirmed she was fine, he let her explain she was just feeling hormonal and tired of being awkward and fat.

After that little incident, whenever he finds her crying, he feeds her chocolate and tells her she's beautiful. Hissa men aren't dumb.

"I think this kid might be a little too comfortable in there," Mian mutters despondently. "If she doesn't decide to leave soon, I'm going to make one of the menders cut me open and pull her out."

"You're so sure it's a female?" Halin asks, ignoring her bloody threat. Mian refused to let the menders reveal the gender of the child so it can be a surprise at birth. Halin wasn't thrilled but went along with it.

"The kid is stubborn, so I'm assuming it's going to be a girl," she answers and then grunts when the baby kicks.

"I would like our young to be female," Halin whispers.

"And if it turns out to be a boy?"

"I'll love him as I love his mother," Halin states without hesitation. "And then I'll insist we try again until our daughter joins us." Mian chuckles at his words and reaches her hand back until it rests on his hip. They stay like that for several minutes, enjoying the comfort of touching each other. After a while, she decides she might as well tell Halin the idea that's been circling her mind since she was told they were scheduled to leave Raider Alley soon.

"I want to be a Range Master," she blurts out.

"After you're recovered from the birth, I'm sure it will be easy to convince the Council to assign you that duty," Halin agrees, and she struggles to sit up, gaping at him.

"You're not going to argue? You're not going to tell me it's too dangerous and you don't want me around all those men and weapons?"

Halin grins at her and pulls her back down. "If I've learned anything over the last ten months, it's that you're a skilled and honorable warrior. Your weapons skills are exemplary, and as a Range Master you'll have the opportunity to impart your knowledge in a controlled environment. How could I not approve?"

Mian eyes him for a moment. "I think the keywords in that statement are 'controlled environment'," she mutters.

Even though she knows she needs to give up the idea of combat for the time being, it's a hard pill to swallow. It helps that according to Council decree, Halin couldn't engage in combat situations either, so they were being treated as equals in Hissa society. In other words, they're both being treated as if any kind of stress might kill them.

She tries very hard to keep from feeling like they're a pair of prized breeding animals being kept safe and secure while they're reproducing. That feeling isn't helped when she found out that the Council issues a report on her health and the progress of their child to the entire Hissa population. She felt only slightly mollified when Halin explained they do the same thing for all the Decanted women on Hissa.

Reading the daily report the Council issues on the other Decanted women, Mara, Lara, and Deena, makes her feel like she almost knows them. She regrets leaving the planet to hunt raiders before Tiran and Mara returned with Lara and Deena, but only when she read about Lara's pregnancy. She almost asked to be taken back to Hissa, the urge to have another woman to commiserate with was that strong.

The need to hunt down raiders is stronger. She thinks of her parents sometimes and knows they would be proud of all her decisions, including the one to stop allowing vengeance to consume her entire life.

Now that she's sure there's a job waiting for her back on Hissa, she slides a glance over her shoulder at Halin and gives him her best smile. "You know, I think the range should be expanded."

"Anything you want," he promises. "Hissa will give you anything you want. Doubling or tripling the range is easy enough."

"Anything I want?"

"Anything."

"Including you?"

"Including me," he agrees.

"You know, I never thought I'd have a family again," Mian whispers, feeling tears prick her eyes. She can go from feeling such joy and contentment to tears in the matter of moments. Damn hormones!

Halin moves his head so he can kiss her. "I never thought to have a female or children, so we share that erroneous belief," Halin tells her. "It's good to be wrong sometimes."

"Yes," Mian agrees wholeheartedly. "No one else has ever been so happy to be proven wrong."

Dear Readers,

Thank you for reading Rescuing Halin. If you want more Hissa Warriors the next book, Buying Tiran, is available.

I hope you enjoyed Rescuing Halin enough to leave a review! As an indie writer without the support of a publishing company, I need all the help I can get. Your good reviews keep me writing.

If you have any questions, comments, or suggestions feel free to contact me via email: Author@RK-Munin.com

Check out my website. You can find links there to sign up for my newsletter and get free novellas!

www.RK-Munin.com

Cheers,
Rye

OTHER BOOKS BY RK MUNIN

-Science Fiction-

Hissa Warrior Series
Rescuing Halin (Mian and Halin)
Buying Tiran (Mara and Tiran)
Tempting Selon (Lara and Selon)
Defying Kilan (Deena and Kilan)
Healing Mavito (Raleen and Mavito)
Claiming Yopin (Mouse and Yopin)
Teasing Woken (Safena and Woken)
Defending Revin (Kamaril and Revin) – Coming soon

Human Pets of Talin Series
Loving Captivity (Sora and Searin)
Escaping Captivity (Lakin and Dalt)
Negotiating Captivity (Nalia and Derani)
Fighting Captivity (Zia and Palforma)
Tender Captivity (Jinna and Holian - This is a novella you can get
for free by signing up for my newsletter)
Craving Captivity (Lasha and Tamerin)
The Twelve Nights of Halloheen: A holiday mashup novella (Isla
and Tisuran)
Stealing Captivity – Coming soon

Origins (A Human Pets of Talin Series)
Creating Captivity (Ari and Bazium)
Gossamer Chains (Rain and Hesarium)
Golden Cages – Coming soon

-Paranormal /Urban Fantasy-

Ours Evermore Series
Two Wolves for Soren (Soren, Kalli, and Quinn)
A Hacker, Vampire, and Chimera Walk into a Bar….(Tobias,
Briar, and Memphis)
When Darkness Meets Dawn (Imani, Lex, and Mac)
Tag, You're It (Short Story)
Kidnapping Their Third (Cora, Pike, and Kimble) – Coming soon
Pastries on a Plate and Blood in a Mug (Novella) – Coming soon

Alpha Series
Alpha Mage (Emma and Kade)
His Alpha Mage (Avery and Jason – Novella)
Alpha King (Cathleen and Lazlo)

New Clan Series
Stray Wolf (Steph and Eli)
Lost Lion (Maeve and Cyrus)
Reluctant Cervid (Tavi and Donovan)
Broken Thorn (Sabina and Theodosius)